THE I-94 MURDERS

THE I-94 MURDERS

Frank Weber

North Star Press of St. Cloud Inc.
St. Cloud, Minnesota

ISBN: 978-1-68201-093-8

This project was made possible by a grant provided by the Five Wings Arts Council, with funds from the McKnight foundation.

First Edition: September 2018

Printed in the United States of America
North Star Press of St. Cloud
19485 Estes Rd
Clearwater, MN 55320
www.northstarpress.com

Dedications:

To my wife Brenda: When we first met, I thought you were a beautiful and insightful teenager with a gracious heart. I felt that if I could be part of your life, I would be a happy man. Today I see you as a beautiful and insightful woman, with a gracious heart, and have the satisfaction of knowing this was something I was right about.

To my parents, Rosetta and Leo Weber, Rod and Janet Brixius (After years of marriage, your in-laws become your parents too.): I have the utmost respect for each of you, as you've traveled a path before me, that I would be wise to learn from. As my journey covers more of your tracks, the learning is easier (I get it), and my admiration for you grows.

Tiffany Lundgren: Thank you for your perceptive understanding of people, your creativity, and the sincere honesty with which you work with me. As a writer (and perhaps for anyone), it's important to have a friend who has my best interests at heart, yet doesn't hesitate to disagree. It is appreciated!

The Beginning

Yesonia Hartman, sixteen
9:30 P.M., Saturday, November 21, 2015,
Buckman, Minnesota

Fall was the worst time to have a sinus infection, and my misery was not going over well with my seventeen-year-old sister. Leah had a big night planned with some guy she'd been talking to online, and she wanted me out of the house. I didn't blame her, but I couldn't move without my head hurting. Leah was being such a *bitch* about it. We shared a bedroom, so I agreed to lock myself in the room for the night and not make a sound. Our parents were out with friends at the Bottoms Up Saloon. I called it the "twerk bar," but my humor was lost on them.

Leah could afford to be a bitch, as people described her as a young Sophia Vergara, while I, on the other hand, was nick-named "Sony," and compared to a flat-screen television. Older boys had been after Leah since she was eleven, and she had fallen so hard for the last one she humiliated both of us by sending him a topless picture of herself. Our parents would freak if they knew boys were now sending it around. If that's what she had to do to get a guy, what am *I* going to have to do? And she was the one who was *mature* enough to have a cell phone. It wasn't fair.

As crappy as I felt, I wasn't going to miss creeping on Leah's first meeting with Cully for anything. I was upstairs, so I crawled next to the banister. If I'd lie on my stomach, I could see down into the living room without being seen.

Leah was primping in a small mirror in the entry hallway—all chocolate brown hair and smooth, caramel-colored skin. Her simple beige dress contrasted with her colorful personality and the bright, but naïve optimism with which she entered relationships. There was nothing understated about her eye makeup. Her signature cat eye involved the use of Kat Von D's raven black, super-thick, winged eyeliner. Leah had amazing hazel eyes—dark brown from our Mexican-American mother and emerald green from our German father, splayed out in concentric circles—which she knew was her best feature. Mine, of course, were just a faded brown.

Over the next twenty minutes, I watched Leah text away on her cell phone, with no apparent reply. She was on crutches, due to a torn ACL. She had a large blue wrap from her ankle to her thigh that was supposed to keep her leg motionless. It was a bit of an ordeal, then, when she periodically got up and glanced out the window. After repeated trips to the window, Leah finally accepted she'd been stood up. Irritated she sought solace on the couch.

Buckman was a town one square mile in area. There were about fifty houses, which meant our house number, 27222, had more than 27,000 unnecessary digits. My eyelids were getting heavy, but as I hoisted myself up to go in our room, I had to tease my sister a little. It's an unwritten rule. She hated it when I sang my revamped version of "Please Come to Boston." Because of that, I deliberately crooned, "Please come to Buckman for the springtime. You can sell your sweet corn on the sidewalk. And tan at a gas station where I'll be working soon . . ."

Potato chips tumbled to the floor as Leah scrambled for a shoe to throw at me. She yelled in warning, "You better hope I don't catch you!"

When I saw she was half crying, I felt badly and apologized, "I'm sorry—I . . ." Realizing nothing I could say would comfort her, my voice trailed off. I got up and retreated to our bedroom. After first slamming the door to let her know I was in the room, I quietly reopened it—just in case. The front of my forehead throbbed in protest of my movements, so I collapsed on my bed and pulled a pillow over my eyes.

I must have drifted off, but I woke to hear Leah talking to someone downstairs. She was asking impatiently, "Why don't you just step where I can see you?"

I pulled the pillow from my eyes, and strained to hear the exchange. The voice of whoever she was talking to was muffled, so I could barely make out him saying, "My phone battery froze, so I didn't get your texts. What do I need to do to prove to you that I'm Cully?" I realized the discussion was being held through our locked front door.

Leah remained silent.

I silently slid off my bed and snuck back to my prone position next to the banister, peering downstairs. *Could a phone battery freeze at thirty-four degrees?*

He spoke again, "Okay, I'll tell you what I know. You tore your ACL dancing in front of the mirror." In spite of the searing sinus pain through my head, I had to giggle over that. Leah had told everyone she had been trying a rock climbing maneuver.

Her hand was on the doorknob of the still-closed door, and she leaned her forehead against the door.

He continued, "You wanted to play volleyball in college, but being five-six, and now having a torn ACL, you feel that's shot. You told me you had two chances—slim and fat—and now you have none. You weighed 125 before the injury, but now you weigh 136."

Leah jerked her head back indignantly, "One thirty-*five*. I'm sure I said one thirty-*five*!"

"Okay, what else? You secretly hope your volleyball team loses in your absence."

"Shhhh," Leah shushed him. She turned around and leaned her back against the door, arms crossed. She turned her face toward the door and suggested, "Tell me about you."

"I hate talking about me—you know that." After thirty seconds of silence, Cully confessed, "Okay. My dad's in prison. My mom's been with a dozen guys who rub her like a bad stain before they completely wash her from their lives. I spend my free time hacking into people's computers and reading about their lives, because my life sucks."

I groaned inwardly. *This is getting pathetic. But I think I'd still let him in. He's got to be telling the truth. Who'd lie about that?*

In an apparent concession, Leah's arms dropped to her sides; she turned again, and her fingers curled tentatively around the doorknob.

"Look, I'll go," Cully offered. "I just want you to know you're beautiful. And soon you'll resume an active lifestyle, with a new appreciation of the freedom of unrestrained movement."

I shook my head gently, careful not to stir up my sinuses. *Wow. Girl, let the boy in.* I guess this guy wasn't a big enough loser to make her roster.

Suddenly, Leah smoothed her hair and reached for the deadbolt on the door as she turned the knob already in her hand. I heard it snick open.

CRASH! Before I had a chance to smile, our front door blasted open, and Leah went flying backward to the floor. A heavy man landed on top of her and straddled her quickly before she could react. I tried getting up, but I felt frozen in place. Leah winced in pain as she reached for her injured knee. He struck her hard in the stomach, knocking the wind out of her.

My headache was pulsing in earnest now and, as if in sympathy with Leah, I couldn't breathe. I tried to yell for him to stop, but only a barely audible whine left my constricted throat and went unnoticed.

Leah fought back with a resilience that made me proud of her. Cully pulled his weight up for a moment and slammed her to the floor. Dazed, Leah moaned in pain. Tears of helplessness began flowing, creating trickles of winged eyeliner from her eyes to her ears.

Instead of conceding, Leah rallied and elbowed him in the face with the raging scream of a warrior. When he raised his body to slam her once again, she quickly squirmed out from under him. Crawling on her hands and her one good knee, her blue-wrapped stiff leg clunking awkwardly behind her, Leah managed to escape his grasp. But Cully caught up with her and tackled her hard, face down, and pummeled her in the kidney with his fist. Then he turned her over, and held her wrists to the floor. He was now firmly in control.

Panting from exertion, he laughed as he told her, "My name is Culhwch, pronounced *Cull-lock* in Scotland, but in America we'll say *Cul-witch*."

Their wrestling had landed them so Culhwch was facing away from me. I dug deep and got myself on my feet. I began slowly and silently working my way down the steps, my eyes riveted on my sister and this monster, with no idea what I'd do once I reached them. Searing pain ripped through my skull when I moved, forcing me to sit.

He grasped her chin to hold her focus. "Just to be clear, you're not telling anybody about this, because I have all those topless pictures of you, and I'll make sure your parents and everyone in your church youth group gets them if you say a word." His head turned my way ever so slightly, so I froze in place. He focused on her once again.

"But you were so nice to me," Leah whimpered. I wanted to hold her head in my lap and gently soothe her, like Mom did when we were little.

Cully laughed at her, "I Googled, 'What do you say to someone who's lost a lover?' I found, 'I wish I had the right words. Just know I care. I can't tell you how to feel, but I'll listen.'"

How humiliating. I felt sick for Leah. I took a few more steps down the stairs, praying I wouldn't hit the one that creaked and had given us away since we were little. The pain in my head once again compelled me to sit back down.

Bewildered with shock, Leah asked, "Why *me?*"

Cully bragged as he continued to pin her arms to the floor, "I went through hundreds of profiles and cut it down by attractiveness, neediness, willingness to put out for a guy, and it all came down to *you.*"

He smirked brazenly, "My process is similar to how people steal cars today. People don't hotwire cars, anymore—they haven't been able to do that since 2000. Instead, they search cars until they find one with a hidden set of keys on the frame—typically hidden under the driver's-side wheel well." His laugh was low and sinister. "You were available and easy."

My experience arguing with Leah told me her blood was boiling, and she was about to say something stupid. I silently prayed she wouldn't. Her gaze shifted past his face, and she locked eyes with me. She shook her head slightly, her eyes warning me off. Then, with venom in her voice, Leah spat, "And now you're going to get your ass kicked by a one-legged girl!" She valiantly scratched and hit, until he got his hands around her throat. Soon, he was choking the life out of her!

An unrelenting rage overtook him, and he unleashed it on Leah. I didn't have the power to stop him.

Leah's panicked resistance just seemed to anger him further, and he tightened his grip. After a torturous minute or two, her ferocity dwindled to a stop. Her good leg stilled. I watched helplessly, feeling that, not only had I abandoned her, but life was now abandoning her, too.

My head swam with agony and, feeling weak, I clung to the spindles as I stood. Instead of coming to Leah's rescue, I retreated back up the stairs. Carelessly, I stepped on the damn creaking step.

Culhwch glanced up, but before turning my way, he caught his own reflection in the living room window. He suddenly pulled his hands away from Leah, as if they were burned by the flesh on her neck. What did he see? He was staring intently at his own reflection in the window. When he turned in my direction, I was out of his line of sight, again lying flat on the floor at the top of the steps.

I could see Leah's carefully applied makeup was smeared about her face like dirt, but she was still sadly pretty. I urged her in my mind, *C'mon Leah. I'll never argue with you again. I promise.* The miserable pig of a man was still sitting on her still body. Suddenly, Leah started coughing and gasping for air, and I felt a surge of adrenaline. She was alive, but now she was scared to death.

Cully mercilessly howled at his good fortune and taunted her, "If I wanted you dead, you'd be dead." Using both hands on either side of her head, he pushed himself clumsily to his feet and stood over her. He lecherously grunted, "I need a souvenir. You told me your dad has a gun. I'll let you go if you tell me where it is; then I'm going to leave, but the gun better damn well be there, or our evening isn't over."

Leah lay as vulnerable as a lamb. It was clear from her expression she truly feared her life was about to end. Her bruised voice choked out, "It's in my parents' bedroom. There's a compartment in the headboard."

Hell. That's exactly where the gun was.

Leah glanced over at her cell phone on the floor and, for a moment, I had a sickening fear she was about to risk going for it.

Cully warned her, "If you tell anyone about tonight, I swear I will find you and finish this—even if it's years from now. Do you understand?"

Leah nodded tearfully. Cully noticed Leah's cellphone on the floor, and snatched it up as he left the room.

I scrambled downstairs to Leah's side. Since she was in no shape to run, I helped her up and, with her arm around my neck, she was able to hobble up the stairs. We moved as quickly as she could with her wounded leg and beaten body, fearing what would happen when he returned with that gun. Once inside our bedroom, we pushed a dresser against the door, hoping it would keep him at bay. We slid to the floor and clung to each other behind the dresser, waiting for the jolt of Cully ramming the door. Instead, we heard the porch door close as he left the house.

I touched her cheek gently, as it was already discoloring with bruises, and looked Leah in the eyes. I urged, "We need to call the police."

Leah painfully pulled my hand from her face, and gripped it ferociously. She urged, "You have to *promise* me you will never tell anyone about this—he will kill me! And if Mom and Dad and everyone at church gets those damn pictures of me, that'll be way worse than tonight. Please, Sonia, let it be over," she breathed painfully. "If the neighbor asks, say it was some guy looking for Trail's Edge"—Buckman's one-stop shop for food, fuel, liquor, hair styling, and tanning.

"But your face and neck—you're already bruising. Someone's going to notice you've been beaten up!"

Leah smiled sadly, "That's what makeup is for, Sonia."

Feeling cowardly, I reluctantly agreed to stay silent. I commented, "He's lucky I didn't have that gun."

There's a shadow on the ground,
So the sun must still be there.
No one's lost that can't be found,
By someone, somewhere.

Jerry Riopelle

1

JON FREDERICK
10:05 P.M., THURSDAY, APRIL 13, 2017,
MINNEAPOLIS

THE ARTIFICIAL LIGHTING on the storefronts in Minneapolis couldn't distract from the eeriness of its bitter-cold darkness. The city was a ghost town tonight—cars lined a street devoid of people, and wisps of steam escaped from manhole covers, evaporating into nothingness. I turned the heat up in my car in an effort to stop the chill, but the arctic wind wouldn't be denied.

My apartment was cold, empty, and dark when I entered. I'd had this fantasy, for three months, of opening the door of my fifteenth-floor apartment to find Serena there with our daughter, Nora. When Serena walked out with Nora, the best part of me left, too. I'd become exactly what I never wanted to be—a part-time father. The last census, in 2010, was the first time fewer than half of American children were living with both their biological parents—it's dropped to forty-eight percent, and now I was contributing to that decline.

My Nora's a beautiful, curly-haired and maybe a little over-inflated, two-year-old. I think of her as my little scientist, as she's always questioning and experimenting. She's like most toddlers, with more confidence than wisdom. Nora is very active, which is enjoyable, but exhausting by the end of the day. Still, it was hard to be away from her. Her mother, Serena, is a petite, brunette beauty. Serena had been a victim of a brutal assault, and the assailant had been killed. She and I were engaged, and we both wanted to marry, but she wanted to work through her trauma, first. She was recovering, and we were planning our wedding. Then her progress suddenly eroded, and Serena took our daughter to our hometown of Pierz, and moved into a house recently built by her parents.

I'm an investigator for the Bureau of Criminal Apprehension—otherwise known as the BCA. The BCA handles all the homicide and kidnapping cases in Minnesota, similar to the manner in which the FBI handles cases that cross state lines. I work out of the St. Paul office, so the distance between us doesn't allow me to see Nora during the week, but I'm always with her on my days off. Whenever I can, I'd pick Nora up and take her to my parents (who also live in Pierz), so I don't have to waste any of my time with her in travel. It's an absolute heart-breaker for me when we're playing and she gets bumped, as she typically says, "I want Mom." I could never take her away from Serena. I just wanted more time with her.

When Serena and I were about seven years old, we were in a play together—*Babes in Toyland*—at Holy Trinity Catholic School in Pierz. It wasn't the best of times, but it still meant something to me. Serena was so adorable with those big green eyes and long dark pigtails. Her dad seemed so intimidating when he told me, "You know how all parents think their daughter is the cutest? Mine actually is." It felt like there was an unstated *so don't screw this up*, in his message. I remembered sweating bullets as I nervously forced out my lines, while Serena handled hers with graceful confidence. At the time, I never thought either of us would change. The world can be cruel to promising young women.

Serena and I were directed to lie in bed together, in our pajamas, "dreaming" while older kids acted out the play. My best friend, Clay Roberts, was first selected to play opposite her, and I was the stand-in when he skipped practices to go ice fishing with his dad. The director thought my shyness and obvious embarrassment over lying in bed with a girl played better with the audience than Clay's hamming it up did, so Clay was booted out. I never realized the level of resentment he held over this until a couple years ago. Today, Clay looked like Brad Pitt in his youthful, long-haired days; I sometimes thought he actually believed he *would* be Brad Pitt, if he had kept that part.

As if I wasn't already uncomfortable enough, halfway through our performance, Serena reached for my hand, and my mentally ill older brother, Victor, stood up and yelled, "Jon, watch out!" Victor was only eleven years old at the time, but he had the misfortune of struggling with childhood schizophrenia. At seven, having a brother who was afraid of everybody, regardless of size or sex, was embarrassing. I was already feeling humiliated over the pajamas I was wearing. My mom wouldn't let me wear the loose-fitting, comfortable pajamas Grandma Kapsner made for me. She didn't want people to think we were too poor to buy clothes. Instead, I wore long-sleeved, cotton pajamas that were too short and so tight they looked like they were painted on my body. Even though they looked new, they were obviously bought at a garage sale since, like most of our clothes, they came without tags or packaging. The Catholic in me felt tremendous guilt, at the time, over allowing this to embarrass me.

Just a couple hours ago, as I was leaving my parents' home, my mom reminded me righteously, "Your daughter has gone long enough with two unmarried parents."

My response was flat, "You should have seen that coming when you made me do that bed scene with Serena when I was a small child."

As I walked to my car, I could hear her yelling, "That's not funny!"

It was a little funny.

After I entered my apartment, I kicked my shoes off and set my phone and billfold on the kitchen table. Then I noticed my extra set of car keys sitting on the counter—someone had been in my apartment. I had no reason to take out the extra set and, when I was alone, I always left my counter clean. I quickly spun around, scanning my space, but nothing else seemed out of place. I cautiously picked up the keys and hung them back on the hook over my mailbox key.

I immediately texted Serena and asked if she had been at my apartment. I received a simple, "No," in reply. It was typical of how little she had to say to me, and it hurt. I'd become the arctic air to Serena—painful when present and nothing of concern after she shut me out.

I am six foot one, and, as they say, "wiry strong." Energized with anger over someone invading my home, I methodically searched my apartment, daring an intruder to be present. I had a solid oak bedroom door (installed by my dad who feared for my safety because of my job) that remained securely bolted, so that space had not been violated. After a walk-through, I was satisfied I was alone.

Okay, who was in my apartment?

The realization that a stranger had walked about my home was unsettling. Even though it was after ten at night, I called Jada Anderson, and she immediately offered to stop over.

Jada was a news reporter I had dated for four years before Serena, and I'd rekindled that old flame. Jada was a confident and assertive African American woman, who was friendly enough that a person felt fortunate to be in her presence. Her willingness to venture out into the bitter night simply to pacify a friend was admirable.

Jada's thick black hair was pulled into a ponytail, revealing her smooth, dark skin and swan-like neck. I hung her red, wool pea coat over the back of a kitchen chair. Jada was dressed in a scarlet cotton top with three buttons open, and dark blue jeans, which was apparently what you wear to meet an obsessive ex down on his luck. Jada's mocha-brown eyes met mine as she said, "You do remember that I returned my key three years ago."

Jada and I never lived together, but we had been close enough that I'd given her a key to my place when we were dating. I honestly wasn't certain if she had returned it, but I hadn't been sure of a lot lately. I trusted Jada.

Jada cupped her hands in front of her mouth, blowing warm air into them. Her eyes smiled as she peered about my spotless apartment, "You could have just said you were lonely." Jada didn't give me time to respond to that, thankfully. She asked, "Have you thought any more about taking on the private-eye work I offered you yesterday? She's a cute little blondie in distress. It's the

Mayers—remember years ago, we attended a posh fundraiser sponsored by Marcus and Angela Mayer?"

I dismissed the offer. "As they say, not my circus, not my monkeys." I gestured toward the countertop and said, "My extra set of keys was sitting on the counter. And the toaster's plugged in."

Jada grinned as she remembered, "And you have to *unplug* your toaster because your mom bought you one with a light on it, so it burns electricity all the time it's plugged in. And, God forbid, you waste electricity." She raised an eyebrow, then changed the subject. "Remember why we *used* to call each other late at night?"

I was momentarily jolted into silence. Amused by my awkwardness, she winked and commented, "You could at least offer me a beer. It's so cold, I thought of asking a cop to tase me, just to warm up."

As I obediently made my way to the fridge, my obsessive brain considered, *What if the intruder touched my food? Beer should be safe. It's sealed. I'll throw out all my unsealed food tomorrow.* I retrieved a cold Surly Furious, rinsed off the top of the can and poured it into a glass to make certain it was the appropriate, untampered color. Jada smiled at the ordeal I made of it as I handed the glass to her. After I closed the refrigerator door, I opened it again and grabbed another Surly for myself and repeated the process.

Jada took a sip. "Mmmm, lots of hops." She rambled on. "Work's crazy. I've got a transsexual assistant. El Epicene. Straight, thick, strawberry blonde hair, black framed glasses, talks like a woman, but seems to have an Adam's apple. Kind of like a young Woody Allen, but with a paunch."

Jada had followed me to the kitchen, and leaned a hip against the countertop next to where I was standing. She continued, "She—he?—compliments me all the time, but I'm not sure which way the door swings, so I just use 'El' as much as I can. In a pinch, though, I say 'she' or 'her,' as that seems to be the way she's leaning. It's more difficult than you'd imagine to not use pronouns, but I don't want to be disrespectful to El's choices." Jada leaned into me and teased, "So, who would break into your apartment and plug in your toaster? Any similar appliance-related crimes the BCA has you working?"

I knew it sounded stupid, but it concerned me. Jada had featured my work on a previous investigation in a WCCO news story, which highlighted how my obsession with details had helped solve the case. I carefully placed my cellphone on the kitchen table, thinking of nights spent hoping for calls from Serena that never came. Instead, I received late-night work calls that mercilessly stole my peace of mind. Nobody called an investigator late at night with good news.

Jada glided to the kitchen table, and perched elegantly on one of the wooden chairs. "So, either it's someone you know, or someone who followed my story." She stared intently at me while she mulled the situation over, then asked, "Why did you call *me*?"

"Two reasons. The first is that you're the only emotionally stable friend I have." I pulled out the chair across from her and sat down.

Jada mused, "That's a scary thought." Using one hand, Jada counted off on the manicured nails of the other, "Let's see, Tony is battling with his paraplegia, Victor is schizophrenic, and Clay is just an ass. When Serena bailed, you lost the one stable leg on your chair, and landed exactly where you're at today."

Like most guys, I had shared all of my distressing thoughts with one woman, so when Serena left, I felt abandoned—like the floor dropped out from beneath me. Getting to the second reason, I said, "Do you think the Mayers may have come here, looking to talk me into taking on the case?"

Jada set her beer down on the table. "It's possible. They were persistent. They have a lot of money, and they're used to getting their way. It could be a nice payoff for you, and if you'll work with me, it may well be the break I need to be a primary reporter in a large market. You could help me here, Jon."

I had intentionally avoided working with Jada over the last couple years, out of respect for my relationship with Serena. I took in a deep breath. Hell, with Marcus and Angela Mayer's money, they may have even paid the landlord to let them in. Waiting for Serena to return hadn't exactly been productive.

It suddenly occurred to me the Mayers could help reduce my misery. I owned some land by Pierz, in a beautiful, wooded area. I'd bought it a year ago because the price was right, and I knew I'd be able to resell it for a profit. If I built there, lived there, I'd have more time with Nora, and I'd be happier, even if I didn't have the job I desired. Maybe I could earn a down payment. I told Jada, "If you think it's a good idea, I'll do it."

Jada leaned back and, in contrast to her usual poised manner, took a large swallow of Furious, leaving a little line of foam on her upper lip. She delicately swiped her thumb over it. Her expression brightened, "Okay. Angela Mayer claims her daughter's innocent of everything but being reckless, and they'll pay a fortune to protect her." Jada placed her hand carefully on top of mine.

Even though I'd been cast aside, the touch felt like a betrayal to Serena. I momentarily tensed. Sensing my discomfort, she slowly pulled her hand back.

My heart unexpectedly sank to a dark and lonely place. To create some distance, I walked back over to the refrigerator and opened the door, pretending to be looking for something as I gathered my composure. I returned to the table and asked, "How are *you* doing?"

Jada had picked up my cellphone and was scrolling through recent calls. Embarrassed over being caught in the act, she said, "I'm sorry. It's the reporter in me. Serena's not calling, but you're waiting for her to change her mind—ruminating over everything you could have done differently." Jada set the phone down and, with one finger, slid it back across the table. She cocked her head and asked, "What are you going to do?"

"Work obsessively. Make enough money so I can build a house close to my daughter." I raised my beer in a mock toast and took a drink.

Jada responded with concern, "You're a great investigator, Jon. Don't throw that away."

"The only time I'm happy is when I'm with her . . ." I tossed back the remainder of my beer, and, mercifully, Jada let the subject rest for the time being.

Jada gave me the contact information for my prospective clients, and after a pleasant but chaste hug, I walked her out to her car. She lightly kissed my cheek, and we went our separate ways. Talking to Jada made me realize there was safeness in our poorly aligned goals. Jada and I drew lines and neither of us conceded, so we were never at risk of being consumed by one another. Serena and I were so closely aligned, we would each lose our sense of self taking care of the other. I couldn't be Serena's *friend*. How could I have a relaxing conversation with Serena, when her every mannerism tore at my heart strings?

When I'd returned to my apartment, I received a text from Serena, "Are you okay?"

I immediately thumbed in my answer, "Yes. Nothing taken."

Serena texted again, "I lost my key. I thought I'd find it, but I haven't. Sorry for not telling you. I forgot about it."

This actually brought me some relief. Maybe someone found it, and only recently discovered where the key could be used. After entering my apartment, they realized I didn't really have anything of significant value . . . *except for Serena's ring*, and that was safe behind my locked bedroom door. Maybe the intruder considered stealing my car but discovered it wasn't there. My mind churned as I tried to make sense of the intrusion.

My phone chirped with another text from Serena, "Had to know you're okay. It's best for me if we don't talk."

In hopeless resignation, I responded, "I love you."

Her response was, "I know." I heard nothing further.

Serena once was good for me. I just wanted her to be okay. It was a hard thing to say, because I missed her immensely. The Tom Petty song, "Walls," played through my brain as I lay in bed. Serena was the most gracious and tender-hearted person I knew. But waiting for months for her return, when she couldn't even commit to a conversation, weakened my resolve. Even walls fall down.

My mind drifted to lying in bed with Serena after the last time we made love. She was lying on her stomach, her beautiful, tanned body on white bed sheets, partially beneath a white comforter. Her long dark curls were flowing down her back. Her captivating green eyes seemed distant, so I'd asked, "What are you thinking?"

Serena turned into me, "I appreciate that you're so responsive to me."

I swept a dark strand from her face and sighed, "Somehow I feel the wrong kind of 'but' coming," I reached beneath the blanket and caressed her derriere.

"This is embarrassing." Serena blushed and pushed the sentence out, "You know I've needed you to be more crude in our, uh, *talk*." During foreplay, we'd spoken of our desires. We were never demeaning to each other, but it had taken harsher terms to achieve the same arousal in her more recently.

She softly asked me, "Do *you* need that?"

"No. Personally, I like it best when we don't talk at all." Although I have to admit, a twisted part of me sort of enjoyed it.

Serena closed her eyes and was silent for a moment before admitting, "It bothers me that I need that. I think I need help." Dejected, she turned away from me.

I didn't know what to say. It was painful to see her so broken. No lottery I could win could make me feel better than moments I'd had with her. I ran my hand through her hair and gave her a deep massage. She closed her eyes. I kissed her shoulder and whispered, "We're just two people who love each other, having fun. Don't read anything into it. Couples try different things . . ."

Looking back, she was turning me into a man who would be easier to leave, and, with blinders on, I followed her lead. I had minimized her misery. I should have said, "We should go to counseling together." Since she left, I'd done my research and discovered she was struggling with "eroticized rage." When victims haven't resolved past abuse, they can experience shameful arousal related to their past humiliation. I wished I would have listened with the insight I have now, but I reminded myself, *Let it go. What's done is done. Continue to learn, and be ready for the next opportunity.*

2

I F YOU ADDED TWENTY DIGITS to every number on a roulette wheel, you'd be spinning numbers from twenty to fifty-six, and have all the possibilities of April weather in Minnesota. There are days in April when the temperature will vary over thirty degrees in the same day. Last night, we were at the low end; today, we were above freezing.

I told my BCA supervisor, Maurice Strock, that someone had been in my apartment, since there was always the possibility it could be associated with my work. With his blessing, I left work to review the camera footage from my apartment. There was no hall camera by my door, but there was one by the building entry. It made me realize I had never seen most of the people who lived in my complex, and the few I recognized, I didn't know well. When I fast forwarded through recordings of people walking, I become aware of behaviors I'd rather not observe, such as how frequently people adjusted their clothing.

I had no idea who had been in my apartment or why, but nothing was taken or damaged, so I had to set that intrusion aside for the moment. I thought about replacing the key fob, but decided to do one better. I carefully carved a space into the sheetrock on the wall, directly across from my door, and installed a motion-sensitive camera behind a one-way glass mirror. My landlord wouldn't be wild about it, but I'd agree to have it patched up before I moved out. It would simply look like an ornate mirror hanging on the wall. I could access the recordings on my cell phone at any time. I wanted to catch the intruder. And I would still be safe behind my bolted bedroom door at night.

2:30 P.M., FRIDAY, APRIL 14, MINNEAPOLIS

I CONTACTED A MAN I had helped from the Rotary Club of Eden Prairie. He was eager to share Marcus and Ava Mayer's business dealings with me. He told me Marcus could be bull-headed, but Angela was always fair in her business ventures. When I contacted Angela and Marcus Mayer, they insisted on stopping at my apartment right away, suggesting the matter was urgent.

Marcus entered with the subtlety of a marching band drum major—big and loud, and used to people following his direction. He looked like a man who would never be seen in anything but the expensively tailored, dark-blue suit he had donned today. Marcus had an extraordinarily large head, and his body seemed to consume the entire doorway. He was over six feet tall, and reeked of power. In spite of his brouhaha, his carefully combed hair did not move with him, as it was securely sprayed in place. Angela Mayer was no small woman, standing nearly the same height as her husband. She strode into my home with confidence, her slacks, blouse, and cardigan all cream-colored. Even her perfectly coiffed, shoulder-length hair was a creamy shade of blonde. One would *have* to be confident, wearing all white in the slushy throes of April. In contrast to Marcus's bluster, Angela was calm and intense, and determined to finalize an agreement.

Angela was all business. "We believe our daughter was assaulted on Wednesday night, and abandoned on I-94, in freezing weather. The police aren't going to do anything, because she agreed to be blindfolded and tied up naked to the bed before the assault. She doesn't know who the assailant was, but she knows it wasn't her partner. We want you to find this horrible man. Do whatever it takes. We will compensate you."

After ten minutes of Marcus's telling me what I should do, I offered, "I have land near Pierz I'd like to build a house on. I've drawn up a house plan, but I don't have the capital to start the project. I know a great builder who happens to be available." I didn't bother to tell them Clay Roberts was available as a result of an argument with a homeowner that ended his current project. I could handle Clay—he was an old friend.

I continued, "If you start this project and deal primarily with Clay, I'll spend every free moment I have helping your daughter discover who assaulted her. No payments will go through me. While you'll initially front the building costs, I'll pay you back, minus my salary, which is $10,000 down, plus the additional compensation Angela feels appropriate for my work."

Marcus objected, "That's ridiculous. We're supposed to fund your entire house?"

I asked, "Do you know where Pierz is?"

Marcus grumbled, "No."

"It's two hours north of here in rural Minnesota, and you can build a nice house for one-third what it would cost here." A benefit of feeling like I had nothing to lose was that I really didn't care if I got this job, and that gave me great bargaining power. I explained, "I've thought about the possibilities this job could entail, and it may be I can only be paid once for it. There are ethical codes for BCA investigators. You both have serious concerns, so I have to consider the possibility the BCA may become involved. If the BCA asks me to help, I can no longer be on retainer by you. I have to put my BCA work first. To be honest with you, I'm not sure that even this offer will fly with the BCA, but I do know for now, it's good, and it would encourage me to work unrestrained. When it's resolved, I'll explain what I did and you can determine how much I still owe for the house at that time."

Angela told me, "If you start immediately, it's a deal . . ."

I HAD DRAWN UP SEVERAL HOUSE plans in my free time since Serena left. Maybe in the back of my mind I knew I'd have to start a new career to be closer to my daughter. I honestly thought it would be much more difficult for me to leave my work, but I felt strangely at peace with this decision. If Serena wasn't bringing Nora back to me, I'd go to Nora. I just had to resolve this case, first.

4:25 P.M., FRIDAY, APRIL 14, EDEN PRAIRIE

CENTURY-OLD MAPLE TREES SHADED the front yard of Angela and Marcus Mayer's multimillion-dollar rose-brick home. Mar-

16

cus and Angela sent me to their Eden Prairie home, hidden in a professionally groomed community, near the Bearpath Golf and Country Club. The neighborhood wasn't advertised. If you were wealthy, you knew about it; if you weren't, they didn't want you around.

Their twenty-one-year-old daughter, Ava, waited for me at the door in a commercially faded, green Eagles jersey, and short, red gym shorts. The moment I saw her, standing with her legs crossed at the ankles (likely because it made her legs look nice, even though it had to be quite uncomfortable), I knew she would be difficult to work with.

Ava was annoyingly cute, at a little over five feet and a hundred pounds. Her hair was short in the back, with long blonde waves in the front, reminding me of Hermey, the misfit elf who wanted to be a dentist on Rudolph the Red-Nosed Reindeer. Ava had big blue eyes, perfectly groomed dark eyebrows, and her skin had the smoothness of soft vanilla ice cream. She presented as a mopey, spoiled teenager who had just lost her best friend.

Once inside, Ava wearily sat back on a white Nella Vetrina kitchen chair, which cost more than my first car, explaining her dating strategy. "I wanted to find my very own Christian Grey— of *Fifty Shades of Grey*. You can't narrow the field down on Tinder, so I had to go to the Backpage of Craigslist. I filtered through a cornucopia of slime balls before I finally found Alan Volt."

My obsessive brain wanted to point out that a cornucopia refers to an abundance of *pleasant* items, but I let it go.

Ava looked away with a brief, wistful memory of Alan. "Alan and I sat courtside at the Timberwolves games. He drove a BMW, knew where to get the best expresso, and wore Armani suits. He had some road rage, and did a little cocaine, but he wasn't an addict. Alan didn't hesitate to spend money on me and was into some light BDSM."

I kept my thoughts to myself—*bondage, discipline, and sado-masochism—when love isn't enough.* Backpage was shut down in January of 2017, after data from Consumer Watchdog suggested ninety-nine percent of the income generated from it was from sex trafficking. Backpage wasn't popular with the younger crowd, so I had to verify, "*You* were on Backpage?"

Ava pouted. "For God's sake, I'm not a prostitute. Alan and I were both looking for a little provocative passion." She chewed the inside of her cheek and sheepishly admitted, "We didn't share much. That was part of the intrigue. We'd communicate like characters from a Jason Bourne movie—making urgent demands of each other. He emailed me Wednesday night and told me to go directly to his basement and be prepared to submit, so I did." Ava grimaced, and waved a dismissing hand at me before I could interrupt. "I know. Stupid—it was just a game."

As I watched her speak, I noticed the skin around her lips had been carefully covered with concealer. I asked, "What's going on with all the makeup around your lips?"

Ava avoided eye contact. "I'm getting to that." She swallowed hard. "I remember pulling up to the house, walking through the front door and down the steps, and that's it. When I regained consciousness, my wrists and ankles were bound to the bed, and I was naked and blindfolded. Loud techno music was playing. It was all about sensory deprivation for Alan. I was to focus completely on anticipation of touch. I couldn't see, couldn't hear. I couldn't move. Alan and I had done all this before, but before, I'd remembered all I did getting to that point. I knew something wasn't right."

Ava's eyes filmed over with tears. "I'm such an idiot. Do you have any idea how helpless it feels to be bound, spread-eagle and naked? When I came to, there was a gross angry man grunting on me. He had man boobs. It wasn't Alan. He smelled like a combination of a factory and ginger. When I yelled for help, he choked me." She shuddered and tucked her hands into her sleeves, "You should see my body. And I don't even know exactly what happened to my mouth—it's just all red and chapped, and stings like hell." She pulled her feet up on the chair and rested her forehead on her knees.

I postulated that Ava's mouth had been burned by a chemical with an anesthetic quality, like chloroform, but not chloroform. It would explain her memory loss. Chloroform didn't burn. A byproduct of ethanol had a similar effect and burned, but the closest ethanol plants were ninety miles away in Little Falls or Winthrop.

I considered. "What was the industrial smell like—oil or fiberglass, or wood?"

Ava raised her head and used the cuffs of her sweatshirt to dry her eyes. She fought back tears as she toughed out the conversation, "More like oil, covered with ginger perfume." She looked at me pleadingly, "There was nothing I could do."

I thought about the variety of auto repair garages, or tool and dye businesses around the metro area. I patiently waited for her to collect some composure before asking, "Anything else?"

She straightened and untucked her legs again, crossing one over the other as she thought over her answer. Her elevated foot began to bounce rhythmically as she sardonically spat, "He had a small dick."

I didn't know how to respond to that, so I continued my line of questioning. "What did he say to you?" Sometimes, the expressions used can help identify a rapist.

She covered her face with her sleeve-enveloped hands, recalling the trauma, her manicured nails peeking out from the cuffs. I noted some of the heavy makeup around her mouth left a smudge of putty-colored foundation on the fabric, along with black smudges of mascara. Still holding her hands against her cheeks, she went on, "He called me ignorant and obtuse. Who uses the word *obtuse*? Then he asked if I had *learned my lesson* about bondage." Her expression was caught somewhere between fear and incredulity. Barely audible, she uttered, "I told him I'd learned."

I quietly waited for her to continue.

Ava succumbed to her restless foot. She stood and padded in stocking feet over to the kitchen island, disinterestedly rearranging the bright-colored, ceramic fruits resting on a multicolored platter, likely collected during worldly travels. She gestured with what I was sure was a hundred-dollar apple, "Then he calmly gave me directions, like we were friends. He said he would free one of my hands, and I should count to two hundred before I removed my mask. He said the keys were in Alan's BMW—told me to drive it on Interstate 94 West, past the Maple Grove restaurants, park it on the side of the road, and hitchhike home. I did as I was told." She smacked the apple down hard enough to break it.

I recalled, "There was a wind chill warning on Wednesday night."

"I don't really remember the weather. I was in a haze. Mom said a very nice woman dropped me off—but I don't even remember what she looked like." Ava studied me to see how I'd respond, "My mom said there was blood on my shoes."

5:45 P.M., FRIDAY, APRIL 14, EDINA

AS WE DROVE TO ALAN VOLT'S HOME, I was bothered by the thought: *Where was Alan when all of this occurred?* After all, Ava didn't see or hear Alan the entire time. I was pleased to see a security camera underneath the eave facing both the porch and the garage. The front door was partially open and loud electronic dance music was thrumming from the basement. When no one answered the door, we followed the music into the basement. A white, fold-up table was set up on the concrete basement floor. Sexual play toys were lined up on a silver rolling tray, like a surgical procedure instrument tray. The tray's contents included what I deduced were nipple clamps, a cloth whip, a crisp black leather belt, a blue permanent marker, and two champagne glasses.

The gray mask Ava described lay on the bed, along with cushioned leather handcuffs, similar to the kind used in mental institutions to restrain unruly clients. Ava's face paled at the mere site of the empty, innocuous bed, leaving no doubt in my mind she had been assaulted there. From that point forward, a flat emptiness settled into her eyes, unnervingly similar to the ghost that haunted Serena before we parted.

Ava turned away and whispered, "There's a pair of metal handcuffs and a black permanent marker missing. Alan and I

21

drew on each other's bodies, in places where it wasn't noticeable with clothes—better than tattoos, right?" Her attempt at light-heartedness fell flat.

I did a quick walk through the rest of house, which was decorated with metal and glass furniture and Salvador Dali art. It had all of the warmth of a Chipotle restaurant. Alan's computer tower was gone, which was terribly disappointing. His security system ran entirely through the tower, rendering his state-of-the-art cameras worthless.

We retraced Ava's footsteps to the unfinished garage. Ava gasped at the reddish-brown splatter on the floor; there was little question for me that the splatter was blood. She closed her eyes for a moment and shared, "It was like this when I left. I remember, but it just didn't register until now."

"You were probably in shock." I felt badly for this trau-matized young woman, who was now standing in a blood-soiled room. I lightly touched her shoulder and guided her to where I'd been standing. "I have one more question, and then I'll get you out of here."

I bent down and pointed to a curiously unstained rectangular shape on the concrete garage floor, the size of a half sheet of paper. It had to have been removed after the blood misted the floor. I drew an outline over it and turned to Ava, "What was sitting right here?"

Ava began vigorously rubbing at the makeup stains on her cuffs, "There was a piece of paper on the floor. Without thinking, I picked it up and threw it in the garbage before I left." Ava was incredulous, "The floor's full of blood, but I had to pick up that piece of garbage?" She retrieved the note from the tin garbage can. Confused, Ava pointed toward the can, "Alan's clothes are in the garbage can. I saw them when I put the note in there, but I didn't give it any thought at the time."

I held the paper at the corners, the backside of which was smeared with blood and seeping through the page. The note read:

Alan Volt kept blaming Ava M. for allowing his denigration of an identity that I see as caring. In just this act, he used her need to submit to the altruistic care stewards of good honor give with everlasting subjective love. He had to save his guilt-less pics in a file anyone networking can now find. So it's time for all pigs needing to hurt girls to die. / Culhwch

I held the edge of the note carefully and would place it in a plastic bag when I returned to my car. The writer was educated, but either struggled with mental illness, or was trying to send a deeper message. I'd revisit this after I had returned Ava safely home.

I had Ava guide me to the location she drove Alan's car. She had pulled over on a busy stretch of Interstate 94, just north of the Maple Grove shops. She remembered pulling over by a sign that read "ST. CLOUD 47 MILES." I've seen that sign a hundred times, and it always seemed like St. Cloud couldn't be that close to the suburbs of Minneapolis. Alan's car wasn't there, so I contacted a Minnesota State Patrol officer and asked where abandoned cars were towed from this location.

I dropped Ava off at Caribou Coffee and told her to call her mother to pick her up, then called Angela to confirm she would come for her daughter. Ava didn't look well, and I didn't want to put her through what I suspected I'd find in the trunk of Alan's car, once I'd located it.

A Maple Grove police officer was waiting for me at Chase Towing. Our breath steamed in the cold air as we made our way across the tar parking lot, through the rows of cars, to Alan's gray BMW. A mist of rusty red speckled the bumper. Because of the recent warm-up in the last twenty-four hours, we were able to catch a rancid scent from the trunk. I reached through the driver's side door and popped the trunk open. Inside, Alan Volt's lifeless, naked body was frozen into the fetal position. I don't believe these were the *shades of grey* Ava had in mind. The ragged, bright red bullet hole in the side of his head looked like a busted paintball.

A series of two-inch lines were cut down the side of Alan's body. There was little blood in the cuts, suggesting Alan's heart was no longer pumping when they were made. I have an obsession with memorizing numbers, and the lines were cut in a manner similar to how a child would count off an amount, so I quickly encoded the lines as numbers into my memory.

I called Maurice Strock at the BCA and explained how Ava Mayer had come to me for help and, in the process, I'd discovered a dead body. Without serious deliberation, I made a major ethical decision. I was already retained by the Mayers, and now my supervisor had just declared me the lead investigator on this same case. In the moment, it made sense. I could work the case as an investigator, and in my off hours, work for the Mayers helping to keep Ava safe. Helping Ava with her trauma could give me better insight into alleviating Serena's pain.

Investigator Maddy Moore's midnight blue, unmarked Crown Victoria quickly cruised onto the scene and she waved me over to join her. Maddy was in her early forties and had shoulder-length brunette hair that curled up, as my dad would say, like feathers on a duck's ass, in the back. The style seemed outdated, but who was I to say? She was an avid runner, with pleasant, round, facial features. Maddy was comfortably dressed in dark, designer jeans and a deep-purple, pullover sweater.

Maddy had risen fast in the BCA, but after being caught having an affair with one of BCA administrators, she was demoted back to investigator status. He kept his status. The personal consequences became even more severe for her, as it first cost Maddy her marriage and, after a long battle, she also recently lost custody of her only child, a son, to her ex-husband. I liked Maddy, even if she always seemed to be spoiling for a fight. I just wasn't in the mindset to deal with her cantankerous nature today.

The scent of her perfume greeted me first when I opened the car door, and before my brain could filter my thoughts, I asked, "What fragrance are you wearing?"

Her first words to me were delivered with a snarl, "You and I will never have sex. We will confine our conversations to work. I'm tired of having to hint at this to every damn guy I've been around since my divorce. If you are sincerely interested in my perfume, which my guess is you aren't, it's Bvlgari."

Sufficiently chastised, I simply said, "Okay."

Maddy realized, by my deadpan response, that I wasn't coming on to her. Embarrassed, she rolled down her window to let some fresh air in. "I wasn't at work when I was contacted. And for

God's sake," she glared at me, "it's not like I'm that much older than you. If a man is fifteen years older, people think nothing of it."

Unsure how to respond, I got to the details of the case. After I told her all I knew, and we processed the scene at the impound lot, Maddy then followed me to Alan Volt's home, where we spent the rest of the evening.

Walking through Alan's house the second time gave me an insight I hadn't caught earlier. His kitchen made perfect sense to me, and almost no one's kitchen made sense in my brain. The utensils, knife block, and pans were all in one area, and the porcelain and glass in another, separating metal from breakables. Even though Alan and I had different tastes in art, music, and dating, I saw an obsessive cleanliness and order, which was familiar to me. It was disturbing to identify with murder victims this intensely, as it was a hard reminder that under different circumstances *there, but for the grace of God, go I.*

Maddy and I reconstructed the most likely scenario. The killer set the note on the garage floor and waited for Alan to return home. After he pulled into his garage, the killer shot him in the leg. Alan was likely directed to undress, was cuffed, and ordered into the trunk. The killer then shot him in the head. The killer had likely invited Ava to Alan's home, unlocked the front door, and then waited for her in the basement. It wasn't a forced entry. The home and garage had a security code, which was likely used. We dusted the security keypad for prints, but it had been wiped clean. Alan wouldn't have wiped the keypad clean.

WHEN I RETURNED TO THE OFFICE, I copied the note and placed the original in evidence. The killer was very careful not to leave prints, and actually wore a pair of Alan's shoes during the killing, then tossed them back into the garage. We had bagged the shoes for evidence, but I was not hopeful for anything useful. The killer had not been sloppy. The removal of Alan's computer tower with the security camera footage was well thought out. This killing and sexual assault was carefully planned, with a note prepared ahead of time. The killer was angry at Alan.

After I returned to my apartment, I found myself staring at the copy I'd made of the note. I booted up my laptop and typed the whole message, then parts of the message, into the Internet search bar, hoping to find some significance. None of the results were helpful. After a couple hours, my frustration saw me pounding harder and harder on my keyboard. I stood up and paced around my space, trying to expend some excess energy. As I walked, I soon realized my brain was registering my every step, counting out the steps as I moved, *one, two, three, four* . . . I stopped short and returned to the note.

I had become interested in cryptography after we studied the Zodiac Killer in a law enforcement course. Zodiac was a serial killer who killed at least five people in Northern California in the 1960s and early 1970s, and his identity was never discovered. The killer wrote the most famous cyphers—notes containing a hidden message—which he sent to newspapers in San Francisco to advertise his killing. Cyphers were also used by international spies, but spies didn't intentionally leave them lying around. It was the type of obsession I couldn't let go of. Cyphers involving numerical sequences were right up my alley. I began to wonder if that's what I was looking at.

A short cypher was difficult. I could use the rules of grammar to solve a long cypher, but, with a short one, I would be stuck trying any number of hit-and-miss attempts. I began by looking for the word "Alan" in the code, since the victim's name would be the name most likely to appear in it. I was facing a long and tedious night, just what I needed to keep my mind off Serena.

3

THE FINGERPRINTS FOUND in the basement of Alan Volt's home all belonged to either Alan or Ava Mayer. I suspected the killer had worn gloves. Maddy Moore and the BCA technology expert, Zikri Abbas, met me at Ava Mayer's home to pick up her computer and discuss our next steps. Zikri or "Zeke," as Maddy called him, was a little overweight and a bit shorter than average. He had thick, black hair and a thin but neatly trimmed goatee. His skin was almost terracotta in color. Socially anxious, Zeke spoke little, and when he did, it was in short, clipped sentences.

Ava told us she had just dragged herself out of bed. She was barefoot and wearing a PINK brand t-shirt with satin white pajama pants. Her makeup and hair were perfect, though, suggesting she was prepared for us. As we spoke in the entry way, Ava kept inching away from Maddy and into me, pushing the boundaries of personal space.

Ava's behavior didn't escape Maddy, who shot me a questioning glance.

Uncomfortable with this game, I asked Ava, "Can we take your laptop back to the BCA lab?"

She crossed her arms petulantly in a genie pose. "Why should I turn my laptop over?"

Maddy feigned curiosity and asked, "Is there something you need to hide?"

Ava's eyes flashed angrily, and her expression hardened as she met Maddy's gaze. She turned to me, and her features transformed into that of a distressed child. She sniveled, "My ex and I used to sext. It's all deleted now, but I've heard you can pull all that back up. I don't want a bunch of horny cops getting off on my personal affairs."

I replied, "That's not going to happen."

Unaffected by Ava's narcissistic hysteria, Maddy continued her line of questioning, "Are there any bondage pictures?"

"No," Ava whispered coyly, glancing at me through her lashes. We waited patiently until she finally added, "I had cuffs on in one."

I considered, "Did the metal cuffs Alan was wearing belong to you?"

Ava gave me a coquettish smirk, "Maybe."

Her efforts to flirt seriously irritated Maddy, who responded in disgust, "For God's sake Ava, Alan Volt died in those cuffs."

Ava spun toward Maddy, forcing us all to back away, shouting, "Get your skanky ass out of my home!"

Maddy shot her a death ray of a look, and pointed into Ava's face, "You and I are not done. Not by a long shot." After

Maddy and Zeke left, Ava handed me her laptop without a bone of contention.

Ava gave a victorious smirk. "She's *such* a bitch. Why can't *you* just help me?"

"Maddy's a great investigator, and she's my partner. Your disrespect of her makes my job more difficult." I considered, "Is there something you need to tell me?" When she didn't respond, I told her, "Ava, you need to talk to a therapist." I left her staring after me, her mouth slightly open in unspoken outrage.

When I left the Mayers' home, Maddy waited for me in the chilly air, still hot from her exchange with Ava. She steamed, "There was nothing in that basement that didn't belong to Alan or Ava. Something is not right with this girl and this whole scenario. This is Jodi Arias all over again."

Jodi Arias was convicted of murdering her boyfriend at his home in Mesa, Arizona, in 2008. After having sex with him, she stabbed him and shot him in the head. There were some similarities, but this wasn't a copycat murder. The problem with referencing history was that it could put a person in a mindset that wasn't accurate. History repeated itself, but never exactly the same way. I pointed out, "Ava didn't ask for what happened to her."

Zeke was your typical introverted computer geek. He was standing next to Maddy in his army green, fur-lined parka. He pointed out, "Ava agreed to be bound and blindfolded, naked, by a man she barely knew. If Alan wouldn't have been killed, I doubt there even would have been cause for an investigation. I'm not saying she wasn't assaulted. I'm just sayin'."

Maddy looked at me accusingly, "What the hell do you have going with Ava Mayer?"

I answered evenly, "I have no interest in Ava outside of this investigation. She's a pain, but painful people get assaulted every day, and it's our job to protect them." My mom would take it a step further and say it was our Christian obligation to love them.

Maddy dug into her coat pockets and pulled out a pair of brown leather gloves. As she was working them onto her icy fingers, she blew out a long, slow breath, in an effort to calm herself. I silently hoped her anger would be carried away with the tendrils of vapor being forced from her lips. She sarcastically commented to Zeke, "Maybe Ava thinks if she's cuffed to the bed, she's technically not sexually active."

I switched gears, "I have a friend I want to talk to about the lines cut into Alan's body—Tony Shileto. He's a former investigator." I didn't add that Tony was paralyzed from the waist down, confined to a wheelchair in a nursing home, after being shot on the job a couple years ago. "He's given me some good insight into cases."

Maddy appeared to have checked her hostility. "I'm familiar with Tony's case. There's always someone who has it worse, isn't there?" Maddy's gave a quick nod, and said, "I'm fine sharing this with Tony. I'll talk to Ava's ex-boyfriend. We'll connect on Monday." She began to turn away, then turned back, looking perplexed, "What do you think the lines mean?"

"The straight lines and the angled lines remind me of an ancient alphabet, but I can't remember the name of it."

"That's an interesting theory," she nodded slightly. "The series of bloody lines looked like the work of a cutter to me. Ava has the over-dramatizing personality of a self-cutter. I think when Alan set her free, Ava killed him, and then cut the hell out of him. Perhaps for the number of times she felt hurt by him."

I didn't bother to share that self-cutters were actually less likely to kill someone than the average person. I countered with, "Cutters typically don't address their anger overtly. Instead they take it out on their bodies—most often the underside of their arms. Ava has no scars on the underside of her arms that I could see."

I turned to Zeke and explained, "There was a note left on Alan Volt's floor with a hidden message." I handed Zeke the copy I'd kept and told him, "At the end of a long night, I discovered the hidden message is 'Alan is just the beginning.'"

Zeke studied it for a few seconds and frowned, "I don't see it."

His lack of interest in the cypher was atypical of an investigator. I wondered if he simply wasn't feeling well.

Maddy reached for the copy and gave it a hard look. "How did you break it?"

"I took a stab at a number of possibilities before I finally tried writing down every thirteenth letter." I pointed to the significant letters and added. "The name Culhwch isn't part of the cypher."

Alan Volt kept blaming Ava M. for **a**llowing his de**n**igration of an **i**dentity that I **s**ee as caring. In **j**ust this act he **u**sed her need to **s**ubmit to the **a**ltruistic care **s**tewards of good **h**onor give with **e**verlasting su**b**jective love. **H**e had to save his **g**uiltless pics **i**n a file anyone **n**etworking can **n**ow find. So it's **t**ime for all pigs **n**eeding to hurt **g**irls to die. / Culhwch

Maddy shook her head, "How in God's name did you know it was a cypher?"

"I wasn't sure," I said honestly. "There were a number of words in common sayings that had been replaced. People say 'stewards of good will,' not 'honor,' and the word 'subjective' is unnecessary. The murder was carefully executed, and this led me to consider that the letter was likely thought out just as carefully."

I had spoken to Tony Shileto about the name Culhwch. I explained, "Culhwch is a cousin of King Arthur in Welsh mythology. It's a tale that dates back to the eleventh century. Culhwch's mother went mad after being frightened by a herd of swine. The pigs raised Culhwch until he was a lad. His mother's madness made him determined to be chivalrous to one particular woman, Olwen. Culhwch became infatuated with Olwen, even though he'd never met her face-to-face, after being told he could never marry her. Culhwch was wise and ultimately achieved thirty-nine seemingly impossible tasks in order to marry her— tasks like taking the horns off a wild boar, which could only be achieved by first killing it. His lover, Olwen, would never have considered him as a suitor in the beginning, but ultimately refused to marry until Culhwch was considered proper by her father."

Maddy said, "And you think Alan Volt was the wild boar?"

"Possibly."

I watched Zeke amble to his car. In his hurry to get to Ava's house, he landed one tire up on the curb. It was a 2012 gray Chevy Impala, license number FPC 835. I have an obsession with numbers and items that are out of place. The plate registered in my brain as **F**oolishly **P**arked **C**hevy, and 835 is how eighth graders write "SEX" upside down on a calculator.

1:00 P.M., SATURDAY, APRIL 15, COUNTRY MANOR IN SARTELL

TONY SHILETO AND I SAT TOGETHER in the dayroom at his rehabilitation center, at a worn, vinyl-topped table—me in a formed plastic chair, and Tony in his wheelchair. Country Manor provided both nursing home care and rehabilitation for individuals with spinal cord injuries. It was a nice place, though I was a bit concerned with how living with the elderly would affect a fifty-year-old man's mental state.

Tony's salt-and-pepper black hair was freshly combed back, and he sported a couple days' growth of matching stubble. His facial features looked Italian, but he was actually Irish. Tony was dressed in a well-worn gray sweatshirt, threadbare charcoal-colored sweats and faded black, corduroy slippers. This man, in his own current shades of gray, once lived, and dressed, like an active and rugged outdoorsman. Now he was steeped in self-pity. The news of my separation from Serena further distressed him. Tony harrumphed, picking at the chipped edges of the old table, "I thought it was fate."

I remarked, "Nothing is entirely fate. Even people who believe in fate look both ways before they cross the street." Trying for humor, I added, "I still believe in love at first sight, though—so much so, I try not to look in to the eyes of homeless people." My effort was wasted as he ignored me.

Tony finally grumbled, "Aren't you a glut of unceasing wisdom?"

"Have you talked to Paula recently?" I asked him cautiously, as Tony and another BCA investigator, Paula Fineday, had once been lovers. Since his paraplegia was determined as permanent, however, Tony had refused to see her, suggesting she "move on."

Sadness cascaded over Tony, his demeanor slack as he shook his head.

I had brought an electronic tablet with a downloaded photo of the lines carved into Alan Volt's body, so I used it to quickly distract him from his melancholy. Tony's eyes flickered briefly over the lines in front of him.

llll .... ///// xx ll 1111.... ll ll .... /////

He glanced at me through hooded eyes and remonstrated, "Don't come here with some bullshit to create pretend work for me. That's not going to make me feel any better."

I ignored his reproach, "Like I have a desire to waste time with some ornery old Celt. Are you going to help me or are you too busy?" I punctuated this by gesturing toward the few elderly folks disbursed about the room, plaid blankets over their frail legs, all of whom were napping.

Tony snorted and made a valiant effort to ignore the lines. It didn't take long, though, before his shoulders straightened, pulling him out of his slouch, and his eyes seemed to brighten. He cleared his throat, and with renewed confidence said, "It's Ogham. It's an ancient Irish alphabet. Once you get a list of suspects, you may want to see who has ties to Ireland."

Admittedly, I brought this to Tony because I recognized the alphabet as old Irish, and I knew Tony was proud of, and entrenched in, his Irish ancestry. I was also desperate to help my friend. Tony needed something to pull him out of his funk.

Now fully engaged, Tony and I spent the next hour converting the lines to the letters, "S,E,R,I,A,L, new word, C,I,L,L,E,R." Tony noted my hesitancy, and said, "There's no 'K' in Ogham." Now that I knew the word, I hurriedly typed "serial killer" into the online Ogham translator, and it revealed the exact marks on Alan Volt's body. Tony and I smiled triumphantly at each other.

I tapped the search results with a closed pen and looked at Tony. "I don't think our killer necessarily has anything to do with Ireland. I think this guy just spends a lot of time on his computer."

He nodded approvingly at the revelation.

I asked, "Are you okay if I drop a bunch of home surveillance footage off for you to go through, from the victim's neighbors?

The corners of Tony's mouth curved up as he nodded begrudgingly, "Yeah, sure." He collected himself, then said gruffly, "Thanks for getting me back in the game."

I couldn't sit on this information, so I called Maddy and shared it with her. She told me she'd search the law enforcement databases for any murders that left the victims with similar lines cut into their bodies. This had possibilities, as the killing and assault were pulled off too cleanly to be our killer's first effort.

10:00 P.M., SUNDAY, APRIL 16, MINNEAPOLIS

I HAD ENJOYED A WONDERFUL DAY with Nora. I loved picking her up and kissing those pudgy cheeks. Once back at my apartment, I double-checked the camera. It was working and showed no one other than me coming in and out.

Jada Anderson sent me a text suggesting I watch the 10:00 p.m. WCCO news. I hurriedly clicked the TV on, just in time to see Ava Mayer in a crisp white, designer Balenciaga parka, being interviewed by Jada Anderson. Ava had agreed to do a brief interview alone, outside of her parents' home, and Jada's questions took advantage of Ava's histrionic nature. Ava primped and swayed to show off her expensive coat like she was on the runway of a fashion show. Her devil-red lipstick, and the manner with which she dramatically bobbed her head, gave her the look of sassy diva.

Jada had done her homework on Ava before she introduced this case to me, and knew Ava was somebody the masses would love to hate—a spoiled, rich, white girl. If Jada could antagonize some drama out of Ava, she'd have a blockbuster of a news story. Ava was too self-centered to notice she was led right into admitting she had been at Alan Volt's home on the night of his murder.

Jada asked her directly, "Did you kill Alan Volt?'"

Ava inappropriately simpered into the camera and quipped, "No!"

Jada had her teeth into this one, and was not going to let go. "But you do acknowledge that the two of you were into bondage and S and M."

It was obvious Ava wanted to talk about this, but to my relief, she kept this desire at bay by biting into her pouty bottom lip with perfectly straight teeth.

But Jada wasn't finished. "People close to the investigation have compared this case to Jodi Arias."

Maddy or Zeke had to have leaked that comment. I felt my teeth grinding together in annoyance.

The little self-control Ava harbored dissipated before my eyes. She smugly retorted, "I'm not Jodi Arias! The son of a bitch who killed Alan has a small dick, so that wouldn't be me . . ."

And, just like that, Ava had exactly what she was fishing for—an outlandish quote that was sure to be trending on Twitter.

4

Jon Frederick
5:15 p.m., Monday, April 17,
Bureau of Criminal Apprehension Office in St. Paul

ZEKE ABBAS'S REPORT WAS on my desk by the end of the day. After a search of Ava's laptop, there was no indication she'd ever accessed Ogham on the internet. Ava was invited to Alan Volt's home, "if she was willing to submit," exactly as she had reported. Zeke was able to determine that the message was sent from Alan Volt's computer. He indicated there were pictures of Ava tied to the bed, which Alan had shared with Ava. I had no desire to view them, and saw no benefit from it, so I headed to Maddy's office.

Cool and composed, Maddy Moore was sitting back in her office chair in a loose-hanging tunic in blurred greens and blues, similar to a Monet painting. I always wondered what Claude Monet's paintings would have looked like if he'd have had better glasses. I don't know that I'd ever seen Maddy in a good mood, but today she wasn't in a particularly *bad* mood. I had a feeling she had leaked the Jodi Arias comment to Jada as payback for Ava's insults. I contemplated the benefits of confronting her.

Maddy interrupted my train of thought by holding up the *St. Paul Pioneer Press.* "Did you see that crime reporter Jack Kavanaugh's article?" He had written a critical article about Jada Anderson's interview with Ava. Maddy started reading, "Was it fair to refer to the killer as a *son of a bitch*? After all, do we know the killer's mother is a dog or inconsiderate and insensitive? And as for the small-penis comment, would we, as responsible and sensitive deliverers of news, allow a comment on the breast size of a female suspect? Shouldn't we be more careful at a time when our citizens are reminded, daily, of the evils of objectification or demeaning others due to their physical attributes—or lack thereof?"

Maddy handed the paper to me. I perused the article and replied, "Jack Kavanaugh and Jada Anderson have taken shots at each other for years, but they still occasionally have a drink together." I set the paper aside.

Maddy stretched her arms up straight, then linked her fingers and settled her clasped hands at the back of her neck. She said, "Ava shows no restraint. I honestly don't believe her 'micro-shaft man' even exists. I didn't find any other murder victims with similar cuts in their bodies, by the way. We're not looking for a serial killer—just a woman who is very clever at deception. She wiped the security key pad on the door clean of prints, to leave reasonable doubt of someone else's presence."

I perched awkwardly on the edge of the chair and defended my instincts. "I saw Ava's reaction to the scene, Maddy. There is no doubt in my mind she was assaulted. If it was Ava, why wouldn't she simply say she was chloroformed, rather than burning herself with a chemical that works like chloroform?"

41

Maddy sat forward and grabbed a pen off the table top. She balanced it on the tips of her fingers, slowly rolling it as she spoke. "I don't doubt something happened she didn't consent to. But Ava's vain. I think after he took the cuffs off her, she got even. The chemical burn was her coupe de grace. It allowed her to not account for her time, and it convinced you she's a victim." She handed me a report. "The ether wasn't from an ethanol plant."

I had already seen the report. "It makes me nervous as hell to think how easily it's made. A chemical used to start cars in the winter combined with a chemical you can buy at any hardware store. We have to sit on this. I absolutely don't want this information out there."

Maddy nodded in agreement. "Do you think this guy's a mechanic?"

"I don't know—maybe. Ava did say he smelled like oil, but I took her to an automotive garage Saturday morning and she said it was more industrial. It may be this killer watches a lot of investigative television. In 1980, Robert Bruce was known as 'Ether Man' for raping women using this chemical compound. I'm afraid this guy is just getting started. He used a minimal amount this time, which allowed Ava to come back to consciousness."

I moved on to the next piece of evidence. "The bullet was from a Colt 45. Neither Alan Volt, nor the Mayers, owns a Colt 45, but there are a lot of these weapons reported as stolen."

California and Connecticut have comprehensive ballistic identification systems. They require gun manufacturers to test-fire the firearms and then store images of the ballistic markings.

They are saved in a data base, so law enforcement can later determine whether a particular gun fired a particular cartridge. Unfortunately, Minnesota doesn't have a similar data system.

Maddy scratched her scalp with the closed end of the pen. "We have no way of knowing what else was on that table, Jon. Remember, Ava took a full *day* before you were contacted. Did you feel the pressure on those nipple clamps?" She shuddered, and protectively crossed her arms over her breasts. "They must have hurt like hell! What the hell is wrong with people that they need to torture someone in order to enjoy sex?"

She probably didn't intend for me to answer, but I did. "You commented earlier that Ava shows no restraint. Is it possible, because her lack of self-control, she enjoys sex more if someone restrains her?"

Maddy apparently didn't have a similar obsessive brain, as she simply looked blankly at me.

5

EL EPICINE AND I LEANED against my car, waiting for Ava to exit from her massage appointment. During our interview yesterday, Ava let it slip that she has a reoccurring massage here on Monday nights. They gave a soothing massage at Elements, and I could've used one right then. The muscles in my neck were tight, and I had a tension headache boring into my eyes.

I told El we should try not to look so obvious tonight, so I wore a faded maroon Gophers hoodie and jeans. El, on the other hand, showed up in what appeared to be a new army camouflage uniform, complete with hat, making El the *first* person anyone would notice loitering outside a massage parlor. The uniform fit wasn't particularly flattering, either. It accented El's belly, as this was the one area it was snug.

I shared with El, "You know how I got Jon Frederick to take this case? I plugged in his toaster."

El smoothed her reddish bangs beneath the hat and looked at me like I was talking gibberish. "What?"

"We used to date, and it bugged him that I always left the toaster plugged in. So, I stopped over and, for a joke, I plugged in his toaster. He thought someone broke in, and it was somehow related to this case, so he hopped on board."

El laughed, "And you never told him otherwise. I like it." El considered, "He didn't go back and look at the apartment footage? It seems like Jon would do that."

"Oh, I'm sure he did. But I had to park behind the apartment building, and there was a young couple moving furniture through the loading bay, so instead of walking all the way around to the front, I entered there. I hadn't thought twice about it at the time." I chuckled for El's benefit, but my insides clenched at my deceit. I wish I would have just told him what I'd done. It was intended as a joke.

Jon and I had once been the toast of the Twin Cities, which I attributed to his being a handsome and compassionate factotum investigator. It didn't hurt that I was a reporter for "the most watched news station." Our work required long and unpredictable hours. We'd crash at each other's places anytime, day or night. I loved knowing there was always someone there, and I was always welcome. We only broke up because Jon wanted a family, and I had too much to accomplish before I could even consider motherhood.

Now Jon had a child, as he has always desired, and was single again. So, on a night I was feeling lonely and vulnerable, and maybe had one glass of wine too many, I wrote him a letter professing my feelings and mailed it. I realized, a day later, it was too soon. I still had his apartment key, so I went to his building to intercept the letter before he got it. I didn't even realize I'd left his extra set of car keys on the counter when I took them off the hook to get his mail key. I plugged in the toaster, with the intention of returning the apartment key fob when he called me on it.

I asked El, "Have you ever done something you wish you could take back?"

El's body jerked with a one-syllable chuckle through her nose. "Are you *kidding* me? Look at me. I do something I regret every damn day."

I lowered my tone confiding in El, even though we were alone. "I took an unopened letter from the mother of Jon's child." I didn't share that I took it out of his mailbox. If I said that part out loud, it'd make what I'd done more real.

El raised an eyebrow with interest, "What did you do with it?"

"It's in my glove box. I'm afraid if I return it, Jon will shut me out and we won't get any more information about this case. I have an in with him, because he respects me and he's single and lonesome. But I don't feel like destroying her letter, either."

El marched to my black Ford Torino and snatched the letter from the glove compartment. Before I had a chance to object, she tore it open and read the letter aloud with a contemptuous sneer that disrespected the intended message:

> *Dear Jon,*
> *People don't understand Posttraumatic Disorder. I would lie in bed at night afraid if I relaxed, someone would kill me, which left me exhausted and irritable all the time. Loving you isn't the issue, so if I don't say it, please understand. I'm just trying to function. I lie awake, trying to sleep,*

knowing sleep will only bring nightmares. When you would leave for work in the morning, I'd be so exhausted I was a disservice to our poor little Nora. I need help. I thought I was doing better, and then creepy pictures and messages started appearing on my laptop. I swore I saw flashing pictures of the man who assaulted me.

Then Mark 5:15 appeared. It's a verse that speaks of Jesus challenging evil spirits. The spirits entered a heard of swine and they ran violently into the sea where they choked to death. I got so freaked out I threw my laptop away, fearing it was possessed. It was so crazy. Now, I'm not even sure if any of it was real. I'm in therapy now, lying low, and I feel like I'm recovering.

I'm sorry, but right now I don't see myself returning in the near future. I'm not sure if it's your apartment, or your work, or… I can't even say it. I'm just so, so sorry.

Love, Serena

El callously remarked, "Sucks to be her."

I added, "Sucks to be *Jon*. I should just—" I tried to think of the right way to say this to El. Man up? Woman up? Person up? Instead, I went with, "Return it."

El took out a cigarette lighter, flicked it, and set the letter on fire. As we watched it burn, she dropped it to the dirt and ground it into ashes with too-shiny, wannabe combat boots. She spat on it, and with a theatrical bow, proclaimed, "Message deleted."

It didn't feel right, but I hadn't stopped El. I told myself a burned letter was a small price to pay for Jon getting involved in this case. The Mayers never asked for Jon. *I* was the one who convinced them Jon Frederick was the very best, and if they wanted their daughter safe, he would be the only one who could guarantee it. I needed Jon to work the case, as he would give me an exposé of the events I needed to take my career to the next level. As if I needed more justification, Jon was also obviously depressed, and I honestly believed the case would pull him out of his funk.

Ava Mayer exited Elements Massage in her beloved white parka and, after a quick glance toward El, sauntered overconfidently toward her Infrared Lexus. If Ava didn't approach us, I was just going to let her be tonight. If she was innocent, as Jon suggested, I felt badly for spotlighting her on the news.

El commented, "Ava has the trashy nymph look down to a tee, but she's like a Marvel comics gal, while you're an Emma Amos painting."

I had to smile, "I appreciate that you know who Emma Amos is, but don't make this weird."

I liked El, but I needed comments like that to stop. "I'm going to give you a lesson in boundaries, because you obviously need one. Now, if you have a romantic interest in someone, but they don't feel the same, and you want to keep working with them, you don't tell them—capisce? Trust me on that one."

I watched a familiar black Honda Accord pull up, and dryly told El, "I care for you as a friend, El, and I like working with you, but I won't if you keep making comments about how I look."

El watched me as I spoke, but I wasn't sure if any of my words were registering. Before there was any opportunity to respond, our attention was diverted to the Honda.

Jack Kavanaugh stepped out of his car and planted himself in front of Ava's driver's side door, just as she was reaching for the door handle. Jack was a tough and aggressive reporter. His nose had been broken at one time, and now rested on his face in an S shape, typically indicating poor health coverage and misguided healing. His skin was pale from long days indoors, writing for the *St. Paul Pioneer Press.* His thick, short blond hair looked like a small mat with a zigzag edge had been placed on top of his head. Even though Jack was cocky, I'd seen him go out of his way to help others. He and I often competed to be the first to cover a news story, and we'd meet with our cohorts at the Town Hall Brewery to commiserate on our efforts every couple weeks. I had no doubt in my mind he intended to steal this story out from under me.

Jack wore a royal-blue, down jacket and an all-knowing smirk as he told Ava, "I've only got a couple of questions for you." He held his hands in the air, "No recorder, no paper, no pen."

As El and I watched the exchange from across the parking lot, he pointed offhandedly in our direction with his thumb, "Not like your friends, there."

Ava glanced our way, and then, to my amusement, growled at Jack, "Get out of my way, jerk off."

Jack held up a business card as he suggested, "Call me. I've only one question—is there any possibility your attacker could have been a woman? Maybe a finger instead of a small penis? You said you didn't see the person."

Ava contemplated and then quietly told him, "He *did* have boobs."

I was shocked by Ava's response.

She looked at me and her voice increased in volume, "And he was wearing woman's perfume. I know *someone* who wears that same perfume."

Jack recaptured Ava's attention by taking her hand and folding it around his card. He repeated, *"Call me."* He then looked our way, "Maybe you're confused because it wasn't a man or a woman. Maybe it was an El." He shook with laughter at his own joke.

El made a move in his direction, yelling, "Go to hell!" I caught the canvas sleeve of the new uniform and looked hard at El. I received a look of frustration and compliance, and El stopped the charge in Jack's direction.

When Jack stepped back, Ava pulled open her car door and dropped into her seat. After she had shut the door, she held his gaze defiantly as she hit the lock buttons, then fired up the engine and tore out of the parking lot.

The three of us stood in the empty lot. With a condescending glance my way, Jack said, "You just need to ask the right questions." Jack retreated from us, by back-stepping toward his car as he told El, "I was just kidding—lighten up! You're the one who doesn't want to be defined by gender."

I called after him, "How did you know Ava would be here?"

With his arrogant grin, he retorted, "Well, I followed you, of course."

I was upset at myself for not being more careful. I wouldn't make that mistake again.

6

THIS MORNING, MAURICE STROCK demanded I report to him. Had he heard about my work for the Mayers? I couldn't afford to lose my job. I'd been sending Serena money to support my daughter out of every paycheck, and it hadn't left me much on which to survive. Still, I wasn't going to lie to him.

Maurice was a white-haired man, who was always clad in a gray suit. The drab gray was punctuated today by a royal-blue tie. He had beady eyes behind wire-framed glasses, which rested on a pointed nose, giving him possum-like features. In his grating, nasally voice, Maurice read me an article from this morning's *St. Paul Pioneer Press*. Jack Kavanaugh's front page story implied that Alan Volt's killer was female. Ava had apparently told Jack during a phone interview, last night, that she had come to associate the scent during her assault with a specific person. She insinuated that, because that person works for law enforcement, she was uncomfortable saying anything more about it to investigators.

Maurice wanted me to question Maddy Moore in the interview room, while he observed behind the mirrored glass. He wanted to know how Maddy knew where to find Alan Volt's body, when the homicide hadn't yet been called in.

When I entered the interview room, Maddy was seated in a crisp white blouse and black slacks. She was a powder keg of angry energy. Her lips thinned menacingly. "Are you kidding me?"

I carefully explained, "I didn't ask for this, Maddy."

Maddy leapt to her feet and shouted, "That crazy bitch makes an accusation, and I get called into the interview room for questioning! *I* suspect a woman of killing Alan Volt, too. I suspect Ava Mayer!" Maddy started to pace, her hands flexing and opening in rhythm with her steps.

It was all I could do not to look away when I asked, "How did you get to the scene of Alan Volt's body so quickly?"

Maddy stopped abruptly. "I received a tip." She looked at me imploringly.

I sat down and Maddy seated herself across from me. "You were on the scene before it was assigned. Who was the tip from?" I kept my expression neutral.

She softly asked, "Where are you going with this, Jon?"

Maddy looked up at the camera, then discreetly looked at me, at my note pad, then back at me, communicating a silent request. I slid my pen and tablet toward her. She wrote, *Kent*, the administrator with whom she'd had an affair. Maddy nodded toward the notepad. "He sent me an email—a murder victim had just been found at Chase Towing in Maple Grove."

"Did you ask how he would have known this?"

"No." Maddy wrote on the paper, *After his wife confronted me*, then spoke aloud, "I agreed to never talk to him again." Maddy circled Kent's name on the paper. "He has a lot of connections. I assumed an officer called him. You can find his message in my deleted emails."

I pressed, "Ava Mayer is claiming the scent she experienced during the assault was yours. She claimed she recognized it when you came to her home." I recalled Ava backing away from Maddy and into me.

Deep in thought, Maddy rubbed her eyebrows with her thumb and forefinger. She finally realized, "When you asked me about my perfume, it was because it matched the description Ava gave you about the scent."

"Yes—ginger."

Maddy closed her eyes, "Now I *really* feel stupid." She was angry, but her eyes pleaded for understanding. "She wants me off this case, Jon."

"Ava claims you were at the Town Hall Brewery, two weeks before the assault, at the same time she was there. You were all by yourself. She believes you were already stalking her back then."

Maddy glowered, but after staring daggers toward the recording devices, she clenched her jaw and held it in. She looked down, resigned. "I was at the Town Hall Brewery two weeks before Ava was assaulted, but I didn't know her at the time. I can't recall if she was there. If Ava was there, it would explain how she knew I wore Bvlgari. That was the night I found out I had lost the final custody appeal on my son. "

Bvlgari BLV wasn't rare, but it also wasn't one of the top twenty-five selling perfumes in the United States. "How much did you have to drink?"

Maddy didn't say anything, but wrote on the pad in front of me, *Too much*, and then crossed it out. Frustrated, she said, "I left the bar and was going to call a cab—I remember that. I went to my car to grab a CD my son had made for me before the cab arrived—I needed that reminder of him—and that's all I remember."

Maddy ran her fingers over her lips. She appeared lost in a memory as she added, "I woke up the next day pretty confused. And when I looked in the mirror, the skin around my mouth was all red—like I had some kind of a burn. I can't imagine where that would've come from."

She studied me, appearing to question if I believed her. "Ask your friend Jada if she saw anything. She was there that night."

This surprised me. I maintained my composure and asked, "What did you do after you left the bar?"

"I got a ride home. I picked up my car the next day."

"Who'd you get a ride from?"

Maddy wasn't pleased with my prying. She wrote on the tablet, *I don't know*. She then straightened up. "I feel like this is unjustified prying into my personal life," Maddy paused for effect and then added, "bordering on harassment."

"Maddy, I honestly don't know what this is. I'm just trying to sort it all out. Why didn't you report it?"

Frustrated, she sternly replied, "Report what? Nothing happened." Maddy stood up. "I'm done with this. I have work to do." She aggressively tore off the page she had scribbled on and walked out with it clenched in her fist.

Maurice, like most people in the office, didn't like confronting Maddy, so he told me to let it go for the time being. He commented, "Ava *did* say her rapist had breasts."

"Man-breasts," I corrected. "She also said he had a penis." It didn't make sense, but I had smelled the gingery perfume.

Maurice was frustrated. "There isn't a damn thing we can do with Ava matching a scent. You work with Maddy every day. Keep me apprised."

Maddy was going to go after Ava full-barrel now, and this was going to put us at odds.

7

JON FREDERICK

8:45 A.M., SATURDAY, APRIL 22,

MINNEAPOLIS

MARCUS AND ANGELA MAYER had followed my recommendation that Ava have bodyguards for the time being. Marcus knew of a company that provided this security. Unfortunately, Ava had been evading her guards on a daily basis, so she could go out "clubbing," which tormented her parents. Ava's parents were suffering the consequences of failing to hold her accountable—ever.

Alan Volt wasn't particularly well-liked, but we hadn't found anyone with a motive to kill him. His funeral was attended by a number of young curiosity-seeking professional men who loved to talk about themselves, but had little to say about Alan. I attended the funeral with Ava. She wore a conservative black dress and was content being in the background, which I appreciated and respected. It was a sober reminder that Ava was capable of acting like a normal, responsible adult. The worst aspects of her personality had emerged in full force after the assault.

Alan's family believed Volt's murder was the result of an attempted break-in, even though nothing was taken that belonged to Alan, other than the computer tower and a black marker.

I REQUESTED OUR FORENSIC LAB perform a VMD process on the bed sheet from Alan Volt's basement. A VMD, or Vacuum Metal Deposition, involved placing the sheet in a chamber and heating a small amount of gold—about twenty cents worth—until it turns into a gas. The same process was repeated with zinc. The gold adhered to the fingerprints, and the zinc made them visible. I was told it would be days, even weeks, before I received the results.

I collected security footage from every home in the neighborhood that could have had a camera aimed toward Alan Volt's driveway and delivered them to Tony Shileto. If Ava's story was accurate, there should be footage of two cars leaving the driveway—Alan Volt's car, with Ava driving, and the killer's. Ava's car should stay out front, where it remained until her parents picked it up the following day.

Maddy had little to say to me the last couple days, so we separately interviewed Alan Volt's neighbors and friends, as well as Ava's friends. No one had knowledge of their relationship. One neighbor had seen a gray Chevy in the driveway but wasn't certain of the exact make.

This morning, Maddy appeared at my apartment door, her expression gratified, holding up the *St. Paul Pioneer Press* newspaper. In her button-down and untucked plaid blouse and blue jeans, she appeared ready to reconcile and work with me, again.

Ava Mayer had given Jack Kavanaugh another exclusive interview. The paper published photos of the purple bruises on Ava's torso. She was quoted as saying, "Bondage is an option for adventurous couples, as long as there are rules." There was a seductive photo of Ava with her face screwed into a mock frown, shackled in handcuffs. Ava had declared that these were the very cuffs Alan wore when he had been murdered.

I called both Jack Kavanaugh and Jada Anderson and asked them to refrain from interviewing Ava further, for her safety. This killer took his name based on a character who had to possess a woman forbidden to him. If this was the case, there was likely an "Olwen" in his twisted fantasy, and I feared Ava was the killer's Olwen. Jada heard me out, but made no promises. Jack admonished me, stating, "Ava *is* the news; I'm just a messenger feeding a public that's starving for her story."

Maddy cracked wise at my frivolous efforts with the media, at least until I told her Jada might have something for us.

12:30 P.M., MAPLE GROVE

MADDY AND I MET JADA AT KHAN'S Mongolian Barbecue. Maddy had a bowl full of vegetables, Jada had beef and vegetables, and I had vegetables, shrimp, and sausage.

When we settled at our table, Maddy grimaced at my choice. "You know what they say—people who like sausage and respect the law shouldn't watch either being made." She busied herself stirring her steaming vegetables and chuckled.

I volleyed, "Where I come from, when someone says she's a vegetarian, people say, 'Maybe you should try hunting with me.'"

Maddy smoothly clipped vegetables with chopsticks suggesting, "Eating with traditional utensils offers the full experience."

I remarked, "The fork was a great improvement over the chopstick. That's why you see farmers in the field with a fork, rather than a pool cue."

Jada looked amusedly back and forth at the bickering between Maddy and me, then moved her sizzling bowl aside to cool. She quickly got to the business at hand, and reached into her black leather satchel. As she gently unfolded a piece of white paper, she said, "I received this letter in the mail at WCCO. The name 'I-94 Killer' was written in the corner of the envelope, but there was no return address below it. I kept the envelope." She carefully set the page out on the table, turning it so we could read it:

Time to educate the ignorant seekers of fantasy, through actual life experience, and with serious action. I have sat by pleading for men playing God, to probably come to understanding that 1 in of maybe only 3 million really desire being loved by someone who accept personal derision. / Culhwch

As I studied the letter, Jada pulled the envelope out of her bag and placed it next to the note. She asked, "Is this guy stark raving mad?"

My immediate thought was there are only two numbers in the code, and if he wanted them to form "13," there would need to be thirteen letters between each significant letter. As I studied the note, I asked Jada, "Did El have anything to do with your first asking me about this case?"

Jada said nothing, but cocked her signature *what the hell?* eyebrow at me. She had such an expressive face. I sometimes wondered why she bothered with words at all. Her message was, *Don't be a xenophobe.*

Ava's small-penis comment had triggered my curiosity about El, so I had done some research. Epicene obviously wasn't her birth name. The odds of a transgendered person being born with a last name that means "transgender" are astronomical. I discovered that El Epicene was born Del Elliot. El had Klinefelter syndrome, which is an XXY chromosome pattern rather than XX or XY on the twenty-third pair. Individuals experiencing Klinefelter syndrome were physically male, but they didn't develop facial hair or a masculine build unless they took hormones after puberty. El apparently opted not to. They also had the same rate of breast cancer women have, which is much higher than XY men. There was a similar syndrome called Turner syndrome, for females who only had one chromosome, the X chromosome, at the twenty-third pair. They also had to take hormones at puberty for further sexual development.

I told Jada, "I'm just ruling out possibilities."

Jada nodded her understanding.

Maddy's eyes narrowed. "The *St. Paul Pioneer Press* has had a great reputation for their writers. I know that they're only working with a skeleton crew now, but the pictures of Ava seem desperate." She stabbed her chopsticks in my direction, "And by the way, if I find out you have something going with Ava, I swear to God I'm coming after you."

With an almost imperceptible twitch of her mouth, Jada reminded me Maddy was present and I needed to avoid discussing anything that would hint toward my financial arrangement with the Mayers. I wasn't at risk of saying anything, but I did appreciate Jada's effort to protect me.

Jada made an attempt to diffuse the tension at the table. "Jon doesn't do blondes—bad experience as a teen. Ava has no boundaries." She threw me an offhand look, and added, "Kind of like your friend, Clay."

Maddy cut in, "Jon hasn't told me about Clay." She looked with interest at each of us.

Jada dismissed Maddy's curiosity with an inward groan and wave of her hand, "Don't waste your time." She turned to me, "Is it that easy to find men who tie women up?"

"Unfortunately, yes. Our cybercrimes unit reports that on B-D-S and M sites, there are four 'master' men for every submissive one, and there are four submissive women for every dominatrix."

Jada's lips compressed as she pushed her food away. "It makes my stomach roil. Part of me feels like it mocks the brutality of slavery."

I sighed heavily, appreciating her point. "I hear you, but we both know these folks aren't thinking that deeply."

Her next bite balancing precariously on chopsticks, Maddy stopped midway to her mouth. She asked, "What exactly is your type?"

Uncomfortable with our conversation, Jada stood up and squeezed my shoulder. "I should take my meal to go." She whispered in my ear, "Call me later." Jada addressed both of us with an afterthought, "Is it safe to leave you two, or should I take the utensils with me?" When neither of us responded, she picked up her bowl and went to the counter for her to-go box, then made her way out the door. She left Culhwch's note and the envelope on the table, and I carefully dropped them into a plastic bag I'd taken from my pocket. Whenever I was working a case, I kept evidence bags handy.

Maddy watched after Jada with a smirk on her face, "She still has feelings for you."

I took in a frustrated breath and gave in, "Intelligent is my type."

Maddy chided, "I told you not to hit on me." I smiled as she continued, "Like Jada?"

I chose not to respond. Eventually Maddy realized I wasn't going to give her any more. She emptied her bowl and said, "Well, I'm sure you've heard all the rumors about *me*. I'm into sleeping my way to the top. And what a catch our administrators are." She tossed her chopsticks into the empty bowl and mused, "I think Maurice Strock should be next on my list. I could live off his pension after he retires next month. Instead of the silver fox, I could call him the gray ferret." Maddy's cynicism slipped ever so slightly, and I saw a flash of pain across her eyes.

I tried to ease her mind by offering, "Sinclair Lewis once said, 'The town gossip is embarrassed that he's the only one in town with nothing to be ashamed of.'"

Maddy softened, her shoulders rounding as her guard came down. "I like that." She appeared to come to a decision and flattened her palms on the table top. "Okay—do you want to know the real story? I was married to a nice guy, and I blew it." She shrugged, "We had a child, and we became two people who loved and took care of the same child, but we forgot about us.

I'd like to say Kent initiated the affair, but honestly, I don't know. The bottom line is, I didn't stop it—so maybe I'm a little over the top with putting a stop to any suggestion of impropriety at work, now. The flirting turned into more, and Kent's wife, Chloe, finally called him out on it." She grimaced at the memory of her infidelity being discovered. "And then Chloe called our supervisor, and HR, and Craig—my husband. I'd gambled everything and lost, for nothing more than a little attention. I *loved* Craig, but he couldn't come back from the betrayal." She sighed and started smoothing her napkin in front of her.

I stayed silent, respecting that this was difficult for her.

"And then, like a storm, Craig came after our son. I won initially, but he's an attorney. He kept taking me to court, over and over, until he broke me and got custody." Maddy's posture straightened with renewed tension, and she said flippantly, "So now I hate him, and I hate his almost pubescent young wife, and the fact that I have to beg them to be able to spend a special occasion with my son. And work sucked, because I was still working with Kent, trying not to talk to him, or even *feel* for him. So finally, I asked if I could go back to being an investigator. I liked being an investigator."

I had finished eating. "You're good at it."

She smiled gratefully and nodded in agreement, "I am."

I appreciated Maddy confiding in me, so in turn, told her, "I see some of the same pain and anxiety in Ava's eyes that I saw in Serena's. I didn't realize, back then, that it was about Serena's trauma. I thought it was about me, so I kept trying harder. I didn't know how to help, and I didn't encourage her to get help. I tried not to show my frustration, but she had to sense it." I swallowed hard and then stood up and said, "I'm going to wash my hands, and then I'm good to go."

Maddy compassionately let the conversation end.

The power of a look in shaming a person is intriguing. My mother had always been a master at this. I should point out this was my issue since, more often than not, I didn't consider the full impact of my behavior until I got *that* look. Jada's piercing glance reminded me I had no evidence to suggest El Epicene was involved, in any way, with Alan's death or the assault on Ava. I *was* being a xenophobe. Transgendered individuals, like El, were more likely to be assaulted than to assault, and were far more likely to commit suicide than murder. If El was struggling with transsexualism, the statistics didn't change significantly. Transsexuals converting from female to male had higher rates of criminal convictions than their sex of origin. However, transsexuals converting from male to female (hypothesizing that El could be in this category) did not. Until I come across some specific information implicating El, I would let go of the notion of El as a suspect.

8:10 P.M., SATURDAY, APRIL 22,
OFFICE OF BUREAU OF CRIMINAL APPREHENSION, ST. PAUL

WHEN I RETURNED TO THE OFFICE Saturday night, I found Maddy in a faded black t-shirt and blue jeans that looked like they'd been fitted just for her. She was going through the information we had retrieved from Ava's computer. There we were, spending our Saturday evening working this case. I pulled out my clunky office chair, cursing at the caster that never seemed to roll, and settled at my pristinely organized desk.

Maddy leaned back and put bare feet up on her cluttered desktop, pushing a pile of binder clips aside with her heel. I registered her chipped burgundy toenail polish. She saw my glance and said with a wave of her hand, "Shut up. It's not sandal season yet."

Maddy began filling me in on her recent discoveries. "Ava's previous guy, Jacob, told me he just couldn't take the drama anymore with her. They dated for two years. Jacob left when she became obsessed with the *Fifty Shades of Grey* books. He didn't want to act out a book—he wanted a real relationship."

Maddy was fit and exuded intensity, even in casual attire. I would never say this to her, but I'd been considering how aspects of hers and Ava's lives were similar. Both had long-term lovers, followed by poor relationship choices and public humiliation. And they hated each other. I think Sigmund Freud would call this projection. The similarities got me thinking about Maddy's comment of having a slight burn on her lips after leaving the Town Hall Brewery. Could this guy be stalking a certain personality type online?

Maddy caught me looking at her and asked, "What?"

"Ava has a hell of a time keeping her mouth shut. Still, she's never made a reference to the cutting on Alan's body. She's never even questioned if there was any additional evidence on the body that would suggest she wasn't the killer." I paused for effect, "I don't think she's aware of it."

Maddy silently tapped her pen on compressed lips as she considered this. "She certainly puts on a good act."

I wanted to ask, *How do innocent people act?* but, not wanting to argue, I handed Maddy the cypher. "The message is, 'There will be thirteen dead.'"

Maddy wrinkled her forehead as she looked at the letter. "How did you come up with *that?*"

"There are thirteen letters between every significant letter." I settled beside her and cleared a space on her desktop for the note, then took the pen out of her fidgety hands. I read through the cypher aloud, and and traced over every significant letter:

Time to educate **t**he ignorant seek**e**rs of fantasy, **t**hrough actual li**f**e experience, and **w**ith serious action. I **h**ave sat by **p**leading for men **p**laying God to pro**b**ably come to un**d**erstanding that **1** in of maybe only **3** million really **d**esire being lo**v**ed by someone who **a**ccept personal **d**erision. / Culhwch

Maddy sat back, marveling. She asked, "Why thirteen?"

"I have a theory."

"Let's hear it."

"Maybe the killer *wanted* me on this case. Jada publicly announced my fascination with numbers in the last case she covered of mine. He sent the letter to Jada, because most people think Jada and I are still together."

Unable to sit still, I pushed my chair back and got to my feet. I began to pace as I continued, "This might be a stretch—stay with me, here. My first case involved the investigation of Mandy Baker's murder. Thirteen is a baker's dozen. I don't believe her murder is related, but it might be his way of challenging me."

I stopped pacing and plopped on the chair alongside her desk. "Or, it might be my own self-centeredness convincing me that the universe rotates around me. But there is one thing I am sure of." Her pen still in my hand, I held it up like the number one, "I am in dire need of a decent night's sleep. I haven't slept well for months." I sighed noisily and slouched in the wooden chair.

Maddy reached over and reclaimed her pen from my grip. She resumed tapping it against her lips, then pointed it toward me while changing the subject. "You filed a ballistic report on the bullet that killed Alan in both Connecticut and California?"

"I did." It was a long shot, but still a shot.

Maddy smiled triumphantly, "Well, you are one lucky man. The report was on my desk when we got back from Khan's. Maurice must've stopped in and left it here. The murder weapon was purchased in California by one Maria Fernandez. She brought it with her when she moved to Buckman, Minnesota, where she married Luke Hartman. The Colt 45 was stolen from their home in 2015—nothing else was taken. It had a silencer. Maria said she used it when she worked as a farm laborer. Why would someone who worked on a farm need a silencer?"

"If you're working on a family farm, the owner might request you use a silencer so the children aren't cognizant of every time you put an animal down."

Maddy's expression softened briefly as she considered this, revealing the compassion she made great efforts to keep in check. "I'm sorry for not calling you, but I thought you weren't working this afternoon." She handed me a report off her desk. "After the report came in, I drove to Buckman and met with

Maria and her daughters, Leah and Yesonia. They're both sweet girls. Leah is an absolute knockout. Her younger sister, Yesonia, is a nervous character, but overall, the Hartmans were salt of the earth, kind and humble people. "

This was a big break. We know where the killer got the gun, which is something the killer didn't realize. I felt energized, and was once again on my feet, bouncing with electricity. I paged through the report and asked, "Was anyone assaulted when the gun was taken?"

"No. The family members claimed they hadn't used it for months, so no one really knows when it disappeared . . ."

12:45 P.M., SATURDAY APRIL 22, MINNEAPOLIS

I RESTLESSLY LAY IN BED CONSIDERING exactly what we had regarding Alan Volt's murder. I finally had to grab a notebook and start writing to make sense of my swirling thoughts. I wrote furiously until sated, then reviewed my notes.

Alan's killer was:

1. An unidentified male
2. An unidentified female
3. An unidentified transgendered person
4. Ava Mayer
5. Maddy Moore

I was leaning toward number one, although it is important to note that transgendered was not a category in past studies. For example, Epicene would have been listed as male, because

El was biologically male. If this person was a serial killer, as the killer suggested, I needed to consider the following statistics:

- ☐ 94% of serial killers are male. This percentage has continued to increase since the inception of the serial killer database in 1900—when 74% of serial killers were male;
- ☐ There were four times as many male serial killers in 2010 as compared to 1900;
- ☐ There were only half as many female serial killers in 2010, as compared to 1900.

It was important to understand this wasn't the worst of times. Even though men were killing more than women, more than ever, there were seven times as many killers (both male and female) in 1980 as there were in 2010.

Another reason I believed the killer was male was that the killer *wore Alan's shoes*. Even though he tried to implicate Ava by having her drive a car with the victim in it, and implicate Maddy by using her perfume and inviting her to the site of the body, the killer *put on Alan's shoes*, a size considerably larger than either Maddy or Ava would wear.

The killer enjoyed this entire ordeal too much to be uncomfortable. I needed to find a camera from any of the neighboring homes that would suggest two cars drove away from Alan Volt's home that night. These details wormed their way into my brain in the middle of the night, and made sleep difficult.

8

FROM I-94, I CUT THROUGH CLEAR LAKE, across Highway 10, past the Thirsty Buffalo Saloon on Commercial Drive, and found my turnoff. Layla Boyd and Asher Perry have a Lifestyle modular home built on a slab just east of Clear Lake.

I guess if your last name was Boyd, you almost have to name your daughter Layla, being that Eric Clapton wrote the song, *Layla*, about George Harrison's wife, Patti Boyd. Most people don't know Clapton actually based the song on a seventh-century Arabian love story, in which a young man fell hopelessly in love with a woman named Layla—a woman he wasn't allowed to marry. Clapton eventually had Patti Boyd, as I will have Layla tonight. Layla is no Patti Boyd, or even an Ava Mayer. Her long, golden blonde hair is parted down the middle and hangs limply about her shoulders, as if she doesn't fuss with it, and her build is average. But there's a warmth in her hazel eyes and petite facial features that pull it all together to make her appealing. Layla's work shift at GLM Displays will be ending at 5:00 p.m.

Asher Perry promised to be home a little after 4:00 p.m. to make dinner. Who the hell names their kid *Asher Perry?* The name means "happy pear tree." Asher's a scrawny character with a thin face and boney nose. I type in the security code, which I've pulled out of a file on Asher's computer (containing all of their passwords), and enter the home. Same modus operandi—wait for Asher to come home, walk him to the trunk and wait for my date with Layla. Asher ties Layla with a standard three-eighths-inch braided, nylon rope. I wonder what the folks at Brigg's Lake True Value would say if they knew that bookworm Asher was purchasing the nylon rope for kinky sex. Sometimes I wonder if I should kill someone in the act of bondage sex to deliver a message. I don't kill women, though. I could tie Asher to the bed when he gets home, put a bag over his head and suffocate him. When Layla comes home I could ether her, and lay her in bed with him. In 2008, Rebecca Bargy was charged with Reckless Homicide after killing her husband accidently during bondage sex, so there is precedent for this. But, stick to the plan. It worked perfect with Ava Mayer. I want the same experience with Layla.

I wander about the kitchen, not sure what I think about the combination of chestnut brown cupboards and a white-washed Elm floor. I open the cupboard to find basic white Corelle ware. I hear a labored breath only a few feet behind me. *Shit!* I have allowed myself to get too relaxed.

When I turn around, Asher Harper is standing there in a white robe, his eyes vacant. Without thinking twice, I pull the gun from the back of my jeans and fire. I didn't intend to, but I manage to hit the middle of his book-spine of a forehead, dead to rights. Asher drops like a tipped milk can and lies there on the

Elm floor, white trash on white wash, with one leg unnaturally crossed over the other.

Asher hadn't made a sound. I was waiting to hear him pull in the driveway. "What the hell, Asher?"

The way he had been struggling to focus on me, Asher had to be under the influence of something. I rush into the bedroom and there's an open bottle of Oxy—the prescription made to Gustov Boyd, date of birth, 07/21/1934. I return to the lifeless body on the kitchen floor with no plan. I don't like looking at dead bodies, so I place a dishtowel over his face.

Okay, I just have to wait until Layla comes home, have my fun, and then I'll drag Asher's body out when it's dark. Fortunately, the combination of the noise suppressor on my gun and the rural location of this home made the gunshot unremarkable. I think a man deserves an explanation first, but he didn't really give me that option. At least he didn't suffer.

I got shot in second grade, and it hurt like a son of a bitch. I wasn't the intended target. Mom and I lived in a crime-ridden area of St. Paul called "Frogtown" at the time. I was on my way home from school when I heard gunshots, and then it felt like a red hot rebar rod was pushed through my shoulder. When I came to consciousness, my mom was holding me in the back seat of a car while one of her psychopath boyfriends was racing us to the hospital. As cruel as mom's partners were, they were cool in a crisis. Looking back, they lived in crisis all the time, so it likely didn't cause them much anxiety. As a result of the injury, I was never able to play high school sports.

I get out the black marker I took from Alan Volt's home to make lines on Asher's torso. I had cut on Alan's body, but after seeing the marker, I liked the idea of drawing on a body better. I don't like messes, and prefer not to touch dead bodies. I had committed to cutting when I arrived at Alan's home, and I don't like to change a plan on location. Deviating from a carefully calculated plan can result in unforeseen errors. After thorough deliberation, I write on Asher's body as planned: 111.111 11111…../////

Where the hell are you, Layla? It's after 5:00 p.m. I need to find Asher's phone and text her. I carefully pat his lifeless body and locate it in his bathrobe pocket.

I text: "Layla, where are you?"

She texts back: "Where do you think? I told you I'm not coming home until you can pass a drug test in front of me. You stole my grandpa's Oxy, you shit. I know it was you."

Son of a bitch! There was no indication of this online. *Okay, how do I get her here?*

I text: "I'm done. It's too late to get into treatment today, but I promise to on Monday. Let's get the ropes out. If you're willing to submit, this will be the best ever." That worked with Ava.

Layla responds: "I'm done with the games. I want a real relationship with a man who's emotionally present."

That's good. But if I can manipulate Layla to come here, she still deserves a hard lesson.

I text: "If you don't come, I'll kill myself."

The threat of suicide would always get my mom to come back. I picture Layla sitting in her car, parked on the side of the road, tears streaming down, tormented over her decision. I remember sitting next to my mom saying, "Don't go back," but she always did.

Layla texts back: "Serious? Please wait."

I don't respond. I don't have to. She's coming. But just in case, I prepare for the worst-case scenario. I bend down and place my gun in Asher's hand and fire a shot into the ceiling. Now Asher has gun residue on his hand. If Layla doesn't show, I'll have to leave my gun, but it's worth it to rid the world of one more slime ball. I begin working on a suicide note.

Maybe someday, had I had the bloody courage to address my demons, you wouldn't deal with this mess. I'm sorry. I would kill myself to set you free love, from my life as I act it. Every childish thing was so painful. It is evident now, had Asher been very committed to acceptance of his unfortunate costly obsession, associated wastefully with drinking, opiates, one night abstinances and sin. Is death better?
Asher

I look at the clock. Over an hour has elapsed and she's still not here.

I text: "Please come now. I fired a shot into the ceiling. The next one will go into my head."

Layla: "Where did you get the gun?"

I respond: "Stole it. Years ago."

Layla: "I'll be right there."

I have to smile over how well I am handling this. I remove the tower from Asher's computer, and place it on the bottom rack of their dishwasher. I then find Asher's iPad and put it on the top rack. I go to Asher and remove the now blood-soaked dishtowel from his face and toss it there as well. I find an unopened gallon of bleach in the laundry room and empty it over the electronics and towel.

I select the heavy duty load, hot, with presoak, and start the machine. When Layla sees Asher's hard drive is destroyed, she'll assume he simply didn't want her to know how frequently he was accessing porn. As I start the wash, I laugh aloud, "Good luck trying to retrace my access to his computer now!"

My dad would be proud—except for the fact that I'm getting rid of slime balls like him. Actually, come to think of it, he'd be proud of that, too—slime balls don't like other slime balls. I find Asher's bondage ropes in a plastic container under the bed and tie them to the posts so they're ready for use when Layla arrives. When I glance out the window, I see a car kicking up dust on the gravel road, and I can't contain my grin—until I realize it's not Layla. It's a squad car. I burst out the back door and sprint to the woods behind Layla's home. Fortunately, the house is between me and the approaching car, so my exit can't be seen.

Aided by shadows from the setting sun, I pass unnoticed through the thick brush. I'm able to see back to the house as I journey toward my hidden car. The police officer now exits the home, and hurries back to his squad car . . . a red Toyota Camry is dusting up the gravel road toward the home. That has to be Layla. Asher's being addressed as a suicide. I'm relieved, but not completely satisfied. I'm not sure why. The goal is to eliminate slime balls and give women a lesson that will make them abandon abusive men. Layla made the right choice. I handled the situation perfectly. I should be happy.

Jon Frederick
9:00 a.m., Monday, April 24, St. Paul

O N Monday morning, I finally received some good news for Ava. There was a male's DNA on the mattress that did not belong to Alan Volt. A search was conducted through CODIS (Combined DNA Index System) to see if this man had previously been incarcerated, but no match was found. CODIS is a national DNA system where you can compare DNA at a crime scene to the DNA of individuals who have been arrested for felonies across the United States. The problem with the system is that some states were months behind in storing data, and some crimes didn't warrant DNA testing.

Maurice Strock warned me the DNA might be unrelated, as it could have come from another male who had simply been in the bed a different time. But Alan Volt was obsessive like me, and I would have washed the bedding after a friend stayed over. I needed to find a way to utilize this evidence.

Tony Shileto managed to find security camera footage that showed the headlights of two cars pulling out of Alan Volt's driveway the night he was killed, which supported Ava's story. Unfortunately, it was dark, and the footage was from so far away it gave no information as to the type of vehicle. Still, it was good news. Tony had now taken on the task of reviewing all of the neighborhood tapes to see if he could find me a gray Chevy.

4:45 p.m., Monday, April 24, Minneapolis

Maddy asked if I would hit baseballs with her son, Miles, after work, at an indoor batting cage in Minneapolis called Game

Changers. Her ex had asked if Miles could stay with her tonight, as he and his new wife were celebrating their six-month anniversary. Maddy wasn't feeling well but was afraid if she declined, he would look to someone else to take Miles when the need arose.

Miles was a typical, awkward and thin eleven-year-old boy—but not a bad baseball player. He just needed to turn his hips when he struck the ball so he could drive it with power. After a couple hours of hitting, we picked Maddy up and the three of us stopped at Cecil's Deli in St. Paul to enjoy a bowl of hearty chicken soup, with perfectly textured dumplings—not too dense, but not too fluffy. After observing Maddy's red nose, the waitress proclaimed their chicken soup had healing qualities and stated with a wink, "It's Jewish penicillin."

It was a balmy sixty-five degrees, which was warm for April in Minnesota. After we returned to Maddy's house, Miles and I sat on the back steps in our jackets, enjoying a glass of lemonade. Maddy was inside taking care of some of her household chores. We lamented the pitching woes of the Minnesota Twins and watched the steady drops of melted snow run off the rooftop.

Miles was clean cut. He had short, dark hair and an innocent smile. He looked like he was wrestling with an internal battle, and finally asked hesitantly, "Have you ever liked boys? I mean, *liked*-liked them?"

I looked back toward the house, hoping Maddy was about to come out. When she didn't, I suggested, "Maybe this is something you should talk to your parents about."

"I asked my stepmom about a month ago, and she said I should ask my dad.'"

"Did you?"

Embarrassed, Miles said, "No. Did you ever talk to *your* dad about that stuff?"

"No," I chuckled softly. "I always felt I was on the verge of getting an ass kicking."

I turned to him, "When you're eleven, there's a big difference between what you think and reality."

Miles nodded with some understanding, then began to retie his already tied shoe laces. He asked again, "So did you like boys?" He was not looking at me, but his shoulders tensed, waiting for my response.

I carefully considered this and decided to be honest, "I don't remember. Some guys are attracted to girls, some are attracted to guys, some are attracted to both, and some aren't attracted to either. You know who I feel sorry for?"

Miles looked up in interest, "Who?"

"The ones who aren't attracted to either. Falling in love has made me more miserable than I ever imagined being. But I wouldn't wish those experiences away for anything. It doesn't make any difference who you're attracted to, you'll get teased in junior high regardless. Everybody goes through it."

He gave that some thought, but wasn't entirely satisfied. "So, when did you know?"

I had to think about that—it was a tough question. Finally, I said, "When I was twelve, I had this fantasy of saving this girl, who was four years older than me. When I realized all of my rescues of her involved part of her clothing being torn off, I knew the direction I was headed."

"So were you ever with her?" He looked at me expectantly.

"No. After a few months I never even thought of her again—until just now." I smiled and bumped his shoulder gently with mine. "That's the wonderful part about adolescence. When you get older, you'll forget about most of the stupid, embarrassing thoughts you once had. I call it moving on; a. A psychologist might call it repression."

I was relieved that his questions appeared to be answered, for now. I pointed out that Sam Bradford, last year's starting quarterback for the Vikings, was of the Cherokee Nation, and we moved on to talking about how the Vikings might have the best defense in the NFL.

Maddy called Miles in to answer a phone call from his father. When I told Maddy of our conversation, she scolded me, "You should have let his dad handle it. This is probably going to cost me some visitation."

I answered evenly, "I just wanted him to know that confusion is normal, and that it'll be clear in a couple years."

Maddy obviously wasn't feeling well and frantically blurted, "I don't want his dad mad at me. I can't give up any more time with Miles." She ran a tired hand through her hair. "I liked it better when kids didn't have a choice about who they were attracted to."

I pointed out, "They still don't."

This conversation heightened my awareness that I didn't belong there. I offered to leave, and Maddy agreed it was best.

A SOFT KNOCK ON THE DOOR brought me to my apartment door in gym shorts and a t-shirt. Jada Anderson was waiting in a flowered blouse and jeans, holding a six-pack of 805 Beer.

I invited her in, and she handed me the beer, explaining, "I had a friend driving back from Morrow Bay. He even purchased it at the brewery in Paso Robles."

I removed two bottles and poured them into pint glasses. My favorite beer, 805 Beer, could only be purchased in California until recently, as Nevada and Texas were now added to the list. It was named after an area code in California famous for lowrider cars and parties along the ocean shore. It was illegal even to ship it to Minnesota. I enjoy the flavor of this smooth lager.

Jada and I retreated to the beige couch in my living room with our glasses and discussed the Alan Volt homicide. I told her, "We have a killer and a victim who both love attention, but while Ava's putting it all out there, the killer remains dormant."

Jada suggested, "Maybe Ava and your killer are the same person."

I sat back, "I don't think so. I also don't believe it was our killer's first effort. It went too smoothly—as if he'd previously had the opportunity to consider all of the risks. I think there may be at least one unreported attempt, but no one's going to come forward with this information if we keep pointing the finger at Ava."

Jada smiled, "I hate to say this Jon, but right now Ava's a better story than your killer. The BCA is sitting too tightly on the evidence. Ava is all we have to talk about."

I savored a swallow of 805 and told her, "I'm going to find this killer—not maybe. It's simply a matter of time."

Intrigued, Jada raised an eyebrow. "How can you be so sure?"

"I developed an algorithm that could change the way homicides are investigated. But I'm not ready for you to put this on the news."

Jada hummed, "You know how to tease me." When I didn't respond, she asked, "Do you trust me?"

"Yes, I do. You've never let me down."

"Then tell me. I promise I'll keep it as your mother would say, 'Sub rosa,' or I'd say, 'in strict confidence,' for now."

"We have a man's DNA, other than Alan's, on the bedsheet."

Jumping ahead, Jada said with excitement, "And you have a match on CODIS."

"No. As a matter of fact, my boss is arguing this DNA could have been from a previous encounter on that bed. But Alan was obsessive like me, and I think he would've washed the bedding."

"I give up," Jada sighed. "How do you solve it?"

"I ask people in the community to volunteer DNA samples, to be used to help clarify the genetic profile of the killer. The original sample helped clarify some ethnic characteristics. My next step is to go to the ethnic group identified, and get samples again."

Jada argued, "The killer will never volunteer his sample."

"He doesn't have to. With each round, I get closer to his relatives, and reduce the number of possible suspects. It may take me a year, but I'll get him. Hopefully, I'll solve this through other means, first."

"Who's paying for all of the DNA testing?"

"I ran it by my supervisor, and the BCA won't strain our budget for it at this time. So, I presented it to Marcus Mayer, pointing out we could do it through a private lab if he'll fund it. He's considering it."

Jada raised her hand and pointed an elegant finger at herself, "Well, I get the scoop if he does."

After a large swallow of beer, I said, "That's all I have."

Jada got up and shut off the living room light, leaving the room only illuminated by street lights shining up through my fifteenth-floor window. She returned and sat cross legged on the couch with her back to me. She asked, "Would you mind giving me a neck and shoulder rub like you used to? I have a headache I haven't been able to shake all day."

As I rubbed, I could feel the tension in her muscles loosen, and she undid a couple buttons on her blouse to bare her shoulders.

Jada elicited a warm pleasant purr, and turned into me and kissed me.

I reciprocated, and then pulled away. Whenever I'm faced with a dilemma, I try to sort out what I want from what is right. I wanted Jada. She was beautiful and compassionate. But this was a decision I should make in daylight, and now that I had a child, I needed to be damn sure about it. I told Jada we needed to call it a night.

10

I loved Serena Bell, but felt like I was falling apart and at risk for making choices I'd regret. I was tired all the time. I needed some feedback from Serena, whether she liked it or not.

I called her, and was pleasantly surprised when she answered. After our initial greetings, I told her, "I'm not doing well. I know this isn't your problem, but I haven't gotten a decent night's sleep since you left. I'd be grateful if you would sleep with me. I'm not talking about sex—just sleep next to me. I feel if I could get a solid night's sleep, I could make the decisions I need to make about my life with a clear head."

Serena asked, "Are you talking about your personal life or your work life?"

"Both."

There was a pregnant pause before Serena asked, "Would you want to make love?"

"It isn't why I called but," I honestly admitted, "yes, I suppose I would."

Serena laughed, "It does seem foolish for the two of us to sleep together and not do the one thing we always did well together."

I should have made this phone call months ago. "Okay, when?"

Serena assented with an "Mmm—how about tonight—under conditions. You need to get a hotel room. I'm not moving back. You need to understand this is just one night. And we will confine our conversations to making love or Nora."

I smiled, "I can do that. Any particular hotel?"

Serena suggested, "If we go to the Radisson Blu, I could shop at the Mall of America tomorrow morning before I head back."

"Radisson Blu it is . . ."

11

I SAT OUTSIDE JON FREDERICK'S APARTMENT, vacillating on whether to pay him a visit. It would be nice to start over with a clean slate. Yesterday, after Jon left, I spoke to Miles about their conversation. I was not sure I would have handled it better. Jon was conflicted, but kind, and he had always been respectful to me. He tried to mask his deep sadness with an obsession over his work, but his expressive blue eyes sold him out every time. Watching Jon joke around with my son gave me a new appreciation of him. Despite his flaws, he loved to make people smile.

Jon suddenly walked out of his apartment building, dressed in crisp burgundy dress shirt and black jeans—interesting attire for a man who claimed to be living like a cleric. *Where's he going?* I decided to trail him at a distance, and surreptitiously followed him into the Radisson Blu Hotel. *If he is meeting Ava Mayer, I will personally kick his ass.*

From behind an ornate pillar, I watched him meet a radiant beauty in a simple, straight black dress. She had long dark, naturally curly hair, tanned skin, and that smile? A smile so contagious, I had to smile—before I realized what he was doing. How does a man go from single one day to having a woman throw herself at him? Jon specifically said yesterday he had no current dating interests. I took a deep breath in an effort to calm myself. A side effect of being a vice investigator was expecting the worst in people. I just had a sense that Marcus Mayer had made some sort of deal with Jon, and I was tortured with the thought that Marcus might have set Jon up with a high-priced hooker.

The investigator in me had to see how this was going to play out, so I went to the desk clerk, flashed my badge, and got his room number.

12

JON FREDERICK
8:00 A.M., WEDNESDAY, APRIL 26,
BUREAU OF CRIMINAL APPREHENSION, ST. PAUL

I STOOD IN THE HALL, READING the results of the VMD test. The testing showed that the only fingerprints on the bedsheet were from Alan Volt and Ava Mayer. When I called Ava about this, she claimed she had forgotten to mention that it felt like the killer was, as I suspected, wearing thin gloves.

Whenever I had a free minute, I continued to check in on Ava to make sure she was safe. Her public advocating of bondage in the paper had me worried our killer would return.

With righteous indignation, Maddy Moore marched right at me, dug her fingernails into my bicep and roughly pulled me into her office. She closed the door behind me. "I followed you last night. I saw the woman you met at Radisson Blu. She's certainly not the type of escort you could afford on your salary. So *that's* the deal you made with Marcus Mayer?"

Incredulous, I stepped back, "Are you out of your mind?" I had no desire to explain my personal life to her.

She gripped my arm tight, demanding, "Answer the question."

"Back off." I jerked my arm free. "First of all, would you go out with anyone Marcus Mayer set up for you? Second, they don't make a wetsuit thick enough for me to sleep with a hooker, no matter how much she costs. As my dad would say, 'Hookers are like manhole covers. All the slime that runs about the city eventually runs into them.' I called a friend because I have a hard time falling asleep at night alone, and I desperately needed sleep."

Maddy's jaw dropped, and she mockingly shook her head back and forth, "Wow, that's a pretty smooth story. I got your room number from the clerk and stood outside the door for a bit. What you asked her to do can't be taken out of context."

I decided not to respond for the moment.

"I pity what that poor young woman had to endure for you."

She was trying to goad me into talking about it, but I wasn't giving in. "You're a hypocrite."

Maddy defensively questioned, "Because I had an affair with a man I thought I loved?"

"Stop." I interrupted. "I've never brought that up once, and you keep throwing it out there like you deserve a purple heart for it. I have never engaged in nonconsensual contact with a partner. I know because I make it clear. You obviously didn't hear our entire conversation. Let's leave it at that."

I was about to exit her office when she had the audacity to add, "I can only imagine what you did with all the lotion."

I grimaced and rubbed my eyes. I had asked room service to send up some extra bottles of lotion. "This isn't any of your damn business, but to set your mind at ease, I massaged her feet."

She sat back and said sourly, "So you have a foot fetish."

For God's sake, will she never shut up? I'm the one who should be angry. "No. I massaged her feet as a symbol of respect. It was a common practice in biblical times, and she greatly appreciated the warm lotion massage." I wanted Maddy to believe in me. She was my partner, and my life would eventually be in her hands. So, I decided to be more specific, since investigators needed details to be convinced. "For future reference, you only have to heat the lotion for seconds in a microwave before it's hot. After I was done with her feet, I massaged her legs and ran hot water over a towel and laid it across her legs. I scratched her back, then rubbed her muscles smooth with the hot lotion. When I was finished, I laid hot towels across her back. I removed them when they cooled, and dried her off. There, are you happy?"

Maddy mouthed *Wow*, but still prodded, "If you're not ashamed, how come you won't tell me who it was?"

"Because it's none of your damn business." I turned to leave, but then stopped and considered the stupidity of maintaining this argument. I needed to work with Maddy, so the best move would be to make a concession. I turned back, "If you must know, it was Serena—my daughter's mother."

Maddy blushed red, "Wha—I am so sorry. I didn't even consider—I mean, just two days ago, you said she wasn't talking to you."

"We spoke yesterday and agreed to meet. She does help me sleep at night."

Maddy said, "I imagine." She chuckled, "That was a good argument that you'd never go out with someone Marcus Mayer set you up with. It would be like having Donald Trump for a pimp."

She tried to imitate Trump's voice, "She's the best—ever! She's fantastic! Tremendous!"

I smiled in spite of myself.

In apparent surrender, she momentarily put her hand on my shoulder, "I am sorry, Jon. I came to your house to apologize for being a jerk and instead doubled down with my stupidity. So are you and Serena back together?"

"No. Before I left, she told me, 'I hope you understand that this doesn't change anything.' So, I guess it was just a mission of mercy."

Trying to be positive, Maddy suggested, "It's better than where you were a week ago. And Serena's a damn fool to walk away. If you ever need to practice rubbing feet, I'm here. I'm not the most pleasant to talk to, so I promise to shut up when you rub."

I appreciated her concession, so I told her, "I'll keep that in mind. I'm going to talk to Tony Shileto," and was about to exit once again when she stopped me.

"Hey, I know you don't owe me any favors, but there's a police officer in Clear Lake who asked to speak to an investigator on the Alan Volt homicide. He said it wasn't urgent—he's dealing with a suicide of a drug addict and wanted to clear up a typo in a report. I've been putting it off, but I thought as long as you're headed that way, would you mind talking to him?"

I reluctantly took the note and said, "I'll stop in and talk to him on my way back."

I drove to Country Manor to see if Tony had anything for me. He was still in bed and unshaven when I arrived. He barely gave me a second glance when I entered. I asked, "Are you not feeling well?"

Tony angrily snatched a notebook off his nightstand. "You know I've tried to avoid talking to Paula since *this*," he waved the notebook over his useless legs. "But I broke down and called her. I had every plate run, and I don't think it's going to give you a damn thing! I took pictures of each car on my phone." His sigh was laden with frustration at his impotence. "It's just a monumental waste of time."

"Can I see the pictures?"

He handed me the phone, and I began scrolling through the pictures. I saw pictures of a couple partial plate numbers, as well. I knew Tony was not one to be placated, so I was careful not to make eye contact as I scrolled through his work. I wasn't sure I could contain the sincere pity I was feeling for my friend. I had offered this work to give him a sense of purpose, not considering the depression that would ensue if he found nothing useful.

I told him, "Thank you for doing this. I've got another way to go at this, so don't lose heart." Suddenly, I stopped at a photo that caught half of the back end of a car. It was blurry, but I could make out almost half the plate.

I showed it to Tony and said, "You wrote 3-3-5, but we only caught half of the first number. Could that be 8-3-5?"

Tony shrugged dejectedly, "Could be."

I dropped next to him on his rumpled bedding and pointed to the picture. "You see that circular tail light? Just like a Corvette. I always wanted to own a Corvette when I was younger. Instead, I'm driving a four-door Taurus with a car seat in the back."

Tony gave the photo a second glance and said, "That's not a Corvette."

I tapped the picture excitedly, "Chevy Impalas have *the same tail lights*. I know this car. Would you say it's gray?"

Tony had now taken interest, "It's hard to say when the picture's in black and white. Maybe."

"Zikri Abbas, our BCA tech wizard, drives a gray Impala, license number FPC 835."

Tony looked at me, fully engaged, "I'd ask why the hell you remembered that, but I know about your thing with numbers."

I remembered Zeke's car up on the curb, as well as his lack of interest in the cypher. "Zeke doesn't live near Edina, but a lot of people go out to bars and restaurants in that area." Arguing with myself, I added, "Still, we know this killer's a computer hacker, and he seems to know something about investigations."

Tony was in. A corner of his lip twitched in semblance of a grin as he said, "Tell me about your other angle."

I revealed, "We have DNA from the bed where Ava Mayer was assaulted."

Tony interrupted, "But it has no match in CODIS."

I conceded, "True, but investigators aren't the only ones evaluating DNA these days."

I didn't want to share my elaborate plan of sifting down the DNA possibilities at this time, because I'd have to share that I'd been paid by the Mayers. Only Jada, the Mayers, and I knew that, and it was best to keep it that way for now. I had also implemented a back-up plan, just in case the Mayers wouldn't fund the DNA testing, so I shared, "I sent a copy of the DNA paper profile report, as if it were my DNA, to Ancestry-dot-com, so they can track down my relatives. They locate relatives based solely on the DNA you give them."

Tony smiled, "And once they send you a list of the relatives they have on file, I could go on Facebook with every name until we can narrow it down to our guy. This is good! But is it even legal?"

"It is in New York, but not in California. This may prove to be a test case for Minnesota. Once we have a better idea of who he is, we can use a variety of ways to prosecute him."

AFTER MY MEETING WITH TONY, I drove to Clear Lake to meet with the police officer, Dale Taylor, at the brick city hall building in Clear Lake. Like most small towns, there was no official police station. People who were arrested in this area were brought to the Sherburne County Jail in Elk River. Dale was a former farm boy like me. He was clean cut with Bobby Flay-like short, red hair. He sat in his dark-blue uniform across the fold-up table from me on an aluminum chair, telling me about the suicide of young man, Asher Perry, last weekend. Asher had struggled with abusing pain killers ever since he suffered a back injury two years earlier. He had threatened suicide one week ago, after his partner, Layla Boyd, had left him to stay with her parents until he committed to getting clean.

I wasn't sure what this had to do with our case, until Dale commented, "Layla kept asking where he got the gun. He had told her he stole the Colt 45 *years ago*. It seemed sort of irrelevant. I knew Asher fired the gun—there was gun residue on his hand, and the Colt 45 was still in his hand. I ran the serial number, and it's got to just be a typo in the report we received, but it matches a gun you were looking for in the Volt homicide. Asher Perry's suicide is an open and shut case, so I'm sure it's a mistake. I called to straighten this out so I can finish my paperwork and close this case."

Now he had my attention. I requested to see the gun and then called our office to confirm the serial number. Once I had the confirmation, Dale opened up a manila folder that contained Asher and Layla's shared texts, along with pictures from the crime scene. The comment that Asher had stolen the gun years ago also interested me. *Had our killer committed suicide?*

As I reviewed a photocopy of their texts, I questioned, "He made a comment about her submitting in the text. Were there any bondage-like items found in the bedroom?"

Dale's gaze dropped to his hands, and he picked dirt from his fingernails as he told me, "No, there's nothing like that."

He looked troubled. I asked, "What's on your mind?"

Dale leaned forward, his rugged facial features etched with concern. "Layla and Asher had been together for almost a decade. Layla's a sweetheart and has recently had sort of a love/hate relationship with Asher. Despite Asher's addiction, she didn't tell anyone she'd left him. She thought they'd work it out. If this is the gun from the Volt homicide, why would Asher steal a gun two years ago from a house in Buckman? Asher was doing fine. He and Layla were close back then—as loving a couple as you'd find anywhere."

A sadness overcame the young officer, and it was clear he struggled with the suicide. Dale said, "I know young men are impulsive with their suicides, and we never get all the answers. But I wish I had something to tell his family. I just hate to see families in so much pain when I have no answers to give, other than drug abuse."

I reassured him, "Sometimes that is the only answer."

As I paged through the folder, I found myself glancing back and forth between the picture of Asher Perry's body on the wood floor and the cartridge residue testing report. If Asher had placed the gun against his forehead, there would be a burn on his skin, and there wasn't. There was no gun residue, at all, on Asher's forehead. A shot fired at close range leaves powder residue. This suggested the gun had to have been fired from more than three feet away. Asher was only five-foot-six—his arms weren't three feet long.

Perplexed, Dale pointed to a picture on the bottom of the pile. "I thought this was a tattoo, but after I looked closer, I think he drew it on himself with a marker."

I pulled out a picture of Asher's bare torso. It had the following lines:

| | |.| | | | | | | |…..// / / /

A chill ran down my spine. Our killer wasn't dead. I took a picture on my cell and immediately sent it to Tony Shileto.

I calmly asked Dale, "Were there any prints on his cell phone?"

"Just Asher's."

I considered, "We need to find out which fingers the prints on his phone came from." Most people don't realize this, but your fingerprints can be different for every finger. The prints may give an indication of whether the phone was used by Asher, or simply wiped clean and then pressed against his fingers.

Dale pulled out a page from the report, "He shot himself with his right hand and the gun was still in that hand. Layla confirmed he was right-handed."

When I saw the suicide note I asked Dale for paper and a pen. I decided to try writing out the suicide letter using the thirteen-letter code used in the previous cyphers.

Maybe someday, **H**ad I had the **Bl**oo**d**y courage to A**dd**ress my demons. **Y**ou wouldn't Dea**L** with this mess. **I**'m sorry. I would **k**ill myself to **S**et you free love, **F**rom my life as I **a**ct it. Every Chi**l**dish thing was **s**o painful. It is **e**vident now, had **A**sher been very **c**ommitted to a**cc**eptance of his **u**nfortunate co**s**tly obsession **a**ssociated was**t**efully with dri**n**king, opiates, **o**ne night absti**n**ances and sin? **I**s death better? **?**

It read: **Maddy like false allegations?** While the killer hadn't yet included punctuation in the code, I was assuming that two consecutive question marks meant it should be used here.

Officer Taylor agreed to find Layla Boyd and to bring her to the scene of the crime so I could interview her. I did a quick walk-through of their small home as Dale and Layla stood like friends, maybe even past classmates, waiting for my questions. Their friendship would explain why Layla called him. If she'd have dialed nine-one-one, the Sherburne County Sheriff's Department would have handled the case, since she lived out of city limits.

The dark circles under Layla's eyes indicated she hadn't been getting much sleep. Her long, honey-colored hair was clean and went well with her three-quarter-sleeved, azure cotton blouse and jeans, which were faded to almost the same blue as her shirt. She wore a simple round charm on a brown leather cord around her neck, and fiddled with the silver disc as we discussed Asher's suicide.

After expressing my condolences I asked, "Did you actually speak to Asher on the phone last Friday? Did you hear his voice?"

Layla grimaced, "No. We texted. I should have just come home. I've played this over in my head a thousand times." She looked at me imploringly, "We didn't typically have guns in the house—I was scared."

"Calling the police was exactly what you should have done," I reassured her. "I'm not convinced Asher committed suicide, so it's essential you're honest with me."

Layla's expression changed to alarm. "Why would anyone kill Asher? People were worried about him, but not angry with him." Her eyes swam with tears; she was incredibly sad.

I softly asked, "What did you think of his suicide letter?"

Layla pondered this. "It didn't sound like him, but he was all drugged up. Ash made fun of people who referred to themselves in third person, so that part surprised me. Even the texts were a little weird, but I wrote it off to his being in a messed-up state."

I turned to Dale, "Has anyone removed anything from this scene?"

"No, sir."

I instructed him, "Okay, wait here. Layla, come with me into the bedroom."

Dale stood ramrod straight, and Layla nervously looked back at him before following.

I squatted down by her low queen bed, and pointed to a slight amount of wear on the bedposts, just above the frame. "Layla, I need you to be honest with me. This is an important piece in this murder investigation. Did you remove anything from the bed?"

Embarrassed and ashamed, Layla looked away, rubbing her necklace charm like a worry stone. Avoiding the question, she asked meekly, "Do you really think it's murder?" I patiently waited for her to answer my question until she said with indignation, "I took some rope off the bed. It's nobody's business."

"Did Officer Taylor okay this?"

"No. Dale was in the other room at the time. Clear Lake is a small town—it would have been all over town once the cops started taking pictures. This is a town where people who don't have a life sit around talking about people who do." Layla rationalized, "Even if Asher was killed, the killer didn't use the rope, so what difference does it make?"

"The rope is why the killer was here." I straightened up, and looked at her directly. "There is no reason for this information to go beyond the investigators. Do you trust Dale to keep it quiet?"

"Yeah, I do." Layla admitted. "If the rope was why he was here, why didn't he take it with him when he left?"

"The same gun that killed Asher was used in Minneapolis, by a killer who let himself into the home of a couple that was into bondage. He killed the man, then tied up and raped the woman, asking her if she'd learned her lesson about bondage when he was done."

Layla looked panicked, "But how could he know we were into bondage? We didn't tell anybody about it and we didn't do it that often."

"Did Asher store any pictures online?"

Layla's cheeks flushed crimson. "He promised he wouldn't show anyone. He wouldn't do that to me. It was just for us."

"Asher didn't have to share it. This guy may have hacked into your computer and found it, so we'll need to look at any electronics you use to access the Internet." I yelled down the hallway, "Officer Taylor!" and he quickly joined us.

I turned to Layla, "Where's the rope?"

"It's in the garbage at my parents' house."

"You're going to go get it," I said, and turned to a now confused Dale. "And Dale, *you're* going to file in your report that Layla removed rope from the crime scene, but once you found out, you had her return it. And, under no circumstances, do you ever let anyone remove items from a crime scene again. This is why cases are not investigated by friends."

Dale started to say, "I didn't see her take—"

I interrupted, "Are you going to tell me you didn't see rope tied around the bedposts when you did your initial walk-through?"

He looked away without answering, the muscles in his jaw flexing in consternation.

"Look, I have no desire to get anyone in trouble," I softened. "Your heart's in the right place. But we have a killer who's targeting couples who are into bondage, and he's finding them by hacking into their computers. My gut feeling is he's tracing people who access BDSM sites."

Layla began to fully grasp the scenario, and she could barely force her words out. "The texts weren't from Asher? He was waiting here for me? He was talking about tying me up—to rape me." She stepped toward Dale for comfort, "Do you think he's still coming after me?" Her nervous hands fluttered back to her necklace.

"I don't know," I told her honestly. "Do you have a safe place to stay?"

"My mom and stepdad are good. I can stay with them."

Dale put a reassuring arm around her shoulders, and added, "I can help keep an eye on their house."

"Good. Dale, you could really help by talking to all of Layla's neighbors. Find out if they saw a car parked within thirty minutes' walking distance of here." I turned to the frightened young woman, "And Layla, for now, you need to stay off any social media that would allow the killer to track your location, just in case he has unfinished business with you."

AFTER WE WENT OUR SEPARATE WAYS, I called Maddy to update her on all I had discovered. I received a text from Tony indicating, "The lines in Asher's body translate as 'Fafnir.' What the hell is Fafnir? Double-checked it."

In a few minutes, I received an email from Tony saying, "I did a little research. In Norse mythology, *Fafnir* is the son of a dwarf king. He was cursed, turned into a dragon and was slain."

It had me thinking about how "chasing the dragon" was a term used by opiate addicts. It referred to trying to recapture the first high they experienced when their brains were still clean. It's simply unachievable. Oxycodone, the drug Asher overdosed on, is an opiate.

13

CULHWCH

9:45 P.M., WEDNESDAY, APRIL 26

ASHER PERRY'S DEATH WAS UNSATISFACTORY. There was a brief note about his death in the St. Cloud news, "Foul play not suspected," indicating I'd fooled those imbecile investigators once again. Asher was a feeble, rather than formidable, foe. So, with a voracious hunger, I quickly prepared for my next adventure. I'm changing my M/O tonight to guarantee both the man and woman are present.

For April, it has been an unusually warm day, so I left in short sleeves and without a jacket. As night falls, the temperature is dropping and I'm regretting being bamboozled by Minnesota—I should know better after all these years. I am forced to turn the heat on in my car as I exit off of I-94 and take Highway 7 to St. Augusta, Minnesota.

Ava Mayer is the most beautiful woman I've been with. Everything went perfect. *Sigh!* She's asking for a refresher course, with her comments about bondage in the paper, but right now she's too well-guarded. Even though Ava Mayer's case is national news, men are still tying women up, and it pisses me off. No doubt there's arousal in challenging the hands of fate. We'll see how comfortable men are with posting photos of bondage after a few more die.

Mia Krunesh is the bait for this predator tonight. Mia is a massage therapist at a mini-mall, and she's living with Brock, her mechanic boyfriend, in an old house at the edge of St. Augusta. The massage you get in St. Augusta is nothing like the massage you get in downtown Brainerd, where the workers wear high heels and miniskirts and smoke cigarettes during their breaks. I slowly cruise the main drag of St. Augusta past the St. Mary Help of Christians Church (*With a few more words in that church title, it could be a complete paragraph*), toward Gaelic Road.

Mia and Brock play the bondage game in the master bedroom, at the end of their one-story rambler; I know this from my diligent reconnaissance. They get at it during the middle of the week, when things are slow at the parlor. They have no close neighbors, so my car sits unnoticed on a gravel side road. I toss an Ambien-laced round steak to their golden retriever, and he devours it without barking. You can train dogs all day long, but all it takes is a juicy piece of meat to derail loyalty to their people—at least for the time it takes to scarf down their snack. I maintain my distance, for now, to keep him silent. Duke's getting the "number one sleep aid," but it's not without side effects. There's a plethora of online stories of people engaging in bizarre behavior under Ambien's influence. Who knows, maybe Duke will wake up with his arm around a skunk.

I'm leery of dogs, ever since I was tore up by a Doberman pinscher when I was five. I had wandered into the neighbor's yard to pet their dog, and it attacked me. Its jaws clenched down on my neck, and tossed my body about like a limp rag doll. But my mom was quickly there, pulling its jaws apart, enough for me to get free. I will never forget the horror on her face as she fought to save me. She loved me. The dog managed to bite into the muscle on my chest, and it still droops some from not healing right, requiring me to wear a shirt when I'm in public. The whole ordeal ended with the thunderclap of a bullet being fired from Dad's revolver. With one perfect shot, the dog was dead.

Mom anxiously skittered away from the dog, as if she feared my dad would now turn the gun on her. Instead, he laughed and said, "We need to get that boy to the hospital."

People say it's not the dog, it's the owner. Maybe it's a little of both. I know a hundred redneck pricks who have a variety of dogs that are all friendly. But unless a Doberman is carefully trained and domesticated, it attacks. Look at how genetics have affected me. My mom was my primary caregiver, and yet her forgiveness simply isn't in me. I'm a good man, but there is no doubt that killing came from my dad's DNA. For a while, Dad was my hero—until I saw him tie Mom up and defile her. I watched through the bedroom door. Dad had punched a gaping crack in the door after a man at the store saw the way he treated Mom and asked her if she was okay. He never intended to repair the damage and wouldn't let Mom cover it. It was a lesson delivered. Mom had that same panic-stricken expression in the bedroom as she had when she rescued me from that dog. I sometimes wonder if my dad would have shot me too, when I was attacked, if Mom hadn't been there.

Brock thinks because they have a reliable hunting dog, they don't need to lock the door. Well, Duke's sleeping now. I stick my nine-millimeter in the back of my jeans and quietly enter. I miss the Colt 45 with the silencer, but I had to give it up to sell Asher's suicide. I'm not sure if I'll steer the investigators to the suicide note or not. It might be fun just to shove it in their faces years from now.

Mia's giggling stops, and I can hear clothes rustling. Brock must be getting her bound. It's a little risky entering when they're both home, but no one's close enough to hear her scream—plus, once Mia's tied, she's useless. Maybe I'll tie Brock up and sedate him a little, so he can still watch before I kill him— no, I like perfect silence. I'll just kill him, so I don't have to think about him. After I sedate Mia, I can drag him out without her silly interference.

Beads of sweat form on my forehead as I slowly make my way down the dark, carpeted hall. I savor the adrenaline rush in anticipation of what lies ahead. After tonight, there will be another slave-maker dead, and another pretty young woman who receives a life lesson. Even if I don't kill Brock, there is no way they could resolve the hatred Mia would experience for him after he tied her up and she was raped. But he'd just find someone else to befoul, and I can't let that happen. Mia may *think* she likes bondage at this moment, but when I'm done with her, she'll understand humiliation, and regret she ever surrendered her freedom of movement.

The bedroom door is open a sliver, and a fraction of soft light spills onto the hall carpet. I quietly push it open another inch and peer in. *What the hell?* The unmade bed is empty. As I'm registering this unexpected sight, a metal barrel presses against the back of my head.

A voice I assume is Brock's growls, "And *you* are?"

Frank Weber

Mia flicks the hall light on. She's fully dressed. She stands in front of me on firmly planted feet, shoulders squared, and arms crossed in defiance. Her eyes narrow as she spits, "We're *hunters,* asshole. You honestly think you're going to creep in and watch us?"

I raise my hands shoulder high and take a deep breath. *Okay, what was the alibi?* I clear my throat, "Wait—there must be some mistake. Piper Bartos invited me over." I asked, "Can I reach in my pocket? I have the address written down. This is Loehrer Drive, isn't it?"

Mia gives Brock a knowing look.

What they don't know is I've read their emails, and Mia has accused Piper Bartos of cheating on her husband. So the intent of my alibi is simply confirm her bias. Loehrer Drive was the only other St. Augusta street that came to mind. "I apologize. She told me to just let myself in, and she'd be waiting for me in the bedroom."

Brock grumbles, "Did you know she is married?"

I quickly tell him, "I did not. Look, it hasn't been easy for me to meet women, so I took the offer. I've never even met her. It's all been online."

Brock lowers the gun and Mia asks, "What's your name?"

Keeping my hands palm up, I say, "Please, I don't want any trouble. I swear, I'm getting in my car and driving back to Rogers as soon as I'm outta here, and never coming back. I have almost $200 in my billfold—I'm hoping you'll take it for your troubles." I reached my hand toward my billfold, "May I?"

Mia remarked in distaste, "Have you ever heard of a coffee shop? Get to know the woman first. What do you think is going on when she won't be seen in public with you?"

I remove all my cash, and Brock quickly seizes it from my hand. He goes to the window and says, "I wonder what that damn dog took off after this time."

I quickly depart.

14

Maddy and I spent a long day in Clear Lake, at the scene of Asher Perry's murder. After a high of fifty-one degrees yesterday, it was a chilling thirty-two today. A cold shiver shuddered through my body as we walked across the dried brown grass extending from Layla Boyd's home. We moved toward a lifeless woods, carpeted with decomposing leaves that had abandoned the trees which once held them in warmer times. The mushrooming darkness from the setting sun seemed to foreshadow an evil we struggled to contain.

Maddy wiped a cold drip from her nose and responded to the latest cypher by commenting, "What the hell does this jerk want from me?"

I asked, "Do you now agree it wasn't Ava?"

Maddy said, "No. I still think Ava's involved. She's surprisingly strong for a little twerp! I spoke to her personal trainer. She works out regularly. Think about it. Most homicidal rapists kill the woman. This killer is murdering the man, more like a woman might do."

The data ran through my brain. I told Maddy, "Most murderers of both women and men are men. Most *rapists* of women and men are men."

"It's all that damn testosterone," Maddy suggested. "Did you know that both male and female Viagra is basically testosterone? And testosterone is associated with aggression?"

I argued, "It certainly is a factor, but most men never sexually assault anyone, so it's a pretty damn poor excuse."

She teased, "I never said it was an excuse. I'm just saying you come from a band of degenerates, but there's bound to be a couple good ones. On the cooler side of the pillow, there are women, and Ava happens to be a bad egg—if you don't mind the ovum reference," she laughed to herself. "By the way, the email I got about Volt's murder didn't come from Kent. It came from the computer lab at the University of Minnesota. Zeke hasn't been able to pin it on any one particular individual." We now had proof the killer was involved in getting Maddy to Volt's body. I didn't know if this was cause for relief or concern.

Zikri Abbas's gray Impala was the only Impala that matched that partial plate number. When I had casually mentioned to Zeke that we noticed his car was near Alan Volt's crime scene, he claimed he was home all night. Still, I had nothing other than a partial plate and Zeke's recent, lukewarm interest in his job. Maddy dismissed my suggestion of Zeke's involvement.

I had a thought that lingered late last night I had to share. "Maddy, I think this killer made a subtle mistake. Why would a killer who left the first victim on I-94 with "SERIAL KILLER" written on the body be content disguising the second murder? Because she or he has a bird's eye view of this investigation."

We both quietly considered the ramifications of this.

Maddy shared, "The bar I was at, when I was ethered, sits at the edge of the University of Minnesota campus. Remember, Ava was at that bar. She and her parents go to the free jazz and symphony concerts at Ted Mann Concert Hall on the university campus, which is about three blocks from that bar."

"I attend those concerts, too," I added.

Maddy stopped short, and looked at me in surprise. "Did you go there with Jada?"

"Yes."

Officer Dale Taylor interrupted us with a call to report a neighbor saw a black sedan, parked on a field approach about half a mile from Layla Boyd's home, during the timeframe Asher was shot. The caller didn't get the license plate, or even know the make of the car. *Could it have been gray and mistaken for black?* The BCA lab crew found that all the fingerprints on Asher's phone were from Asher's left hand. They were directly on the glass, which is an impossible position to hold a phone. This suggested the phone was wiped clean and pressed against Asher's fingers. He was right-handed.

10:30 A.M., FRIDAY, APRIL 28,
ST. PAUL

ON FRIDAY, MADDY AND I RESPONDED to a call from news reporter, Jack Kavanaugh, and met with him on the seventh floor of the Pioneer Press Building in St. Paul.

Jack was clean shaven, and had thick, short blond hair. He was in his early forties and relatively fit. He wore loose-fitting clothing that didn't hide his stocky physique.

We sat across from his desk, and he held up a manila envelope. The return address on the envelope was, simply, "The I-94 Killer." It had been postmarked in Minneapolis.

Jack pulled out the contents of the envelope, and as he dropped them onto his desktop, he speculated, "Whoever wrote this letter must have read my article on Ava Mayer. It came in the mail addressed to my attention today. Any idea what this means?"

I used my index finger on the top corner of the page, so I could turn it toward me. Maddy leaned in, brows furrowed, and read it with me. The note read:

The people who think they can unearth me, prefer at present for me to be free to pass the time as is preferred, as we are working as friends against zealouts who slay the gentle. / Culhwch

I feigned ignorance with a casual shrug of my shoulder, "No idea. We need to take it to the lab and have it dusted for prints. We'll probably need your prints to rule them out, based on the way you're handling evidence right now." I attempted to take the envelope.

Jack slid the envelope out of my reach, and I grimaced at his carelessness in touching it. He insisted, "This person seems to think the investigators are purposely dragging their feet, because she—or he—or whatever it is, makes our city better in the

long run. That's the clear message to me." He repeated, "We, suggesting he and law enforcement, are working as friends against
zealots who slay the gentle."

I wanted to let him in on the fact that the note was a
cypher, but I didn't trust he'd keep it out of the news. I responded, "I assure you, we're not dragging our feet."

Jack pressured, "So, no breakthroughs? Nothing? You
still have nothing?"

Despite his condescending tone, I remained polite, "I'm
sorry, but I don't have anything I can share."

Jack looked at me silently, his tongue pushing against the
insides of his cheeks as he acknowledged the gravity in my tone.
"You're taking this seriously—so this letter is the real deal. What
is it about the letter? Is it the name?" He was studying me intently, poised to infer all he could from my expression, and unin-
timidated, I held his gaze.

Maddy sensed the intensity of our standoff, and with a
karate chop-like motion between our locked stare, she intervened,
"We're taking *all* the information we get on this case seriously."
She placed a firm hand on my forearm, until I broke away from
Jack's stare and looked over at her. Maddy's eyes widened as she
silently told me to let it go. Without looking his way, she said,
"Jack, thank you for calling us immediately." She stood to leave.

Mollified, I also thanked Jack. As I was turning to leave
his office, I added, "I'm sorry for telling you to back off the interviews with Ava. I'm trying to keep her out of harm's way." It
was sort of an apology but, at the same time, an attempted ma-
nipulation. I was hoping if he believed my intentions were protective, he would back off.

Jack didn't show any sign of concession, as he leaned back in his chair and casually expressed, "You were just doing your job, and I am just doing mine."

15

JON FREDERICK

9:30 A.M., MONDAY, MAY 1,

"FROGTOWN," ST. PAUL

FULHWCH'S LATEST CYPHER revealed a name—"Thea Esparza.""

The people who think they can unearth me prefer at present for me to be free to pass the time as is preferred as we are working as friends against zealouts who slay the gentle. / Culhwch

Fortunately, there weren't many Thea Esparzas to choose from. Zeke discovered a Thea Esparza, who had been unknowingly recorded naked in her bedroom, through the use of the webcam on her laptop. Some creeper had posted the video on the internet back in February, so why was he taking credit for it now? The slander of Thea Esparza occurred months before the attack on Ava Mayer. It seemed the killer felt the need to take credit for a past crime, instead of taking the risk of committing a new one. Something had made our killer nervous and tentative. A call to Thea made it clear she wasn't going to be cooperative, so we had to resort to using her probation status to search her electronic devices. Thea had electronic theft charges as a result of pilfering from her last two employers.

Thea Esparza lived in a racially diverse area of north St. Paul called "Frogtown." The story behind the name is that Arch Bishop John Ireland referred to this area as Froschberg, or "Frog City," after hearing a chorus of frogs at night. Frogtown was the poorest area of St. Paul. Most people who lived in the area rented, rather than owned, their homes.

Thea was a bitter, overweight woman in her forties, who had obviously lived a hard life. She wore black spandex leggings so tight I expected to hear the squeak of rubbing a balloon when she leaned against the doorway. I don't like seeing all the curves and dimples on anyone's body, regardless of weight. She had short, dark hair, dark eyes, and a scar extending from the side of her mouth across her cheek ending just shy of her earlobe. Maddy had stayed home with her son, who was suffering from the flu, so Zeke Abbas and I went to the Esparza apartment to retrieve Thea's laptop. Zeke stood next to me in his black St. Paul Saints jacket. I couldn't help thinking his jacket should read St. Paul "Wali," the Muslim word for *saint*, but didn't say anything because I knew I was just being my obsessive self.

After handing Thea the search warrant for her laptop, I asked conversationally, "How'd you get the scar?"

Thea stared hard at me, vibrating with anger. "Go to hell," she spat and skulked off to retrieve her laptop.

I attempted kindness in response. "I'm sorry you had to go through this. We want to figure out who violated you like this."

Thea cut me off and snarled, "Listen pretty boy, I don't give a damn. I swear, you pervs just like looking at this shit." She aggressively shoved the laptop against my chest, her fleshy chest rising and falling with each indignant inhale through her nostrils. We left her standing there, fists on hips, staring daggers after us.

LATER THAT AFTERNOON, ZEKE CALLED me into his office. He stepped behind his desk, but remained standing. Zeke ran his nail-bitten fingertips through his thin moustache in anxious frustration as he prepared to confront me. He finally blurted, "Maddy told me you think I'm dragging my feet. You know how investigations are. You go a long time with nothing, and then it pours in. Today, it poured in."

So basically, Maddy jacked him up and threw me under the bus in the process. I tried to appease him. "Look, I'm struggling myself, so I shouldn't criticize anyone. I'm sorry." I asked, "What do you have?" I sat on a chair facing his desk, trying to encourage him to calm down.

Zeke slowly sat as he continued, "Thea Esparza was catfishing on the internet. She was pretending to be an eighteen-year-old college freshman. Sometimes she pretended to be a woman, sometimes a man. When she got her targets to send a nude photo, she'd then request $200, or threaten to send the photo to all of their relatives. See this girl," Zeke turned his monitor toward me and pointed to a headshot of a teenaged Asian girl on his computer, "Cua Kuam Peb couldn't produce the blackmail money, so our friend, Thea, forwarded the naked pictures of her to all of Cua's email contacts. Unable to live with the shame of her exposure, Cua attempted suicide."

I leaned in closer and looked at a photo featuring Cua's expression, pre-Thea, full of light and innocence before she came into contact with corruption. I imagined her wholesome features would now be forever changed because of Thea.

Zeke was unaffected by the girl's victimization. He continued impersonally, "You may find it interesting that her brother, Kub Kuam Peb, is a computer science major at the University of Minnesota." With an air of vindication, he smirked under his wispy mustache. He handed me a file with hard copies of everything he'd just shown me.

"That's great work Zeke." We needed to locate Kub Kuam Peb and find out where he was when the email was sent to Maddy.

10:30 A.M., TUESDAY, MAY 2,
ST. AGNES CHURCH, ST. PAUL

MADDY'S INTERVIEW WITH CUA KUAM PEB this morning revealed that Cua was a sweet, sixteen-year-old girl who was naïve and trusting. Her brother, Kub, was livid over the shame the photos brought to their Hmong family, but Cua told Maddy that her suicide attempt had abruptly stopped Kub's daily, incessant rants.

Zeke and I couldn't find Kub Kuam Peb yesterday, but managed to track him down in Frogtown this morning. Thea's blackmailing of young people who were looking for love was loathsome. When I realized she likely knew Cua from her neighborhood, it seemed even worse. St. Paul has the largest Hmong population of all cities in the United States. The Hmong had fought as U.S. allies in the Vietnam War, and many came to Minnesota to avoid persecution when the U.S. pulled out of Vietnam. Kub was a community activist; he worked with volunteers who were trying to create a community garden on one of the vacant lots in the neighborhood. Kub was shorter than average, and husky in stature. He had round facial features, and his thick, black hair was shaved short on the sides.

It was about fifty degrees today, which is tolerable. Kub wasn't in any hurry as he meandered along in a black North Face jacket, jeans, and a white Twins baseball hat, with the blue and red "TC" in the front. Kub was carrying a white garbage bag, picking up litter near St. Agnes church. I paused to appreciate the white, limestone church, with its red-tiled roof and beautiful, oxidized green copper tower. The tower was picturesque, soaring 250 feet into the sky.

As we discretely followed Kub on foot, I spoke quietly to Zeke, "This is not exactly what I would expect from a killer."

Zeke shrugged noncommittally, "There may be an underlying religious motivation to his behavior, based on the way this guy writes. He humiliates women, but he doesn't kill them."

I considered this and countered, "The killer wants people to think he's making the world better, but he's just another sociopath. Regardless of what he tells himself, he killed Alan so he could sexually assault Ava." Religious motives for murder are greatly exaggerated in books and movies. The vast majority of killers we deal with have no religious involvement.

Kub Kuam Peb stopped and turned in our direction, studying us as we approached. He remained motionless and silent.

I identified Zeke and myself as BCA agents, then asked, "Do you know Thea Esparza?"

Kub feigned interest in a passing car on Thomas Avenue and unconvincingly shook his head. He asked, "Why?" Kub's lack of eye contact could have been evasive, or it could have been cultural.

Zeke cut straight to the point, "Someone circulated nude photos of Thea online, and we have reason to believe this is connected to another investigation. After discovering what she did to your sister, we're going to need to look at your computer."

Kub nodded as if he understood he did not have a choice.

I asked, "Did you post the naked pictures of Thea Esparza online?"

With a knowing smile, Kub smirked, "No."

I continued, "But you've seen the pictures."

"Yeah, so?" He now made eye contact and challenged me, "Where were you guys when my sister got humiliated?"

Zeke interjected, "Was this retribution for Cua?"

Kub pointed at Zeke, "Why are you protecting Thea Esparza, when you didn't do a damn thing for my sister?"

I told him, "We're not protecting Thea. I presented the information to the Ramsey County attorney, and he's drafting charges against her. Whoever retaliated will probably never be charged for posting the pictures. I simply need to know who did it." I didn't bother to tell him the person wouldn't be charged because he'd be facing Murder One and Criminal Sexual Conduct in the First Degree charges, instead.

Kub was pleased with this and assented, "Good, but I didn't do it. I thought about retaliating—I was even planning on it, but when Cua tried to overdose, I realized I was focusing on the wrong person."

Zeke commented dryly, "Yeah, it still doesn't absolve Cua's responsibility."

I interrupted because I wasn't comfortable with where Zeke was going with this. "Cua was just a teen who thought she'd found love."

Kub nodded, "Yeah. She thought she was acting out of love. Thea acted out of hate. And if I retaliated, I would've been just like Thea. Thea probably has something she's retaliating against, too. But I can't say I felt bad when Thea got humiliated. It's karma."

I changed course, "Have you ever heard of Fafnir?"

Kub jerked a bit at the question, then responded, "Yeah, he's the bad guy in SMITE—the multi online battle arena game. He drops the hammer on his enemies. He's a playable antagonist in the game." He looked a question at me, trying to figure out my reasons for asking.

Zeke stood silent and dug his hands into his jean pockets.

I continued, "Have you ever played Fafnir on SMITE?"

Kub smiled. "I'm sure I have, but I'm more of a World of Warcraft kinda guy."

Zeke slid the conversation away from SMITE by asking, "Have you been in the University of Minnesota's computer lab? The hack into Thea Esparanza's computer came from there."

Kub's head didn't move, but his eyes shifted from Zeke to me as he responded, "Do you have any idea how many computers are in the lab? It's a *building*. It wasn't me." He searched our faces for understanding. "I pray for Thea . . ."

I asked, "Any idea where you were on Wednesday, April 12? It was about three weeks ago."

Kub flatly said, "No idea. I don't know what you're accusing me of, but I'm not wasting time I could be spending helping others, looking back at every day in my life. You go ahead, take a look at my computer and we're done. I'll be home in a half hour. You can get my laptop then. My address is—" Kub stopped, "I'm sure you have it." He resumed picking up garbage.

I reminded Kub to stay in town in case we needed to talk to him again. As we walked away, I glanced back to see him staring after us, white garbage bag still clutched in his hand. I wasn't sure what to make of Kub's obstinacy.

When we neared our car, Zeke pointed out, "You know we're not getting anything off of his computer. His willingness to give us that one piece suggests he's been using a computer other than his own for criminal work. As a computer science major at the U, Kub would not only have access to hundreds of computers, he could also get guidance from some of the best computer minds in the world. Just sayin'."

12:45 P.M.,
BUREAU OF CRIMINAL APPREHENSION, ST. PAUL

AFTER A THOROUGH SEARCH OF KUB'S LAPTOP, Zeke was unable to find anything incriminating. I still wasn't sure what to do with Zeke's denial of his car being in that videotape. It *had* to be his car. I needed to address this in the near future.

My nature required me to pull out my notebook and record my statistical concerns. The recent data on serial killers in the United States strengthened the possibility of either Kub or Zeke as legitimate suspects. In spite of the information drilled into the viewer's heads on television and movies, most serial killers in the U.S. were not white—otherwise known as *Caucasians* or more recently, *European Americans.* I jotted down some demographics from 2016 to consider:

POPULATION	% OF U.S. POPULATION	% OF SERIAL KILLERS
European Americans	77%	31%
Chicano	18%	7%
African American	13%	60%
Asian American	6%	1%
Native American	2%	None Reported

I preferred to use the term *Chicano* over *Hispanic*, because no individuals of Spanish or Mexican ancestry I've met refer to themselves as Hispanic; this is predominantly a term adopted by Caucasians—or *European Americans*—as I'd recently heard was the new thing. If you were to take into account that serial killers were most likely to strike in their neighborhood, where they could walk about generally unnoticed, consider that Alan Volt's neighborhood was mostly made up of European Americans, with the next largest racial group being Asian, the races of both Kub (Hmong) and Zeke (Malaysian).

1:12 P.M., TUESDAY, MAY 2

I WAS SURPRISED TO HAVE A VOICEMAIL from Serena, especially when she asked, "Would you be interested in taking a 'time-out' from our separation? I didn't think you'd be able to do this, but after you asked me to help with one night's sleep last week, I'm thinking you can. I don't have any plans on returning, but I'd love a few hours of our old life together. You could get a decent night's sleep. I could get a massage . . ."

10:00 P.M., TUESDAY, MAY 2,
RADISSON BLU, BLOOMINGTON

SERENA AND I WERE LYING UNDER the covers at the Radisson Blu. Her head rested on my chest while her luxurious curls curtained down her bare back.

Serena prodded, "Talk a little about work."

I smiled, "I'm not going to say anything that jeopardizes nights like tonight."

Serena peeked up at me, "I can hear about your work during our time-out nights. If you don't talk about it, I'll never know if we can live together again. You obviously have a case that's bothering you. Who are the suspects?"

Resigned and somewhat grateful to stop keeping the case at bay in my mind, I began. "Okay, I'm chasing a killer who's after couples who practice bondage. He finds them on the internet, and is computer savvy. He kills the man, uses an ether-soaked cloth on the woman to sedate her, and then rapes her."

Serena sighed against my skin, "He feels powerless."

"He's intelligent," I could feel my flesh tightening with energy as I laid out the scenario to Serena. "He tried to frame my partner, Maddy Moore, by sending an email that appeared to be from work. The email directed her to a murder scene before it was actually called in. The killer even wore Maddy's perfume to the first murder scene."

Serena propped her elbow on the bed and rested her cheek on her hand, "Maddy's the one who had the affair with an administrator, right?"

"Yes. Maddy thinks it's Ava Mayer, but I don't. The killer seems familiar with investigations, and familiar with the investigators. Just between you and me, I'm sure our BCA computer expert's car was close to the scene of the first murder, but he denies it. We also have a couple leads that point to a computer science major at the U named Kub Kuam Peb."

Serena considered this, then asked, "Is the number thirteen significant? In Hmong, Kuam Peb means 'thirteen' . . ."

16

I'VE CHANGED MY MODUS OPERANDI since being caught by Brock and Mia in St. Augusta. I always have a backup plan. They believed me because they already had formed their opinions about the unwitting Piper Bartos.

There is a cold chill in the air tonight. I was prepared this time with a light jacket. Even glamourous and untouched Eden Prairie can feel possessed with evil on an overcast night in early May, when all the foliage is struggling to come back to life. After my failed efforts with Layla and Mia, I'm being extra careful tonight. I've been down these streets twice in disguise. Keeping my distance from Ava's home, I find the telephone line and cut it.

Tonight is carefully planned—no male in the house. All of Marcus Mayer's success hasn't given him the knowledge that his security cameras shut off when the phone line is cut. I miss Ava. I'm banking on the fact they changed all of her passwords, but not her parents'. Ava had shared their security code in an old email. I quickly make my way to the house and enter 1-8-1-2, and the door unlocks. There is no one inside to greet me. I enter the alarm code so I'll be alerted if anyone returns.

If Ava is still on her old schedule, she should be in the shower now. I've stayed off her computer since Alan Volt's death. I believe the only way they can catch me is if I access her computer when they're waiting for me, and I'm not that stupid. I don't take chances, as there are a lot of geeks out there who know more than I do. My genius is in laying the story all out and planning for all the possibilities.

I can feel the blood pumping in my chest, and I find it exhilarating to know Ava could be around any corner. I make my way across the luxurious carpeting. *Where are you, Ava?* Time for a teachable moment. The guard left twenty minutes ago. I can hear the shower running in the bathroom. I had initially planned to wait for her to come out of the room, but this is better.

I turn the knob and find the bathroom door unlocked. This is risky. Is she setting me up? I don't think so. I think Ava's going to cash in on being a victim for as long as possible. My adrenaline continues to escalate as I patiently wait. Holding my nine-millimeter pistol, I decide to chance it, and step inside the bathroom.

Ava stares at me like a deer in the headlights. I've caught her naked and defenseless in her pearl gray, terrazzo walk-in shower. This is the perfect killing chamber—she has no weapons and nowhere to go.

I can see her clearly, and if I shoot her through the door, there's no blood splatter back on me. For the first time since I've known her, fear renders Ava silent. The water continues to cascade down her beautiful, petite body. Culhwch completed thirty-nine tasks before he won Olwen's love. This lesson for Ava is one more of those tasks. Is Ava my Olwen, or someone I simply need to silence after her failure to learn from her first lesson?

Ava continues to stare blankly back at me and nervously adjusts the water. Through the glass, I see goosebumps of fear cover her typically smooth skin.

My frozen stare is finally interrupted by the soft beep of digits being pressed into their security system—someone is about to enter the house. I need to be quick.

17

THE REPUBLIC WAS A LONG, dark, saloon-style bar. Maddy and I were side by side on cushioned bar stools, half watching the bartender work her magic. I sipped on a cold glass of Fulton Ale, while Maddy tapped the copper cup holding her Moscow Mule. Maddy had put on makeup and changed into a classic v-neck, fitted black top and designer jeans. The neckline was lower than I'd have liked, as it accentuated her cleavage, but she wore it unapologetically. I wasn't entirely sure why she insisted we stop. She took her cellphone out and showed me Cua Kuam Peb's Facebook page. There was Cua, long black hair and an inhibited smile, wearing a white, St. Paul Fighting Saints hockey jersey. When she suggested it was similar to Zeke's Saints jacket, I pointed out that the St. Paul Saints, and now the defunct St. Paul Fighting Saints, were two distinct franchises in two separate sports.

Clay Roberts unexpectedly sauntered in and came straight for us. He was wearing fitted, Rock Revival jeans and a tight burgundy, pullover shirt. Clay immediately spoke of the hundred-dollar jeans he purchased at the Buckle. Even though their styles are geared more toward younger men, he pulled it off and it only added to his youthful, soap-opera-star looks. It didn't take long for me to realize Maddy had invited him. Clay's eyes flicked approvingly to Maddy's bosom as he hopped onto the stool on the other side of her. He nodded a greeting at me. His designer cologne was overdone, as usual.

Without greeting Clay, I looked at Maddy skeptically and asked, "What is this about?"

Clay and I had been through a lot together, and he had stayed by me in the worst of times. But he slept with Serena, back in the day. It shouldn't have surprised me, as he always had terrible boundaries. I wasn't with Serena at the time, but I was trying to be with her, and he knew it. We had severed our friendship because of that. Still, I was cordial, and careful, with Clay. I didn't hate him. Serena was beautiful. I got it. I simply could not remain in a friendship with him after this betrayal. Even though there was a distance between us that wouldn't be traversed in the near future, I had entrusted him to build my house.

Maddy slid off her stool, announcing a trip to the restroom. When she was out of earshot, Clay leaned toward me, balancing a calloused hand on the seat of Maddy's stool, and reported on his progress, "We're off to a running start with the house. By showing a little of the Mayers' money, I've got people to work us into their schedules, and I've got great help. And, just so you know, I have not, and will not, tell Maddy about the house."

I nodded, "Thanks." I believed Clay. He was typically dishonest with women.

Clay continued casually, "Hey, I'm not the one who should be telling you this, but Serena's seeing another guy."

Always a fist to the gut with Clay. "Not you . . ."

"You're kidding me, right?" Clay leaned away from me, incredulous. "I wouldn't wish the hell she's put you through on my worst enemy." He innocently shrugged his shoulders and said, "Sorry, man, just being honest. That's what you want, right? I thought you'd want to know." He suddenly became very interested in the bartender's mixology.

I wanted to say, *When I needed you to be honest with me you weren't*, but I let it pass. I nodded affirmatively and turned away.

Maddy returned and slid back on her stool, effectively separating us like a much-needed referee.

As I scanned the bar, trying to process Clay's latest news of Serena, my gaze settled on a young woman standing at the end of the bar. She was thin and fit, wearing black skinny jeans and a white t-shirt under a caramel-colored leather jacket. She was about the same age as the other college students in the bar, and something about her was familiar. With brown eyes, she may have been Latina. Her long, brunette hair was straight and glossy. Though her body was "bellied up to the bar," her head was turned, and she was staring directly at me.

Maddy raised a penciled eyebrow and subtly tipped her head in the direction of the young woman. "It looks like somebody's interested in you."

The woman didn't hide the fact that she was studying me, like I was some sort of unusual specimen she'd discovered in the lab. And then an insight occurred to me, so I turned to Maddy, "You didn't post something on Facebook about us meeting here, did you?"

Maddy smiled guilefully and sipped her drink. "Some people won't go into the police station to share information, but they will go to a bar. I wanna know if someone out there has something. Anything. We need help." She held my gaze, daring me to challenge her.

The bartender squeezed a lemon into a drink in front of us, giving us a brief but refreshing reprieve from the alcohol and perfume-scented saloon. Maddy's Bvlgari and whatever cologne Clay was wearing were competing for space and, combined, they were nearly overpowering. I casually slid my eyes back in the young woman's direction. Unlike everyone else in this place, this woman wasn't socializing. Her eyes seemed to be pleading for help. *What was her pain about?*

Maddy swore as she realized, "That's Yesonia Hartman."

I left Maddy and Clay, and made my way over to her. I planted my feet in front of her and introduced myself. "I'm Jon Frederick."

She nodded, "I know." Her voice was so soft and weak when she spoke, I had to lean closer to hear her over the din of the saloon. "I'm Yesonia."

My interest peaked, I clarified, "Yesonia Hartman, daughter of Luke and Maria Hartman?"

A silken strand of hair had escaped from behind her ear. She swept it out of her face, and nodded.

"I've been hoping to get a chance to talk to you. The gun stolen from your home was used in a homicide. Who would have taken that gun? You must have some people you suspect."

Yesonia had her foot propped on the brass rail across the bottom of the bar. She studied her camel-colored ankle boots with intensity and raised a shoulder, "How would I know?"

Her uncertain posture was reflective of her youth and of her underlying fear. I quickly calculated that she wasn't even old enough to drink in this place, yet here she was, alone. "You were in high school when the gun was stolen. You must have some friends you suspected."

Yesonia stiffened and looked squarely into my eyes, "*My* friends weren't like that. You should be talking to my sister, Leah." She held my gaze, as if trying to communicate something she could not speak aloud.

I pressed, "Why would Leah know?" I looked down the bar at Maddy, who was now sitting particularly close to Clay.

"Guys have always loved Leah," Yesonia stated, as if it was common knowledge. "No one ever came over to see *me*."

My phone buzzed. I held up a finger to Yesonia and turned away to answer it. I'd instructed Ava's bodyguards to buzz me when she ditched them.

Ava Mayer's bodyguard, Jeremy, reported in his clipped baritone voice, "Ava asked me to go home. She called her dad and talked him into ordering me out, so she could have some *alone time*. Feels she's being smothered. I'm still down the block. You asked me to call, so here's the call."

"Stay where you're at," I tensed, my grip tightening on the phone. "I'll stop over and see if I can talk some sense into her." More often than not, Ava didn't answer phone calls, and I wasn't even sure she would answer the door. "Do you have any idea what the home security code is on their alarm system?"

"No, I haven't been privy to that. I do know she makes some vague comment about 'oral' every time she enters the code."

After hanging up, I turned back to Yesonia. She was looking at me expectantly. I wrote my phone number on a bar napkin and pressed it into her hand. "Call me if you have anything that will help with the investigation."

As I was about to leave, I had an afterthought, and was about to gently touch her arm to get her attention, when I decided against it. I don't like to touch anyone unless permission has clearly been offered. So, I awkwardly waved, and when she glanced my way, said, "Stay off line. Whoever is doing this is a computer master. Stay off Snapchat in particular, and tell your sister the same. People can use Snapchat to identify your exact location."

Yesonia tucked her hair behind her ear and quietly said, "Thank you."

I had planned to tell Maddy I was leaving, but as I approached, she slid off her barstool to her feet, so close to Clay that any space between them was erased. Maddy's eyes met mine for a moment. She shrugged her shoulders in a *why not?* gesture.

I waved goodbye and left for Marcus and Angela Mayer's home.

I tried calling Ava on the way, but not surprisingly, she didn't answer. Knowing Ava's trashy sense of humor, and being a man who has a history of making stories out of numbers to remember them, I began to work out possible, four-number codes for their security system. By the time I arrived, I thought I had it—"1812." If you change the "1" to an "I," and say the numbers out loud, you have, "I ate one too." When I arrived and entered the code, the door opened.

As I entered the house, I heard the back door slam. I yelled, "Ava! It's Jon!"

"I'm here," Ava's voice wailed faintly from the recesses of the hallway. Light spilled from the bottom of the bathroom door, so I made my way in that direction, tensing with apprehension. When I pushed open the door, the bathroom was full of steam. Ava was crumpled on the floor next to the shower door. A bath towel had been pulled down and draped over her body. Her skin looked scalded and bright red. I asked, "Are you okay," as I ran some cool water over a hand towel.

Ava nodded weakly, "Yeah."

I handed her the cool towel. "Here—this will feel good against your skin. I'll step out and find you some clothes." Back in the hallway, I called nine-one-one, and then Jeremy, the body-guard, to look for the person who had just exited ahead of me. Jeremy told me he hadn't seen anyone leaving, which didn't surprise me, as he was parked in front of the house. He agreed to look around.

I returned to Ava with sweat pants, socks, and underwear for her, and one of her dad's extra-large Tommy Bahama t-shirts. She wouldn't want anything that clung tightly to her scalded skin. Ava appeared to be experiencing heat exhaustion. She was shaking uncontrollably, and stuttered, "H-he stood there ready to sh-sh-shoot me. I was in the shower and had n-no place to go!" She clutched at the cool towel and continued, "I turned the water as hot as I c-could, to steam up the stall. I planned to move as f-far as I could to one side, right before he pulled the trigger—I h-hoped he'd miss—but he heard you come in and didn't shoot."

I set her clothes on the counter and held her towel in place as I extended a hand to help her up. I very intentionally maintained eye contact with her and said, "You found a way to survive, with almost no resources, and that's amazing! Who was it?"

Ava sighed, "I don't know. He was wearing a black stocking cap, black gloves, and all black clothes." Ava was still shaking.

"Are you going to be okay to dress if I step out?"

Ava nodded. "Thank you."

I called Maddy, and then Zeke, but neither answered. I couldn't abandon Ava to search. I had to give her credit for making a decision to obscure the shooter's view with steam. The fraction of uncertainty the shooter had, over whether he would deliver a kill shot, might have been enough to keep him from firing. He couldn't risk verifying she was dead if he planned to escape the scene alive.

I RODE WITH AVA IN THE AMBULANCE to the hospital. She spoke little during the commute, and I let her have peace. After her parents and armed guards arrived, I called Sean Reynolds, who was working the scene of the crime. I was blessed to have Sean arrive, as he was one of our best investigators. He been occupied handling the fallacious killing of Philandro Castille. Sean knew part of the reason he was assigned to the case was because he was an African American investigator, and the public demanded to have a black BCA agent working the case. Sean reported there were no prints from the intruder at the Mayer home, and no video footage. I drove to the Mayers' and we finished working the scene together.

18

Like a ghost, Ava's intruder had come and gone without leaving a trace of evidence. On Saturday afternoon, I called Jada and offered to buy her a calzone at Broders' Pasta Bar in Edina, if she'd be willing to talk a little shop with me. Broders' has a quaint café with spices and jars of spaghetti sauce for sale on shelves when you enter. Jada's mustard yellow blouse contrasted pleasingly against her dark skin. We ordered at the counter and took a small table by the window. It was almost seventy degrees, and the sunshine beaming through the window gave her coffee-colored eyes a warm glow.

When I asked about being in the bar with Maddy on March 6, Jada groaned, "I remember that night. El was upset that three transgendered women had been killed in New Orleans in the past month. While El and I were at a table commiserating with some of the local reporters, Maddy was going on and on at the bar about her terrible ex. By the time I was ready to leave, Maddy was in bad shape."

"Any idea who gave her a ride home?"

Jada laughed, "She doesn't remember?"

The waitress delivered our calzones. Our conversation was on hold until we could assure our waitress we were fine.

Jada still made me wait a moment before revealing, "I did. When I went to the parking ramp, Maddy was passed out just inside the entrance. Her lipstick was smeared all over her mouth." She shook her head, recalling the image. "She'd only left the bar a couple minutes before me. I was thinking, *Girl, what the hell were you doing?*"

I asked, "Do you think she was assaulted?" I thought about the redness and considered it may not have been smeared lipstick.

Jada shook her head, "I don't think so. I was only minutes behind her. After she stumbled out, I wanted to make sure she wasn't driving. She was so limp, it was all I could do to get her into my car and home. I felt like I'd lost a wrestling match when I was done." Jada cut into her calzone and steam and red sauce oozed from it. "I left her fully dressed on her living room floor. I locked her house and mailed the keys back to the address I got off her driver's license. I didn't bother to write a note—what do you say? It was fun?" Jada chuckled without humor, "Well, that explains why she never thanked me."

Jada closed her eyes in appreciation of the warm sun shining through the window. She opened them and looked seriously at me. "Jon, you're being paid by the Mayers. I don't know how you eluded an investigation into that, and I don't particularly care. I'm not going to tell anyone about it, but you're not going to stop me from covering this case. I was the one who opened the door to this media circus with Ava. Don't ask me to stop doing my job. You saw what happened—when I backed off for one second, Jack Kavanaugh stepped in and filled the void. I could have had those interviews. Ava is a career-making story. I can't abandon it." Jada softened, "Nothing personal. This is my chance."

"I understand." I smiled. "I've always felt you deserved to be on the national news. I'm just trying to keep Ava alive."

Jada took a sip of tea before responding, "Maybe there's a good reason she doesn't fear for her life. She's still the only one who's seen the killer—or claims to have."

"Ava didn't kill Alan." When she looked at me doubtfully, I continued, "I'm right on this."

Jada gave a half-smile. "First, it was a guy with a small dick, now it's a woman—maybe even an investigator. Is there any evidence to suggest she *isn't* guilty?"

"We have DNA indicating another man had been in the bed where Ava was assaulted. A masked predator broke into her parents' home last night when she was there alone. I heard him leaving when I entered the house. Fortunately, Ava wasn't hurt."

I wasn't going to give up the evidence we had about the cutting, as this could ultimately be important to prosecuting the killer, but I wanted to give her something. We needed some fresh information on this case, and we weren't going to get any if everybody assumed Ava was the killer. "Remember Ava's story that there was a third person at the scene?"

Jada brightened, as visions of another breaking news opportunity flashed through her brain. "You're going forward with the DNA study."

"I'm still trying to talk the Mayers into funding the study. I want you to write about the algorithm I've created. I haven't been able to convince people how significant this DNA study could be. I would be creating an outline of genetic patterns in Minnesota we could use for every future crime involving DNA. I've been trying to convince Marcus Mayer this study could be a lucrative private business."

Jada furrowed her eyebrows, "Why isn't the BCA paying for this?"

"It's expensive. I've been told we simply don't have the funding."

Jada took out her notepad and said, "Please explain the process again."

I explained, "It involves a series of DNA tests. I'd go to a variety of ethnic areas and get sample DNA tests. I don't need a lot of people to volunteer—just some. There's nothing illegal about it, since it involves volunteers. The process keeps narrowing down potential suspects until it could only be a handful of candidates. Then we just have to confirm alibis. It may take as long as a year to get this done, but I'll get this killer. My goal is to catch him through another means before then, though."

Jada savored the rich traditional sauce in the calzone as she pondered, "So who's your best suspect?"

"Honestly, I don't have a decent suspect." I thought about Kub Kuam Peb. "We do have a suspect we're trying to match the DNA to, but I don't know that he's our guy." It seemed odd that a killer this intelligent would use "thirteen" for the code if it was his last name. But, Kub had also refused to give a DNA sample.

Feeling it was too early to implicate Kub, I diverted the

conversation to some information I received from Tony Shiletio. "There's surveillance tape from a neighbor down the road from Alan Volt, indicating two cars pulled out of that driveway after the murder, as Ava suggested—first the murderer, then her in Alan's car. Unfortunately, the video wasn't clear enough to even identify the vehicle."

"I owe you!" Jada leaned into me and kissed me on the cheek, wrapped up her calzone, and then took off to prepare her story.

10:45 A.M., MONDAY, MAY 8,
BUREAU OF CRIMINAL APPREHENSION, ST. PAUL

ON MONDAY, MAURICE STROCK CALLED me into his office and told me Maddy had filed a complaint against me. By sharing information supporting Ava's innocence, I had poked a mama bear who had lost her cub. In chemistry, they say for every action, there's a reaction. I was about to get mine.

Maurice directed me to be seated, then stood in front of me, his wild, white hair swaying as he waved a finger at me. "Maddy believes you're being paid by the Mayers to provide them information relevant to our investigation. Do you understand the seriousness of this allegation?"

"Maurice, I told you from the onset that the Mayers asked me to look into an assault on their daughter. Since I've accepted the role as lead investigator on this case, I have not taken even one red cent from them." The twist of words didn't make the deceit easier to voice.

Maurice railed, "Jada Anderson's report on the news last night sure supports Maddy's claim that you're working for the Mayers. She spoke of the DNA of a man, other than Alan, being on the bed where Ava was assaulted. I told you it could have come from another time."

I interjected, "We also have a video of two cars pulling out of the driveway, as Ava reported."

Maurice's aging hands trembled with frustration as he argued, "We don't talk to the media at this stage of the investigation."

In an attempt to de-escalate Maurice's angst, I asked, "Do you think it's fair to crucify Ava Mayer in the news when Kub Kuam Peb is currently our best suspect? We kept the murder of Asher Perry and the attempted attack on Ava out of the news to help our investigation. It's left a troubled rape victim with a big target on her back."

Maurice ran gnarled fingers through his too-long white hair. "You should have run it by me first."

I countered, "Who referred to Ava Mayer as the next Jodi Arias? I didn't. It was all over the news." We both knew it was Maddy. "Ava needs a reprieve from being in the spotlight. It's not good for her, and it could get her killed."

Maurice ignored the comment. "Maddy and Zeke are following Kub, waiting for him to rub his DNA on something they can grab as evidence. We'll get him." Maurice's face scrunched in perplexity. "Maddy said you think Zeke broke into your apartment and plugged your toaster in."

I had shared with Maddy that I had concerns about Zeke, that my apartment had been broken into, and that someone had plugged in my toaster. Somehow, that went from being three separate events to one thing, but I elected not to argue.

Maurice softened paternally, "Are you losing your mind? Have you spoken to Marcus separate from this investigation since you took over the case?"

"I have. After you told me the BCA wasn't going to fund the DNA algorithm I created, I went to Marcus and asked if he'd fund it."

In resignation, Maurice finally flopped into his desk chair. "The algorithm you developed is genius. I'd love to say we'll pay for it, but I can't find the money. We both know that a private lab will do this and ultimately we'll pay through the nose for their results. It's damn near impossible to get people in the state system to fund an idea that won't show a payoff for a year."

Maurice took a deep breath. "I made a mistake by asking you to interrogate Maddy over how she arrived at Alan Volt's body so quickly. It created unnecessary friction between partners. But I've known Maddy for a long time, and she isn't vindictive. I'm taking this seriously. You need to take some time off, away from this investigation. That is *not* a request—it's a direct order." Maurice proceeded to tell me I was suspended pending further investigation.

I wasn't as nervous about losing my job as I should have been. Nothing mattered as much as my longing for time with my daughter and Serena. Typically, when someone vilifies me and they're right, I'm angry because their criticism exacerbates my own shame. But I wasn't upset at Maddy. She expressed a legitimate concern. This meant I was either maturing or simply falling apart—maybe both. It did help that it was paid leave. I offered to open all of my financial affairs to the investigation, and Maurice suggested this was wise.

WHEN I LEFT THE BCA BUILDING, I called Marcus Mayer and told him I couldn't be around to protect Ava until my investigation was cleared. I'd be in further trouble at work if anyone knew I was talking to the Mayers when I was told to be off the case.

Marcus responded with arrogance, "*I* decide when this is over. You're the only thing keeping Ava sane right now. She needs to talk to you every night. Either you protect her, or I'll let them know I'm paying Clay Roberts to build your house."

My first reaction was to tell Marcus to go to hell, but I opted to carefully consider my options before making a decision that would end my career as an investigator. Two years ago, when I asked a woman involved in a previous case why she didn't collect child support, she told me, "If you take their money, you've got to take their shit."

I'd taken Marcus's money; there wasn't going to be an easy way out. I had told him from the onset that my BCA work had to be a priority. That apparently didn't matter to Marcus Mayer. I asked him to give me a minute and I'd get back to him. I closed my eyes and tried to focus on the best moral path. Regardless of my dislike of Marcus, Ava needed protection, and the only way I could realistically protect Ava, was to keep her close.

My incredibly kind parents, Bill and Camille, agreed to take Ava into their home, with the understanding she would surrender all of her electronics first. This would take Ava off the killer's radar and keep my parents safe. I brought Clay Roberts along when I presented this plan to Ava. His model-like looks, combined with an offer to drive her to Pierz, sealed the deal. I would stay in the basement of the home I was building in Pierz, so I wouldn't be in the same residence, but I'd talk to Ava face-to-face every day. The running water and plumbing had already been installed in my unfinished home. I called Serena to let her know I'd be staying in Pierz for the next couple weeks, and I wanted to see Nora every day, if possible.

Serena quietly agreed before asking, "Can I ask why you're being suspended?"

I offered, "Are you ready to talk about us—otherwise, why bother asking?" I wanted to bring up Clay's accusation that she was seeing another man, but didn't want to admit the gossip was getting to me—and I loved her, so I didn't want to argue with her.

I revived the dead air between us by saying, "I'm sorry for being a jerk. I'm dealing with a lot right now."

19

THIS WAS THE LAST DAY I COULD help Clay work on my house, as I was being called back to work tomorrow. I'd enjoyed my time with Nora. She was a spunky, defiant two-year-old, which, come to think of it, were descriptors Maddy Moore might use about me. Nora had a keen awareness of other's emotions, and since she was the only child, she was very comfortable interacting with adults. One morning, my parents were having an argument and had nothing to say to each other when they sat down for breakfast. Nora carefully looked them up and down, and then asked, "Are you doing okay?" They both started laughing and began talking to each other.

I'm not going to pretend Nora was easy all the time (like kids on TV). She reminded me she was two, with declarations like, "I'm not taking a nap, ever," but as exhausting as she was, it was all endearing to me. I knew it was much easier being just a part-time dad, but I wanted more.

Ava was busy with my mom every day, performing her volunteer work during the day and gardening in the evening. The small-town baseball games, Wednesday fresh-bologna days at the Red Rooster Bar, and classic cars parked along Main Street on Thursday nights didn't match the glamor of the Minneapolis night clubs. Still, Ava stayed. Her major attraction was Clay. Clay knew he looked good, and he didn't hesitate to show off his muscular build with tight, white t-shirts. He particularly enjoyed removing them at times, in her presence, because it was "too hot." While I made it clear to Clay that Ava was off limits until she was out of my parents' home, it didn't keep the two from flirting.

My dad taught Ava to drive a four-wheeler (which she loved), so Ava delivered lunch and beverages every day to our work site. It gave me the opportunity to see her differently. My parents' expectations of Ava gave her a sense of purpose and she became slightly more likeable. Still, she was inconsiderate and condescending to my brother, Victor, who lived with my parents, so no one was particularly disappointed that she was leaving with me the next day. Ava didn't like conversing with anyone who could be perceived as less than ideal (when it wasn't in context of charity work), even though Victor worked hard at being considerate to her.

Clay was a few feet away from me with a nail gun, framing the shower in the master bathroom, while I was laying a seal of wood glue along the upstairs frame corners of my home. From my past participation in a model bridge-building contest in high school physics, I knew the glue was stronger than wood, and I wanted my house to be solid. I was close enough to converse with Clay but staying out of his way. Clay was an outstanding builder, so I had primarily been labor for him.

Clay was complaining about the Pierz state championship baseball game of the day before. "Our first baseman is right there to make the play—the ball hits the damn bag and skips over him, and we lose the state tournament." When I didn't respond, he continued, "I don't know why we make such a big deal of the state championship. They're going to be better people if they lose, anyway."

I interjected, "Maybe that's why they only let one team win."

Clay shot six nails into the frame and then roughly countered his own rant, "Although, it didn't seem to taint that Zahurones girl when she won Dairy Queen. She's still as gracious and kind hearted as people get."

"Dairy Princess. Dairy Queen is ice cream. Mary was Princess Kay of the Milky Way."

Clay looked over at me and grinned, "Do you have to be lactating to win that?"

"No, but that would be 'of the milky way,' too." I looked up at him sharply, "*Lactating* is a new word for you, and you used it correctly. You're dating someone with a baby!"

Clay swiped across his forehead with the back of his hand, pushing his longish, sun-streaked hair out of his eyes. "A couple weeks ago, I went out to eat with this woman. Suddenly her shirt started getting wet by the nipples. I was thinking this woman has some sort of superpower—this could be a wild night! Instead, she was embarrassed and went home."

I commented, "Well it *is* a bit of a superpower."

Clay shot a couple more nails. "What does it taste like?"

I looked up, "Are you seriously asking me what Serena's breast milk tastes like? Isn't that a bit of a bad boundary?"

Clay shrugged, "I'm assuming she doesn't have her own special flavor. You had a baby. You must have tasted it."

"And *that's* a conversation we are not having." I focused on the gluing again, closing the subject.

Clay shot four more nails and said, "Hell, we didn't win a state tournament and look at us."

I laughed, "And what prizes we are. I'm suspended from work. My relationship tanked, and you can't make a relationship last for more than a month."

He smiled and sighed, "But we've dated some beautiful women."

"Most women are beautiful. It's a matter of not having exclusion criteria."

Clay curiously tilted his head to the side, playing along. "And what would that look like?"

"Like not wanting children. Not being spiritual."

Clay whistled and shook his head, then shot a couple more nails. "You're a disturbed man." After a beat, he said, "Maddy Moore's been asking about you. I like Maddy. How old is she?"

"Forty-five. What did she want to know?"

Clay was still now, watching to see how I'd react. "If you're doing okay."

"And you said?"

"I'm a busy man. I don't have time to babysit you. I told her you seem to be doing fine." He checked the load of nails in his gun and added, "As far as obsessive nut jobs go."

Clay had a history of pursuing women I knew. He was really a crappy friend, for the most part. Still, we had a friendship that was forged slowly over time and was difficult to break. While I'd never set a friend up to date him, I knew he would help me, with no questions asked, any time.

I stared hard at him until he looked up at me and told him, frankly, "Maddy's a good person, with a son, and she's my work partner. I'd prefer you didn't mess with her anymore."

Clay smirked, "She's the one who looked me up—to gather information about you. Don't worry, I'm the big winner in this house payoff. I'm not saying a damn word to anybody. But I am going to miss ordering you around and insulting you now that you're headed back to your real job."

11:30 P.M., TUESDAY, JUNE 20,
PIERZ

AFTER I WAS DONE PLAYING with Nora for the night, I spent my last night in my new home. I had put a bed in the basement. I think everyone needs to have comfortable shoes and a good bed—when you're not in one, you're in the other. I was drifting in and out of a light sleep when I heard the deadbolt unlocking upstairs. I waited to hear where the subsequent footsteps led. Soft footfalls padded down the basement steps and approached my bed. In the darkness, I watched the silhouette of a shapely and petite young woman remove her blouse and sway her hips as she slid out of her form-fitting jeans. I opened up the bed sheet. Serena crawled into bed with me. I pulled her close as she spooned against me. I pushed aside her long dark curls and kissed the back of her neck. She turned into me and we passionately kissed, as I melted into the warmth of her body . . .

Being the obsessive character I was, it'd been difficult to avoid addressing the rumor that Serena was dating someone else. I didn't want her to think I was having people report to me, and I felt our relationship was so fragile that initiating an argument would smash it to smithereens. I'd been focusing on "mindfulness" or, in other words, carefully observing thoughts and feelings without judging, and I couldn't complain about the results.

Serena had developed a routine of stopping by, nightly. On nights we didn't make love, I poured Eucerin skin-calming lotion into a glass and put it in the microwave for a few seconds and then massaged her feet, legs, and back with nice warm lotion. It was one of the few brands that didn't become too sticky when you rubbed muscles smooth. Serena was often tired, as she was working as well as caring for Nora, so she just relaxed and enjoyed it. I rubbed the tightness out of the muscles in her back and her backside. She had been assaulted face down. I had researched counter conditioning, which involves replacing anxiety-provoking contact with pleasant and desired touch, so I was prepared when this opportunity arose. I didn't bother to tell her I had planned this out. I wanted her to simply be at peace with it. She still hadn't resumed conversations with me during daylight, but I just needed to be patient.

20

WE HAD BEEN ON A STREAK of beautiful weather—mid-seventies, no wind, but still enough clouds to keep it from getting too hot. After the investigation cleared me, Maurice Strock asked me to take Maddy back as a partner. I had no issue with her, since she hadn't done anything wrong. A stakeout on Kub Kuam Peb, while I was out, had failed to produce any useful information. Maddy was quick to point out that there were no new crimes during my absence.

Maddy and I were soon in her unmarked car headed to Zikri Abbas's home. She avoided eye contact with me as she drove. Maddy had this terrible habit of setting her phone on the console. At the first turn, it slid to the floor, requiring me to pick it up.

In a soft voice, she offered, "Look, I'm sorry. Somehow, I'd convinced myself you'd been paid to steer the investigation away from Ava Mayer. All of my instincts told me this. But obviously, I was wrong. And now people might be reluctant to work with you, just because of an unfounded allegation."

I didn't have the heart to tell Maddy our colleagues weren't going to have any problems with me. After all, no evidence was found to confirm what she alleged. But they might have an issue with her for reporting one of their own. "Maddy, I have no issue with you or with what you did."

Maddy digested this. She suddenly swerved the car to the side of the street and violently threw the gear-shift into PARK. She turned to me, straining at her seatbelt. "Son of a *bitch*, you did take money, didn't you?" Maddy's dark eyes were all but piercing through me.

"What if I had? People get paid to do side jobs all the time. I would never let anything interfere with my BCA work."

Incredulous, Maddy shouted, "Do you hear yourself? There's no way for you to know with certainty that Ava had nothing to do with Alan's death. Have you stopped to consider she still may be the puppet master in all this—pulling some guy's strings to punish men? You're a crooked investigator." The muscles around her lips twitched with unspoken epithets. "You might be the worst person I've ever worked with. Being unfaithful can't be as bad as being bought off when you're performing a job based on public trust. Peoples' lives are at stake, here, Jon! How do you make this is okay in your brain?"

I rubbed my forehead and turned to escape her fiery stare. I focused on the texture of the dashboard. Nothing was okay in my brain right now.

Maddy's nostrils flared as she fumed on, "It's always some ass like you who thinks he deserves more than the income he agreed to work for. Stop feeling sorry for yourself and man up. When I go to bed at night, I can feel good about what I've done, because I did my job the right way."

When Maddy realized I wasn't arguing with her, she pulled away from the curb abruptly. The tires chirped as they bit into the pavement, as if surprised by the sudden movement. Maddy drove on, adding, "At least until I remember I'm alone, and I was robbed of my child, and everybody at work looks at me like I'm something they found stuck to the bottom of their shoes."

I honestly reflected, "I'm sorry I put you in this position." I then went on to explain that I had tried talking Marcus Mayer into funding an exploratory DNA study I created, which would eventually identify the killer, but had failed.

Maddy felt some consolation over having gotten through to me and she respected the DNA algorithm. Her demeanor warmed to that of concern. "There isn't anything wrong with helping Ava, but it can't be your job—not while you're investigating for the BCA. The DNA study—that's brilliant. You're basically creating a noncriminal data bank that will help link DNA samples to families." When I didn't respond, Maddy continued, "Any time with Serena during your break?"

"There were a few nights in Pierz when I had a late night surprise," I confessed. "I slept sound, and she was gone by morning. She told me the last night that, tomorrow, we go back to how it was before I returned to Pierz."

Maddy reached over and maternally patted my arm. "Don't feel bad about it. You take what you can get when you love someone. Believe me, I've been there. It's humiliating, but scraps look good when you're starving. Try to keep your kind heart. It's easy to be angry."

It felt like a good time to let that subject rest. We rode in silence for a bit, as Maddy maneuvered the car through the city.

I mused, "I've had a lot of time to think about this case. I think we need to pay less attention to what this killer is handing us, and more attention to what we have. I feel like he implicated Ava by directing her to drive away with her boyfriend's murdered body in the trunk. There isn't any way Ava could have responded that didn't make her look guilty. There were pictures on her computer of her engaging in bondage with Alan. If she hadn't told her parents, Ava would be incarcerated right now. She was lucky they sought out an investigator. I'm not sure she would have done so independently, even if she was innocent."

As Maddy pondered this, I continued. "And then he gave us you—invites you to a murder scene, and wears your perfume. And now, he gives us Kuam Peb. It's too easy. I did some more reading about Culhwch and Olwen and, by the way, it isn't exactly a quick read. Do you know what Culhwch's superpower was?"

Maddy smiled, "No, but I have a feeling I'm going to find out."

"I'm sorry for bombarding you with all of this. I've had a lot of time to think."

Dimples appeared with Maddy's grin, "I missed working with you—always flooded with information. Okay, I just need to ask, what is Culhwch's superpower?"

I told her triumphantly, "The ability to continue to work when everyone else is sleeping

"Well, good ol' Cully might have met his match with you." Maddy's expression became serious. "My frustration lies in the last cypher. What was he falsely accused of?"

After some silence while we both mulled this over, I added, "I can't let go of Zeke denying his car was in the area of Alan Volt's murder."

"I don't know, Jon." As Zeke's home came into view, Maddy pondered, "What if Ava gave me a ride home from the bar that night? She could have noticed my perfume and set me up."

I shook my head. "Jada Anderson gave you the ride home that night. She found you passed out in the parking garage."

Maddy's face was impassive as she worked through this information. She didn't speak until she was parked in Zeke's driveway next to his grey Impala. She turned off the ignition, but didn't move to get out of the car. The only light on in the house was a dim lamp in the living room. Maddy turned to me carefully, "Jada knows a lot about investigations—you were with her for four years. Ava is still my leading suspect, but consider this—maybe Jada was already stalking Ava in the bar that night. You have blind faith in Jada. I doubt you'd even notice if she was manipulating you."

I respected Jada, but didn't completely dismiss Maddy's concern. I opened the car door, then looked back at Maddy. "Jada left the bar shortly after you, to make sure you were okay. She's an amazing person. You need to *thank* her . . ." I wasn't sure why the comment bothered me so.

I gathered my composure and circled back to Maddy, who had just exited the car. I told her, "While our killer may know computers, he's just another psychopath who rationalizes assaulting a completely vulnerable woman. The rapist wasn't Ava, and it damn sure wasn't Jada. I don't see any pent-up anger in Kub Kuam Peb, so that brings us to Zeke—the only suspect we have right now who wasn't handed to us by the killer."

I scratched an itch behind my ear. Maybe I was hoping to instigate a neural connection in my brain that would set in motion a series of answers.

I asked, "Is this killing about intimacy?"

Maddy considered quietly, "This has been my belief since the beginning. Killing is the only intimacy this killer has in her or his life. This is why we're getting letters and messages on bodies."

"This killer has spoken to us directly," I postulated. "I'm not using a metaphor. I mean actually spoke to us. This killer is too attention-starved to just be watching."

Maddy stared straight ahead, deep in thought. "I agree. Let's run through everyone we've talked intimately with about the murders. We know it's not Layla Boyd. She had a solid alibi at the time of Asher's death. She was on camera at work. The Hartman sisters—Leah and Yesonia—are a long shot, unless that gun was never stolen."

I interrupted, "Here's another thought. We know the killer is college educated and he's made the trip from Minneapolis to St. Cloud on I-94. This corridor connects the two largest colleges in the state, the University of Minnesota Twin Cities campus and St. Cloud State University. Is it too much of a stretch to consider that the killer attended one of these campuses and works in the other city? Where did Zeke graduate from?"

Maddy grinned sardonically, "The University of Minnesota—in Duluth. So he drove I-35 rather than I-94. But we have Kub Kuam Peb at the University of Minnesota Twin Cities Campus." She said, "Okay, let's run with this thread. Where did Jada go to college?"

I answered, "The University of Minnesota, Twin Cities Campus."

"And didn't she do some free-lance writing for the *St. Cloud Times*?"

I conceded, "Yes, she did."

Maddy continued, "And how about Ava?"

"Augsburg."

Maddy frowned until I told her, "Her dorm sat right on the edge of University of Minnesota campus. She lived closer to Ted Mann Concert Hall than I do."

She urged me on, "And how about El Epicene?"

"St. Cloud State University."

Maddy murmured, "Mmmm, interesting. Okay and let's see who else is associated with this case—Jack Kavanaugh?"

"St. Cloud State University."

Maddy teased, "How about Opie, that red-headed, Clear Lake cop?"

"Dale went to Central Lakes College, and then Minnesota State University in Mankato."

"Sean Reynolds?"

"Vermillion Community College in Ely."

Maddy laughed, "Are you kidding me? He headed to great white north?"

"Sean loves the boundary waters. Then Hamline."

Maddy considered, "And you went to SCSU too!"

"Yes. Maddy, that leaves you."

She kept me waiting a moment before sharing, "I went to a college that flows off people's tongues with pride. When you ask someone about a state college, they always offer an explanation like, 'It was affordable.'"

"Did I say that?"

Maddy shared with deep pride, "The University of St. Thomas."

"They say you can always tell a Tommie, but you can't tell 'em much."

With a light condescending tone, she whispered, "It's tell them."

Kiddingly, I added, "We forgot about Maurice Strock," our elderly supervisor. "Where did he go to school?"

She laughed, "Stonehenge."

I suggested, "I think we can dismiss Maurice."

"Agreed."

As silly as the exercise seemed, it made it increasingly clear that we were dealing with a small number of people who had inside information on this case. Maybe the answer was closer than it seemed. I became serious and Maddy now listened intently. "Zeke's somehow connected to this. The killer's been throwing darts and we've been chasing them rather than creating our own leads."

Maddy wordlessly walked by me toward Zeke's door, and with a nod, said, "Then let's do this."

Zeke answered the door in a worn black, Foo Fighters t-shirt and dingy blue sweatpants. He squinted at us warily, waiting for us to state our business.

There was no point in small talk, so I firmly stated, "Zeke, I need to know what you were doing on the night Alan Volt was killed."

Zeke was nervous. "I don't have to answer any of your questions." His eyes began darting wildly about.

Maddy interjected with a hand up, "Look, Zeke, we've known each other for years. Let's just get this cleared up."

Zeke stared hard at Maddy, as he realized he didn't have much choice in the matter. He turned and led us into the entryway and closed the door behind us. He crossed his pudgy arms, blocking any further entry into his home and said defensively. "I was home. Alone."

I said, "No alibi?"

"Why are you harassing me? Maybe I should talk to HR. People change jobs all the time. You've been giving me crap about my work on this case, when I've generated our best leads. Neither of you is doing any better than me, so get off my ass."

Maddy asked, "You're switching jobs?"

Zeke's face tightened, but he didn't respond.

I was losing patience. "I don't give a crap about you leaving the BCA. I may leave, myself, when this is done. Do you realize it took over an hour to get ahold of you on the night of the murder?"

Appalled, Zeke opened his mouth to yell, but nothing came out. He looked away and looked back at me again, arguing, "You didn't need me immediately."

I pressed, "Give me an alibi for the murder."

Resigned, Zeke waived us unceremoniously into the living room. We found ourselves standing in front of a large-screened television, paused with the cartoon image of a woman displaying ample cleavage, wearing a red and gold Wonder Woman type of outfit. She had long blades for fingernails and a gold tiara with a green emerald on her forehead.

Maddy laughed and said, "Wow, is she on her way to the Abu Dhabi beach or does she work for the Justice League?"

Zeke was defensive as he explained, "I'm trying to become a professional SMITE player."

I thought out loud, "Smite means to strike with force."

Annoyed, Zeke said, "It's a video game. SMITE stands for Suspected Malicious Insider Threat Elimination. It's one of the most popular MOBA's."

Maddy looked confused, so I shared, "Multi online battle arenas."

Zeke rolled his eyes and explained, "Look, I have to play six hours a day to hone my skills. You have to be in the top point-one percent to go pro, and I'm just outside of the cut right now. You can win $150,000 for one of these championships. I'm close to having sponsors. SMITE consumes all my free time, so I don't always stop and answer the phone."

I told Maddy, "While I'm not familiar with SMITE, I've heard the MOBA League of Legends is paying $500,000 for a championship."

Maddy was equally impressed and incredulous. "That's crazy."

Zeke was becoming more energized. "You know who Marcus Samuelsson is, right?"

I nodded, "Yes, top chef. Born in Ethiopia and was adopted by a Scandinavian family. Does charity work in New York City."

Zeke continued, dropping onto a worn leather recliner, the end table beside it covered with various game controllers and empty energy drink cans. "Marcus talks about there being ten chefs in the world who are a step above even your best chefs. It's the same in the computer industry. There are guys who are that good. This killer is out of the league of any of our state computer experts. We're not going to catch him through computer work. I'm sorry— I'll keep trying, but that's the reality of it."

Maddy and I remained standing. Maddy said, "If you were playing SMITE, you should be logged on during the murder. There should be some record of games, right?"

Zeke nodded, "Certainly. It's not like anybody could just fill in for me. There's nobody else in the state who plays at my level."

"You knew what Fafnir referred to, on Asher Perry's body, and you didn't say a damn thing." I asked, "Why didn't you tell us Fafnir was a SMITE character?"

Zeke looked away, "First you claim my car was there. If I would have told you that," he hesitated, "I don't know—someone's setting me up. As a Muslim, I'm an easy target, so I decided to keep my mouth shut."

"Your car was in Alan Volt's neighborhood the night he was killed."

Zeke offered, "Maybe you read the plate wrong."

Maddy pointed out, "We have it on video. It's your car, Zeke."

Zeke argued, "Well, you're wrong. My gaming history will prove I was right here."

I tried to imagine any other possible explanation. I considered, "Do you keep an extra set of keys on your car?"

He nodded, "Yeah, under the driver's side wheel well. And I always leave it outside . . ."

21

LIGHTNING BOLTS CUT JAGGED TRAILS through the night sky, while thunder pounds in the distance. A spatter of rain weeps as I cruise through the darkness to the home of Nina Cole and Bo Gere in rural Princeton. Bo Gere's truck is at work, as planned, so there will be no surprises tonight. The investigative shows don't bother to show how many times a great serial killer goes out and comes home with nothing. I've had eight weeks in a row of people not being home, having guests over, or neighbors barbequing outside too close to the targeted home for me to escape unnoticed. It's time for me to end this dry spell. Tonight, I selected a house in the middle of nowhere.

I park my car down the road from Bo's rural weather-battered home. One ragged window had simply been covered with plywood, rather than replaced. When I approach the front door, I find it has already been unlocked, as Nina is expecting Bo home from work in an hour. I toe my shoes off and quietly slip inside. Dirty dishes are piled up on the kitchen counter, and my socks peel off the sticky linoleum as I cross the floor.

I can hear Nina whimpering, softly and repeatedly, "No, Bo," as I quietly make my way up the steps. I draw my gun. Bo shouldn't be home yet. I could leave, but I want Nina, so I wait for a minute and then continue my ascent. The second step to the top creaks under my weight, and Nina's soft cries stop.

She calls, "Bo?"

I realize she must have been dreaming. I grunt in response.

I can hear soft footsteps approaching on the other side of the door. I hastily snug the gun into the back of my pants, pull the rag out of my pocket, and wet it with ether . . .

I now have Nina unconscious and restrained, "Bo Gere style," in bed. With half-inch wide, black leather straps, Bo tethers Nina's wrists to her ankles while she lies flat on her back, in bed—right wrist to right ankle and left wrist to left ankle. With two additional straps, he then ties each ankle/wrist bind to the frame of the bed, rendering escape impossible. Nina has small breasts and scrawny, chicken-like arms and legs—not the picture she portrays online. There are purplish bruises around her breasts where Bo must have previously tied some type of ligature. By lamplight, I study her and realize she was experiencing an aftereffect of meth use, called "the shoulder." After the immediate rush, the user slides into a pattern of repetitive phrases or behavior that can last for hours. The ether has silenced her. *She's mine now . . .*

I STILL HAVE AT LEAST TEN MINUTES before Bo's home, so I turn the bright light on in Nina's bedroom for a moment then, disgusted by her pale, scabbed body, shut it back off. Nina's going to die in a matter of months from using.

I wrap my hands around her throat and consider putting her down. Why prolong her agony? I tighten my grip, but I'm embarrassed that Bull (my dad) has taken control. I loosen my hold on her and resume self-control once again. I have to give her a chance to change, like I've given the others.

I abandon Nina and find the gun safe stored in a closet. I selected this home because my reconnaissance revealed that Bo has a Taser, a Maxim nine-millimeter pistol with a built-in silencer, and a stockpile of toys I'll be using in the future. I break into homes *because* there are guns in the home. The safe requires a key, which Bo must have on him. As I check the clock, I realize Bo has either stopped at a bar, or has a friend he's spending time with. Where else do you go after midnight in Princeton?

I find some of Bo's homemade DVDs and put them in the living room DVD player. I cringe as I watch Bo beating a bound Nina with an electric chord. He has two ex-girlfriends who have complained online about how he didn't stop the S&M, even after the safe word was expressed. Bo will soon have his comeuppance.

They stop serving alcohol at 1:00 a.m., so shortly after 1:00, I walk out into the dark and wait for Bo to pull into the driveway. It's damp and warm outside, but no longer raining—a calm between the storms. I shut the yard light off. With the cloud cover, I should be able to get very close to Bo's truck unnoticed.

I could have Nina again, but I don't think I will. I used a condom, to avoid possibly catching herpes. I'm still angry. Nina

Cole was no Ava Mayer. The plus with Nina is the ether worked perfectly, although she was probably too wasted to give the police anything of value, anyway. But Ava's smart enough to figure things out.

I look forward to making Maddy Moore aware of the suicide cypher that reads, "Maddy like false allegations?" After my freshman year of college, an alumnus came forth with a full-ride scholarship for a student of high potential. I was the top candidate until another candidate suggested I had taken advantage of a high school senior I had been assigned to guide through a tour of the college. I never dated much, so when she gave me her phone number, I called. She was eighteen, and visited me when I was alone in my dorm on a cold winter's night. For God's sake, is a work-study freshman really in a position of power over another consenting adult?

A professor later asked her if I made her feel uncomfortable and she said I did, and that was the end of my scholarship. I went back to her and asked her why she said this, and she told me, "It felt a little weird that you asked me to lie still during sex." I had asked her to lie still because I'm not too big and I wanted it to work. "Not too big" is different than "a small dick," as Ava Mayer suggested. A bolt only needs to be the size of the nut, so Ava's comment is more of a criticism of herself. Trust me, Ava will get another lesson, yet.

Tonight I need to remain calm. The best is still yet to come. I'm not running. Before the night's over, there will be a dead investigator near Princeton, and my work will finally receive the national attention I deserve.

22

O N EARLY THURSDAY MORNING, I woke to my ringing cell phone. The body of a male had been found three miles south of Clearwater, on Interstate 94, between Minneapolis and St. Cloud. Fortunately, the responding officer had read the memo we sent, stating the BCA was looking for any murder or suicide victims with odd sorts of lines marked on the body, so we were contacted immediately. The man was apparently still dressed, but his shirt was cut, and line markings were observed on the side of his body. I quickly dressed and was waiting outside my apartment when Maddy pulled in to pick me up.

Maddy told me there was a body, but no vehicle this time. She suggested we have officers secure the crime scene and drive directly to the victim's home. "This guy seems to know exactly how we're going to respond. He's smart enough to not use his car to haul the body, so maybe he's on his way back to the victim's home. The responding officers can secure the scene. My concern is there's a woman still tied up there."

I called the officer at the scene, and he pulled the victim's driver's license from his pocket. Bo Gere—Princeton address. Maddy's siren wailed from her midnight-blue Crown Victoria as it cut through the darkness toward Princeton. Maddy handed me her phone, and I gathered what I could from the officer before we ended the call. I had him email me some pictures I could access on my secure work cell phone.

Approximately three miles south of Clearwater, in a dark and unpopulated stretch of Interstate 94, state troopers were standing over a large ape of a man, whose body was carelessly discarded beneath an overpass on the side of the road. Scanning through the pictures sent to my email, I could see his long hair looked oily, and he was covered in tattoos. He appeared to have been pushed out of a vehicle onto his side and had partially rolled onto his back. He wore a red-and-white sleeveless flannel shirt that was blood-soaked from his being shot in the shoulder and twice in the head. The victim had a tattoo of *Sons of Anarchy*'s "Tig" on his right bicep. In the show, Tig was a biker with a proclivity for bizarre sexual behavior and the use of unwarranted violence. A closer photo showed his shirt had been cut open down the side, and lines were drawn on his skin by what I presumed was a black marker. The black lines gave the following transcription: *////. ///*

I forwarded the picture of the markings to Tony Shileto. It was early in the morning, but Tony could very possibly be awake, since he no longer had a schedule. Even if he was sleeping, Tony would be angry if I didn't send this to him immediately—he lived for this.

This corridor of Interstate 94, from St. Cloud to Minneapolis, was one of the busiest stretches of road in Minnesota, so dropping the body was a gutsy maneuver. The killer took advantage of the fact that 3:30 a.m. was the least busy time of day. Even though he found a window of opportunity to dump the body unnoticed, he was bent on this body being found. State troopers were pulling cars over and searching vehicles on I-94, since the freeway would be the fastest way to escape from the scene.

I pulled up a map of roadways running from Princeton to the stretch of I-94 where the body was found. Interstate 94 ran north and south in this part of the state. This meant the killer had only driven with the body on I-94 for a stretch of three miles. Now, we had three bodies in a fifty-mile stretch of I-94, deposited north of Minneapolis and south of St. Cloud. The killer had to be familiar with this drive. Even though Asher Perry's body wasn't directly on I-94, it was only a couple miles off the Clear Lake cut off people took from I-94 to St. Cloud.

Apparently, I was right about Tony being up. I received a text from him, stating the Ogham translation meant "Drang." I called my mom and got her out of bed to define Drang. It sounded German, and my mother was of German ancestry and an avid reader. She explained Sturm and Drang was an eighteenth-century literary movement, characterized by works containing rousing action and high emotionalism. It literally meant *storm and stress,* and was now used as a synonym for turmoil. Mom believed it could also be used to describe motivation. Our killer had a fascination with words—perhaps an English major or someone who spoke more than one language.

I turned to Maddy. "This killer might be going on a rampage tonight . . ."

23

I HAVE HIT THE JACKPOT. After I dump Bo's body on I-94, I return to his home and load Tasers and ammunition into my car. Bo's best gift to me is a Browning semi-automatic rifle with a thermal night vision scope. Using my new night scope, I keep my lights off as I head back on the narrow gravel road that runs by Bo's home. The only way out is to backtrack on 112th Avenue. As I reach the turn, I can see squad car lights approaching 112th from the highway, so I simply drive through the T in the road. The gravel road I'm on, which crosses 112th, has dead ends at both ends, so I'll have to come back after the car passes. The squad has to be headed to Bo Gere's home.

I pull my car into a field approach grown over with weeds and walk with my rifle and scope back to the curve. I haven't anticipated the cops would be here this quickly. I take my rifle and night vision scope and lay in the ditch to stabilize my shot. Maddy Moore's unmarked Crown Vic is approaching. I have a male passenger in the crosshairs. It has to be Jon Frederick. I have the ideal opportunity to get him off this case. I patiently wait for the car to slow at the curve and, with a perfect head shot, pull the trigger, exploding a lethal bullet into the night. "So much for your algorithm . . ."

24

MADDY AND I TURNED ON A GRAVEL ROAD, 112th Avenue, west of Princeton. Our headlights hit the front of sinister branches and bushes, the limbs of which swayed eerily onto the road. Thunderheads lit up the night sky as another storm approached. I couldn't shake the feeling that a dark shadow of evil had already been down this path once tonight. *Has it left?*

Maddy was feeling it, too. Her voice was thick with unease as she commented, "I am not feeling good about this."

I asked, "Do you want to wait for backup?"

Still skittish, she softly mouthed, "No."

I had never considered not going in. It was my job. But we were in a death trap, in a vehicle all lit up on a pitch-black road.

We reached a T in the road and turned right onto a path that was even narrower. Maddy nervously reached for her cellphone but knocked it from the console onto the floor on my side. As I had done so many times, I reached down to pick it up.

BANG! A blast rocketed through my passenger window, and our car plowed into the ditch. We hadn't rolled, but we were now at a forty-five degree angle, low on the driver's side. I quickly took inventory and saw that Maddy was bleeding from her neck. Her expression was confused as she put a shaking hand to her wound and then looked at the slick of blood across her palm. I quickly took her hand and placed it back against her wound, keeping my hand firmly on hers to apply pressure. With my other hand, I radioed in, "nine-nine-nine, ten thirty-three, 112th Avenue, west of Princeton," then dropped the receiver and drew my gun. "Nine-nine-nine" was the code for *officer down*, and "ten thirty-three" was code for *need immediate help.*

Where was the shooter? Was he heading toward the car? Slouching as low as I could, I told Maddy, "Keep your head elevated, keep applying pressure. I'll get the emergency kit from the trunk. Help is on the way."

Maddy's eyes were wide with panic and shock. They seemed to be pleading, *Please don't let me die.* At the rate she was losing blood, I needed cloth to help stanch the bleeding. I was wearing a t-shirt under my button-down, so quickly shed both shirts, pressed my t-shirt under her hand, and shrugged back into my outer shirt. I was afraid if I tried exiting Maddy's door, the shift in weight would roll the car. Even though the bullet came through my window, I needed to risk exiting my door to retrieve the survival kit from the trunk. I reached over Maddy and popped the trunk open.

I felt blindly into the backseat and found Maddy's powerful Maglite. I pushed my door open, while shining the flashlight directly to where the shot had originated. The illumination would make it harder for the shooter to pinpoint us and would render a night scope worthless. I left the light sitting on the dirt road, facing the shooter's direction.

I held my breath as I made a quick dash to the back of the car. I retrieved the emergency kit and returned to Maddy's side of the vehicle. Standing in the ditch on the driver's side, I yanked the door open and immediately dressed Maddy's wound. I placed her hand over her neck once again and reminded her to apply pressure. My hands were sticky with blood.

I assured Maddy, "I'm going to get us the hell out of here."

She nodded in appreciation. We both knew that her odds of surviving a gunshot were fifty-five percent better if someone at the scene drove you directly to the hospital, rather than waiting for an ambulance.

Keeping a tenuous hand on her neck, Maddy slid over the console to the passenger seat, and I climbed in behind the wheel. I steered the car out of the ditch, careful not to tip it, then cut the steering hard to the right and gunned it so I could spin the back end around on the narrow road. The rear-wheel-drive Crown Victorias made this maneuver easy. I then floored it, and with the tires spitting gravel projectiles into the night, I headed toward the Princeton hospital.

It was chilling to be sharing space with someone who was realizing death could be moments away. She couldn't risk saying anything because any movement would increase the bleeding. I spoke to her evenly, "Keep applying pressure. Hang on, now, Maddy—you're going to be okay." This was bad. I was hypersensitive to every bump.

As we exited the gravel road, I swore I saw a shadowy figure cloaked in darkness. I didn't have time to waste thinking about it. I glanced over at Maddy and her glazed eyes were fluttering shut. I urged her, "Hang in there. You can do this for Miles." Maddy was a loving mother who dedicated her life to making certain justice was served. I silently prayed for help as we rocketed down Highway 95.

MADDY SURVIVED THE TRIP to the hospital, and was quickly wheeled from the ER drop-off into an emergency room. I was told by emergency room staff the goal was to stabilize her and then transfer her by air ambulance to Fairview in Minneapolis. This basically meant if they could keep her alive for an hour, they'd try to transport her. I contacted Maddy's parents and gave them the grim news. I also called the Mille Lacs County Sheriff's Department and had them send a deputy to Bo Gere's home. I warned the officer of the shooter and told her I understood if she wanted to wait for back up. I wasn't immediately returning to help. I couldn't let Maddy die alone in the sterile and empty hospital room. Like many of our brave officers, the deputy told me she was going to Gere's home immediately, for the potential victim's sake.

MADDY WAS UNCONSCIOUS. Her father had arrived, indicating Maddy's mother was close behind. Knowing she was no longer alone, I arranged to have an officer posted outside her door, and drove to Bo Gere's home in Maddy's bloody vehicle.

5:15 A.M., THURSDAY, JUNE 22, PRINCETON

A LANKY FEMALE DEPUTY WAS LEANING on the hood of a Mille Lacs County Sheriff's car when I pulled into the dirt driveway. The house still had the original asbestos, cement-wall siding, and it must have been years since the windows were clean. My tennis shoes screeched noisily, sticking to the dirty linoleum floor as we made our way through the entry and up the stairs. The second floor held only one room, as the roof angled up from the first floor.

A pale meth addict sat on the edge of the bed looking like a plucked and famished crow in her black Ramones t-shirt. The deputy had draped a blanket over Nina Cole's shoulders but it didn't hide that she was tweaking, scratching her arms raw beneath it. The skin around her mouth and nose was reddened and raw, so I knew she'd been subdued in the same manner as the others.

The deputy joined me as I stood before Nina. "It's not the first time I've seen Nina like this. She's called the police about Bo before, but never follows through with charges. So I set her free from her restraints and told her to dress while I waited for your arrival. She's still pretty out of it."

I attempted to interview Nina, but she couldn't explain what had happened—she had no memory of it.

Nina finally slurred, "Is Bo okay?"

I gently informed her of our discovery, and after I gave her time to process this, asked, "Do you feel like you've been assaulted?"

Nina shivered out, "Yeah." She touched her bruised neck while I studied the hand print on her throat.

I kept my tone low and kind as I spoke to Nina, "We're going to have an ambulance pick you up so they can treat your injuries at the hospital." I didn't bother to tell her that they'd probably place her in detox as well, because it wasn't my call. As a result of her drugged-out state, she was going to give us little of value.

Resigned to cooperating, Nina nodded, "I'm so cold . . ."

I STAYED AND PROCESSED THE SCENE until daylight. As I was preparing to leave, a long-haired hillbilly-type character pulled into the yard in an old Chevy truck. After seeing me, he was about to back away when I ran to him and yanked open the driver's side door. I flashed my investigator's badge and introduced myself.

He had a whiney Southern drawl when he spoke, and his age-creased lips sank inward, no longer supported by front teeth. "I'm Bo's dad, Harley. I heard the news about Bo, so I thought I'd pick up some stuff I'd left here." With this, he spat a gob of dark-brown tobacco juice onto the ground, closer to my feet than I'd have liked. I took a casual step backwards.

I nodded slightly, then said, "While you're here, we should get your fingerprints if you've been in the home, so we can separate them from our killer." Honestly, I wanted as much information as I could get on this character.

Harley swore under his breath and said, "I have a couple of past assault charges. Just drunken bar fights." His lips worked perpetually as he moved his chew around his gums. "You know how they say the lights are on, but no one's home—that's not Bo.

Bo's home, he just ain't answering the door. That boy was cantankerous from the day he was born. I never knew who or how, but it'd be a lie to say I didn't see this coming."

AFTER HARLEY WAS PRINTED, he led me into the home. There was no honor among criminals. Harley had come to his son's home to take possession of his weapons. When he saw the safe was empty, Harley grumbled in an accent so thick I could have cut it with a butter knife. "Ah shit!" With his twang, one could have mistaken it for "Aww sheet."

"Bo had a Browning semi-automatic rifle with a thermal night vision scope, a nine-millimeter with a built-in suppressor, ammo, and Tasers." Bent down and showing more of his back end than anybody needed to see, he studied the safe further. "Hell, his hockey mask is even missing." Harley straightened up slowly, wincing at the effort, and turned to me, "Your killer is now loaded for bear, son."

AFTER BEING INFORMED THAT MADDY was airlifted to Fairview in Minneapolis, I contacted her parents again, and her father assured me her brothers, sister, and son were now all there for her. Maddy had lost a lot of blood, but the bullet had missed both her carotid artery and her windpipe.

As I drove back to Minneapolis, I decided not to call Serena and tell her someone had tried to kill me. Serena was already hesitant about being around me. I called Jada, but after some cursory comfort, she told me, "I've got to get to work," and she was gone. So I called the person I should have called immediately after family—Clay.

25

I RECEIVED A CALL FROM FAIRVIEW HOSPITAL in Minneapolis, requesting I come in. I had only been asleep for a few hours, but, expecting the worst, I didn't hesitate.

Various family members stood in the hall conversing when I arrived. I greeted Maddy's father briefly. Then a thin, gray-haired woman approached me and introduced herself as Maddy's mother. When I replied with a handshake and told her my name, she squeezed my hand with surprising strength, and said, "She's asking for you. We've been told to let her rest, but she's insisting she needs to talk to you before she falls back to sleep."

As I made my way toward the room, I caught sight of Miles, sitting away from the rest of the family. He looked up forlornly, and I gave him a slight nod, trying to convey strength.

I stepped into the room to find a pale-looking Maddy, half-awake, with tubes hanging from an IV stand by her bed.

Maddy didn't waste a moment. Through a pained, raspy voice, she croaked with intensity, "I remember him. In the parking ramp—he put a rag over my nose and mouth. He told me, 'You gave away a stable home for your son, for sex. We'll see how important sex is to you after tonight.' And then everything went black."

I silently thanked Jada for interrupting what could have been a much worse experience for Maddy. I sat in a cushioned chair next to her bed, "It was a man?"

Maddy closed her eyes for a moment, searching for the memory, "I think so. I didn't see him. It's weird. I remembered this coming out of anesthesia. I know it wasn't a dream, but why would I remember it then?"

"It's called state dependent memory. The tracers to that memory occurred in an aestheticized state, so when you returned to that state, the memory came back. It's the same reason some people tell the same story every time they're drunk. That state brings back the memory."

Maddy closed her eyes and leaned her head back into her pillow, her burst of energy having drained her. "That's all I have."

"Do you want me to go?"

After a bit, Maddy opened her eyes and with a painful smile, shared, "You know why he shot me, don't you?"

I played along, "Why?"

"'Cause I'm funnier than you are. Watch any horror movie—they always go after the funny one. What's that you always say?"

I shared, "The world hates comedians. What's the first thing a mugger says? 'Don't try anything funny.'"

She reached her hand toward me, and I took it. She softly told me, "You're all right, Jon."

I suggested, "Just relax. We'll have plenty of time to give each other grief when you return."

With her eyes still closed, she shook her head.

I'd thought Maddy drifted into a light sleep, but then she peeked one eye open and asked, "Do you think Clay's cheating on me?"

My first thought was, *probably*, but I honestly told her, "Not that I know of."

She sighed painfully, "It's okay. I haven't dated in a while, and I just want to know where we stand. I bet you and Clay were studs back in that small town."

I laughed, "Did Clay tell you that?"

"No, he just talks about how smart you are."

I told her, "Neither of us graduated in the top ten in a class of *ninety*. Neither of us made the top ten king candidates, out of about forty guys. We both drove cars that were so crappy they didn't heat up enough to melt the snow on the floor in the winter. We both came out of poverty. Mine was financial, his was emotional. We both had angry dads, but my mom was around, and I had an older sister to balance it."

Maddy commented drowsily, "Clay needs a better wing-man."

With a smile, I cautioned her, "I'm not done. Clay is a self-made man. He's made himself one of the best builders I know. He owns a beautiful home and a new extended cab, four-wheel drive truck. My point is, he became who he is without a lot of help."

Maddy's last words before she drifted off to sleep were, "Just like our killer."

I was about to tell Maddy that we know this killer. He writes on the murder victim's bodies, and sends cyphers to the press. He leaves bodies along I-94. It all screams, "Give me attention!" At some point, this killer has spoken to us face-to-face. We just didn't see the killer inside.

I found myself revisiting the term "eroticized rage." I'd bet our killer witnessed sexual violence when he was younger, and even though he perceives himself as saving these women, he's too aroused by the abuse to walk away without reenacting it. Therapists refer to it as a trauma bond. My extensive reading on trauma therapy, since Serena left, has taught me something.

11:30 P.M., THURSDAY, JUNE 22,

MINNEAPOLIS

AFTER A LONG DAY OF WORK, I stood in front of my living room window, looking down at the streets of Minneapolis, fifteen stories below. The dazzling beauty of a lit-up Minneapolis was lost on me tonight. The ghost out there who'd killed three men, and attempted to kill our only coherent witness, had now put an investigator out of commission. Sean Reynolds did me a favor last night. While I was waiting at the hospital, I asked Sean to find Kub Kuam Peb. He did. Kub was working in the computer lab at the University of Minnesota. There were witnesses. Kub had a solid alibi. I was wrong when I theorized the number thirteen had something to do with me. It was all about trying to set Kub up. Our killer loved manipulating the investigators, which gave me the impression the killer was close enough to observe our struggles.

I missed Serena. There was once a sense of magic in our intimacy. We'd stand in front of this window together, wishing the rest of the world could be as content. *How could she walk away from that?* My phone buzzed and, for a moment, I had a sense of hope.

I was greeted by the gruff voice of a police officer from the Minneapolis Second Precinct, "Remember that girl you had me run a check on about a month ago? She was just found dead in her apartment. I remember her because it was such an odd name."

"Yesonia Hartman? Give me the address—I'll be right there!" Panic and despair overtook me. *I should have prevented this.* I called Maurice Strock and told him our killer might be cleaning house, so he agreed to have officers find Nina Cole and keep her safe. I also asked him to make sure Maddy was protected. Culhwch's strength was his ability to continue after others fell asleep, so I wanted everyone to be on guard. I called Ava and Angela Mayer. Ava was safe at home with security guards still in place. I called both Layla Boyd and Dale Taylor in Clear Lake.

When I arrived at Yesonia's apartment by the University of Minnesota, a handful of college students milled about in the hallway. I turned to the officer on the scene and said, "Get all their names off their IDs and keep them in a room until we can interview them. If anyone has anything to offer you deem important, let me know right away."

I stepped around them into Yesonia's apartment.

A pretty Chicano woman with long dark hair lay dead on the couch. Based on her state of dress—an oversized t-shirt, the logo of which was "Empty Without Reason," and just underwear—

it appeared she had been tucked in for the night when she was attacked. My heart sank. It was so easy for people to be evil, and it was so hard to stop it. I made my way over to her for a closer look. Hematomas in her eyes and a red mark on her neck indicated that she had been choked to death. The killer had likely broken the hyoid bone in her neck. The hyoid was just below the chin and over the throat—it was the only bone in the body not connected to another bone. Fracturing the hyoid was the most common way a woman was killed during a sexual assault. The girl looked like Yesonia, but she wasn't Yesonia.

I looked around, "Who called this in?"

One of the officers approached me and answered, "Her neighbor heard what she thought was a physical fight. She locked herself in her apartment, called the police, and hid until they arrived."

Suddenly, a frantic Yesonia Hartman burst into the apartment, flanked by an officer who struggled to hold her back. Yesonia was screaming, "Where is she?"

Yesonia tearfully identified the victim as her older sister, Leah, age twenty-two. Leah had been staying with her to get away from her abusive boyfriend. *Had he found her?*

Investigator Sean Reynolds arrived at the scene. The BCA was taking this seriously, and Sean was one of our best. He was a clean-cut African American whose black slacks always held a crease, and his white shirt was crisply pressed. Sean told me he studied Maddy's notes on this case and was ready to work. After viewing Leah's body and briefly scanning the apartment, Sean approached me and pointed to Yesonia. "Get her out of here. Put her someplace safe. I'll process the scene."

I gave Yesonia a moment to look over the scene with her sister, so she would leave with me willingly rather than my having to force her out the door.

As we exited the apartment complex, Yesonia wept so hard her body went limp. I pulled her close to keep her upright. Once we made our way past the flashing blue lights of squad cars, we headed toward the darkness where my car rested. Cars were parked up and down the street. I helped Yesonia into the passenger seat, and she asked to lie down, so I put the seat all the way back and as flat as it would go. Yesonia turned on her side, facing me, and slumped into a fetal position.

I carefully observed approaching headlights as I pulled away from the curb. Concerned that this could potentially be the killer, I directed Yesonia to stay down, just in case. As I turned to her to make certain, a shot blasted through the passenger side window and out the windshield in front of me. Odd thoughts occur to me during stress. *Gun it!* was my immediate reaction, based on reading a forensic study of John Kennedy's assassination. Our only Catholic president had been killed partially because his driver hit the brakes after the first shot, making the ensuing shots easier.

I put the pedal to the floor, holding Yesonia down in her seat as my Taurus barreled down the block. I took a sharp left around an apartment complex and without looking at Yesonia, asked, "Are you're okay?" The entrance and exit trajectory of the bullet made it clear she hadn't been hit. When she didn't respond, I added, "Be careful, but I think you're safe now."

Yesonia frantically shouted, "How can we be okay? You've only been driving for ten seconds!"

I reassured her, "Long chase scenes are for bad drivers. Unless he has a gun that can shoot through a three-story building, we're good. The shot didn't come from that oncoming car. The shooter was behind us. There was no car approaching us from behind, so he was on foot."

"How do you know it didn't come from that car?"

I pointed to the holes in the windows. "When a bullet first enters it still has its shape, but it flattens out with every object it hits, so the exit hole is bigger." I was sure our killer was excited to use his new weapon with the night vision scope again. I studied Yesonia for a moment and considered the scenario. Yesonia's seat was back, and she was still sitting so low she was basically invisible. That shot may have been intended for me.

There were no more shots. I called for assistance. My colleagues had heard the shot and were responding. I gave them our exact address at the moment the shot was fired. I could hear Sean yell in the background, "Get her the fuck out of here. We'll deal with it! And don't tell anyone where you're taking her." Sean had to have the same suspicion I had. The killer was close to our investigation.

Yesonia and I were both quiet as I headed north. After twenty minutes, she asked me to pull over. We were in a brief lull of traffic around us, so I complied. She stood on the shoulder of Interstate 94, demoralized, staring out at the freeway. The bright colors in her floral, off-the-shoulder blouse were incongruent with her misery.

I listened on the scanner as the police unsuccessfully searched for the shooter. I called Sean and told him I wanted the officers to find that bullet, as I needed to verify this case was related to the other two murders, and not simply the result of a jealous boyfriend.

Maybe I'd been thinking about this case wrong. Culhwch was trying to kill me. He wanted me off this case. Why shoot at me only when I was strapped in a car? For the same reason he sexually assaults bound women. Strapped in, I was no threat. If I stopped thinking of the break-in to my home as related to the killer, it made sense. He knew how to use a rifle, but was not a marksman—he'd missed me twice. He knew computers, but was not an elite expert as Zeke had suggested. If he was, he would've been showing off instead of destroying hard drives. The I-94 Killer was a college student or graduate (based on his cyphers). He wanted Maddy on the case because, like the other victims, she had engaged in something he perceived as shameful—infidelity. Like the others, she was argumentative and attractive.

I observed a flurry of headlights approaching in the distance, so I quickly exited the car and ran to Yesonia. I carefully guided her back to the car, brushing remnants of shattered glass off of the passenger seat before helping her in. I turned the scanner off when we turned onto Highway 25 to head north to Pierz. We were now driving into the darkness of rural Minnesota. No more streetlights and no more billboards, just the blackness of the night on a road that sliced through a forest of pine trees.

Yesonia turned on the radio. A classic rock station was playing, "Sharing the Night Together," by Dr. Hook. Despite my frustration, a sad smile, reminiscent of past pleasantries, came over me, and I reached over and shut it off. This wasn't the time.

Yesonia's voice was weak when she asked, "Do you have a problem with light music? Because I'm feeling a little tense right now." She looked it, too. She was rigid in her seat, hands clasped tightly between her legs. Yesonia looked haunted in the limited dashboard lighting.

I turned the song back on softly, and said, "Do you hear this tacky part, where the girl is whispering in the background, 'Would you mind, sharing the night?'"

She nodded.

"My dad listened to Dr. Hook, so this song was on when a girl I was crazy about was over. She whispered along with the song, in that same tacky tone, 'Would you mind, sharing the night?' because she knew it embarrassed the hell out of me."

"What was her name?"

"Serena. We have a daughter, but we're separated now." There was a method to my madness. I chose to share, because I wanted her to talk to me.

As the song ended, I shut the radio back off and said, "I can't ignore the fact that the killer came to your apartment. Who is trying to kill you?" With my lights on bright, I habitually scanned both sides of the dark road for deer or other creatures that ventured out on rural Minnesota roads at night.

"I'm not sure. I've had this creepy feeling that somebody's been watching me lately."

"Did you get a glimpse of who it was?"

Yesonia shook her head, "No." She took a deep labored breath, as if she could burst into tears at any moment. She quickly forced out, "I first noticed it about an hour after you left Republic that night."

I was uncertain of her honesty, until she said, "He has an odd smell. It was in the bar tonight, again. I wanted to make sure no one followed me home, so I stopped at a friend's apartment before I went to mine. When I got to my apartment, you guys were there." She covered her face. "It's my fault! I didn't know Leah was there. I would have warned her. She comes over when she's arguing with her boyfriend. It's happened so much lately, I just finally gave her a key. Leah had this love-hate thing with every guy she's dated. They'd treat her like crap and she'd hate them, but all they had to do was apologize, and she was back in love again."

Yesonia was unintentionally describing Maddy Moore, Layla Boyd, and even Ava Mayer. It occurred to me that it wasn't a physical type this killer was after. He was talking online to these women and was attracted to the antagonistic and crisis-seeking characteristics of Borderline Personality Disorder. Borderline Personality Disorder involved serious instability in interpersonal relationships and alternating between extremes of idealizing and criticizing lovers. They struggle with chronic feelings of emptiness, and an unstable sense of their own identity.

The night was overcast, dark. I dimmed my speedometer lights so my eyes would adjust and see further into the night. I let Yesonia experience her grief uninterrupted, until she emitted a sad laugh.

"Everybody *loved* Leah. She was so beautiful. Even that dick of a boyfriend was envious of the fact that people loved talking to her. People are going to blame me because she was killed at my place—like maybe I had something to do with it. I was just thinking the one positive thing is that I was shot at. Maybe if people realize he was trying to kill me too, they'll forgive me." Yesonia propped her elbow on the door's armrest and rested her chin dejectedly in her hand.

I softly consoled her, "You didn't do anything wrong. Don't for a moment think that anyone, beyond that psychopath who killed her, is responsible for this. If it was up to you, she'd still be alive."

Yesonia closed her eyes and whimpered with haunting grief that cut right through me. She loved her sister. She finally spoke again. "James Cider was such a jealous prick. He knew nobody could ever love him like everyone loved Leah. He was destroying her. It wouldn't surprise me if he killed her. If he did, I'll kill him . . ." Her voice trailed off into inaudible words.

I asked, "Why did Leah pick abusive men? People who do this usually have a past trauma. What happened to Leah?"

Yesonia took a little too long to answer, "I don't know."

I had struck a chord, and I decided to play off-tune and make her correct me. "It happened to you. Leah's been hiding a secret for you."

Yesonia became defiant, "I would never ask her to live with that."

I considered her response, "But Leah asked that of you." When no response came forth, I revealed, "The other murder victims were shot. She may have been strangled because the killer wanted information—like who she might have told. There is no secret to keep for Leah now."

Yesonia's head was bowed for a long time before she nodded, and seemed to come to an agreement with herself. "Two years ago, Leah invited over some guy named Cully she had met online. He tried to rape her. She had one leg in a cast, and she still fought him off. That's what she was like. I was upstairs peeking down the steps—too afraid to move. I didn't do a damn thing.

I didn't even get a good look at him. The stair railings were in the way."

"And that's the night the gun disappeared."

Yesonia nodded.

I had to wonder how differently things would have gone if she would have just told someone back then. Buckman was a close-knit town. Someone would have identified his car. The rapist went to using ether after Leah defeated him. He wasn't going to risk losing another fight with a victim. I offered, "Thank you for sharing. Please tell me anything you can remember."

Yesonia's voice hardened in determination. "He was fat— he wasn't in very good shape. And when Leah and I hugged after he left, there was this smell—not a strong smell, but a unique smell. I hadn't even thought about that until I caught the smell again in the bar, but it was there again tonight. I immediately panicked and left. I didn't want to know—I just bailed."

"Did it smell like ginger?"

"No. Sweat and something industrial."

He must have added the Blvgari after he met Maddy. He wanted the investigators to turn on her. Now that Maddy was no longer a suspect, he had no reason to keep wearing the perfume.

I handed Yesonia my phone so she could call her parents. They had already received the devastating news and were on their way to Minneapolis. After their long, painful conversation, Yesonia sat in silence, still holding the phone.

I asked, "How badly do you want to live?"

Yesonia looked at me as if the question was absurd. "Bad."

"Bad enough to surrender your cell phone and all your internet use? You'd have to live with my conservative parents and schizophrenic brother for a couple weeks and not tell a soul."

She didn't agree, but she didn't say no.

"It's the only way I can guarantee you'll stay alive. Maybe my dad will even teach you to fire a gun. But Yesonia, you can't contact anyone—not even family—not over the internet. I'll get you a burner phone so you can call them. This guy is tracking everyone over the internet. If you go online, he'll find you."

We drove through Yesonia's hometown of Buckman, and her tears started flowing more freely as we passed St. Michael's church. She sobbed, "I love the Buckman choir. They'll sing at Leah's funeral, and the church will be packed."

I shared, "There's a stained glass window in St. Michael's, titled *The Descent of the Holy Spirit*, which features Mary in turquoise blue and pure white that glows when the sun shines. To me, it exudes grace."

Yesonia bitterly replied, "Why Leah? She was a drama queen—there's no denying that. But she excelled in every aspect of her life, aside from her relationships. She always had to have the bad boy."

I shook my head, "I'm no expert, but I have a theory. I think some people who have experienced trauma divide the world into victims or offenders. Victims don't want to be with someone who is as anxious and afraid as they are. Because of this, they pick partners with vices they think they understand. They don't trust healthy people because they've forgotten what it's like to be healthy."

Yesonia processed all I'd said. She returned, "It makes sense. I briefly dated a good friend, when Leah was dating James. When Mom told Leah she should find a guy like the one I was dating, she told our mom, 'At least I know what James's vices are.'" After a pause, Yesonia asked, "What are your vices?"

"I'm obsessive, and I'm beginning to realize I'm also arrogant. I think I deserve Serena, who is beautiful and kind. I don't stalk her or threaten her like James Cider, but it's still a little arrogant, isn't it?"

Yesonia's bitterness quickly dissipated, and she murmured, "You love her. Love is something." I was having a hard time keeping up with her shifting moods but attributed them to her grief.

"It's something painful when it isn't shared."

Ahead of us, an unexpected orange glow seeped into the blackened sky. My first thought was a farmer was burning a brush pile.

Yesonia, resigned, said, "I'll stay with your parents, but could you bring some of my clothes?" When she noticed the intense light out of place in such darkness, Yesonia pointed. "Maybe it's a sign."

As we came over a hill, Yesonia gasped at the fire surrounding us. The ditches had been set ablaze and generated a bright orange, hellish glow on the charred black prairie around us.

Yesonia shrieked, "We're trapped!" She frantically began looking out all sides of the car.

I soothed her, "We're okay. It only appears we're surrounded. The road curves ahead. The farmers around Pierz burn the ditches every spring. The theory is that the land will be productive more quickly, but honestly, I think they just like burning things. Controlled burning prevents large fires from spreading, since it eliminates the dead brush."

Yesonia stared at me incredulously, looked around at the fires again and muttered, "Jesus," under her breath. "This is where you're from?"

I nodded affirmatively. I could hear a long exhale as she collected herself for a moment, then commented, "Tonight it feels like the devil won. I can't imagine ever being happy again." She slumped into her seat, having now used up the little energy she had left.

The fire didn't bother me, except when I considered we were driving a gas-powered vehicle through an area with flames all around us. The burning was done annually. I'd driven through it before—a lot of people had—and I'd never heard of anyone being hurt from doing that. Yesonia was silent for the rest of the journey.

1:20 A.M., FRIDAY, JUNE 22,
PIERZ

WHEN WE ARRIVED AT MY PARENTS' HOME, they didn't hesitate for a moment to take Yesonia in. My mother, Camille, gently guided a mute Yesonia toward the kitchen, murmuring soft assurances and condolences to her as they moved down the hall. I knew there would be homemade bread sliced and served with jelly preserves, and chamomile tea brewing in no time. As comfort went, Yesonia couldn't be in better hands.

I quietly discussed the dangers Yesonia was facing with my father, to ensure he had a solid grasp of the situation. As safety went, my dad was your guy. He once nearly shot Serena, as he was tucked away with his rifle protecting his home and those of us in it. I knew he would do what it took to make sure no harm came to Yesonia.

My schizophrenic brother, Victor, looked on from the living room doorway, watching both scenes unfold, processing everything in a way only Victor could. After dealing with Ava's insults, he was understandably hesitant, but seeing Yesonia's shaken state, he eventually conceded to another guest and returned to his room. As a paranoid schizophrenic, Victor never minimized anyone's fear. As listeners went, Victor was one of the best. He would sit and listen to anyone who wanted to talk to him, for as long as they wanted to talk. Sometimes, I'd ask Victor later what a conversation had been about and he'd shrug and say, "I didn't understand it, but they needed to talk, so I listened."

I respected Victor for his kindness. It was painful to imagine what it was like for him, to constantly have ideas no one else understood, or to have a legitimate insight into an issue that others dismissed because of his mental illness.

26

I CALLED YESONIA EACH NIGHT to check on her. My parents loved her—she was humble and respectful. Sensing her growing boredom with country life, my father made attempts to introduce her to the more interesting landmarks in the area. On one such day, he took her on a drive to the wooded area East of Buckman, which borders Hillman, where abandoned homes sat lifeless on weed-ridden, forgotten plots of land.

My father pointed to a particularly odd grouping of shacks, and explained with a laugh that this was where the infamous Gwiasdowski brothers once lived as hillbillies making moonshine. They got in trouble one time for soaking the wool sheared off their sheep in used crank case oil, so they'd get more for it when it was sold by weight. Two of the brothers lived in train boxcars they had bought and deposited in the woods. The remaining two built a house with a ceiling one inch higher than the tallest brother, to prevent waste. Later in their lives, the brothers ended up at St. Mary's Villa, and swore like demons any time they were asked to bathe. Dad remembered one of the brothers telling him, "They expect us to bathe every week, whether we need it or not."

My dad got such a kick out of that story, his laughter grew heartier as he told it. Soon Yesonia was chuckling with him. She especially enjoyed the part about how they had the meanest dog alive and stored all their money under the doghouse. The home and boxcars were now gone, but there was still a haggard old hunting shack on their wooded land.

TODAY, OUT OF THE BLUE, my mom insisted I come and get Yesonia, as she was kicking her out of the house. I couldn't imagine what Yesona could've done that would have resulted in this about-face from my mother.

My farm home was like a time warp. If Dad was home alone, the music filling every corner of the home would be that of Credence Clearwater Revival or Lynard Skynard. If my mom was home, you'd be tapping your foot to Roseanne Cash or Emmy Lou Harris.

Today, there was no music when I entered, a clear sign of trouble. Bill and Camille had taken one side of the rectangular kitchen table, while Victor and Yesonia sat across from them. Dad wore his usual flannel shirt and tattered jeans, his rugged features leathery from a lifetime of outdoor work. Mom had long, reddish hair with a hint of gray. She wore a sensible, forest green button-down shirt with jeans. The expressions on both of their faces were anything but warm.

Victor's thinking was so far outside the box, sometimes you'd simply hope he could find his way back to it. He had long, dyed-blond hair and a brown moustache. He wore a black t-shirt that read, *What if the Hokey Pokey Is What It's All About?* Yesonia was clad in an off-white peasant top, with smocking at the neckline and billowy sleeves. Her jeans were fashionably faded and intentionally ripped. When I saw the two of them holding hands, Victor, age thirty-three, and Yesonia, age nineteen, my first thought was Yesonia must be comforting him.

Camille started, lips pursed in pious consternation. "Jon, ask your brother what he was doing this afternoon."

Bill sighed and rested a calloused hand on her arm, in an attempt to calm her, "Don't be so hard on him, now, Camille. This might be the most normal thing he's ever done."

Victor smiled at Dad's approval, turned to Yesonia and said, "Just say yes."

She grinned with embarrassment and turned toward me defensively, "We're both adults." Yesonia shot a look at me that was briefly pleading, and I steeled myself for the rest of the story.

Camille turned to Bill, "Enough of this tit for tat. Let's show a united front."

Victor turned to Mom and casually asked, "In that saying, what does *tat* mean?"

Camille sat forward, a shrill tone cutting through her usual kind voice. "I will *not* have that under my roof! I will not advocate premarital sex." She sat back and roughly folded her arms over her chest.

My dad looked to me for assistance. While he was trying to keep a stern expression to support my mom, there seemed to be a glint of pride in his eyes. He surreptitiously winked at me, then resumed his impassive demeanor and scooted his chair closer to Mom's.

I stared dumbly at Victor, then at Yesonia, trying to process what I was hearing. I struggled with my own conflicts. Victor had always been on the outside looking in, due to his mental illness. None of us expected him to ever have a "normal" relationship, so to speak. I never would have predicted that something would occur between my brother and Yesonia. A part of me was a little happy for him. The other part was the law enforcement official in me, having trusted that Yesonia was there to be protected and not be put in a position of involvement in any kind of romantic tryst. Furthermore, having a child out of wedlock made me the wrong guy to give anyone a lecture on premarital relationships.

I pleaded with my parents, "I don't have another place to hide Yesonia." I turned to my brother, attempting reason. "Victor, could you agree to not have sex with Yesonia for a week?"

Victor was gloating. He gave this about two seconds of thought and said, "Absolutely not. This was the best day of my life. I read if two people want to be together, they will find a way to make it work. So it'll be work, but we'll make it together."

Yesonia affectionately squeezed his arm, "You're so funny, V."

I didn't think he was trying to be funny, but I didn't want to rain on his parade. An ill-managed chuckle escaped from Bill, and Mom threw her hands in the air in disgust. Camille scolded her husband, "You are of no help!"

In a soft, respectful voice, Yesonia intervened. "I know this seems so irresponsibly impulsive, but it wasn't. I mean—I know it's only been a week, but Victor and I walk together and talk for hours every day. Not any of that pretend internet stuff. I'm talking about face to face, sometimes holding hands, honest reflection."

Camille's eyes narrowed, "When do you walk?"

Yesonia glanced down, obviously embarrassed over sharing more than she intended. "Late at night. We walk through the woods, along the river, about the farm. Victor taught me I don't need to be afraid of the dark. It's still the same farm. It's just that the lights are off. And, by the way, I'd like to be called Sonia now. Leah always wanted me to go by Sonia, so it makes me feel like she's still with me."

Lacking an appropriate understanding of social cues, Victor shared, "On hot humid nights, we dip into the river." He was making no effort to hide his glee, and, secretly, I didn't want him to.

Attempting to maintain reverence for my mother, Sonia shared, "Even my therapist tells me V's been good for me."

Camille lamented, "Well that explains why you take a nap every night after supper."

I saw the expression on my mother's face. I knew what was coming. Morality was not negotiable with Camille.

Mom told Yesonia, "I am deeply sorry for your loss, and I am hoping you continue to come over and help me with the food drive, but you can't sleep here anymore."

Victor asked, "Then why can Jon and Serena stay?"

I could see a trace of tired guilt on Mom's face.

Dad knew Mom and quickly said, "Because Jon and Serena are a *family*, and they *will* be married." He narrowed his eyes.

"You're asking us to be a hotel while you're learning to date. We can't do that."

Camille patted Dad on the arm as if to say "good job."

Ever the supportive husband, Bill straightened up and cleared his throat. He didn't look at me when he directed, "Jon, you need to find another place for this young woman to stay."

Having no other choice, I left to find a place to keep Yesonia safe. I considered my options. I couldn't have Sonia stay with Clay, as he'd be sleeping with her in less than a week. I trusted Jada, but she was never home—and the fact that she had been at the bar the same night Maddy was drugged with ether put her too close to the killer.

I swear, everybody in my family is nuts—myself included. But honestly, I was happy for Victor. Nobody should have to be alone forever. I found myself knocking on the door of Serena Bell's parents' home. Serena answered, wearing a black blouse with a simple white floral design around the edges and slim white pants. Her beauty almost made me step back, it struck me so. Her emerald eyes glistened like sunlight reflecting on Alexandrite—the most valuable of all colored gems. Serena's chocolate-hued hair had caramel highlights, and with its natural curl, it just looked delicious. Her petite form was soon joined by our pretty little Nora at her legs, so I scooped up our daughter and held her close. I missed her so intensely at times my heart hurt, but holding her was instant gratification. I treasured that moment, then said to Serena, "I have a favor to ask of you . . ."

27

I'D BEEN ANXIOUS TO MOVE OUT of my parents' home for some time, so I didn't mind Jon inviting me to live with Nora in the home he was building near Pierz. I agreed to take my furniture out of storage and, with Jon purchasing a few items, the home was made functional.

My guest, Yesonia, was kindly playing with Nora while I unpacked and found places for necessities. Jon had just finished assembling the shelving for the bedroom closet and joined me in the kitchen.

I set a mug down on the island countertop—it was made of black granite with Micah chips that reflected rainbows on the kitchen ceiling when the sun was shining. It was one of a thousand little things Jon researched and did right, making my need for distance from him that much more difficult. I told him—or maybe was telling myself, "You know this move is only temporary."

Jon wryly retorted, "None of us is going to live forever."

I confronted him. "Tony told me someone tried to kill you—twice. He said we should be safe in Pierz. This is exactly why I can't have Nora with you in the city."

"I get it," Jon responded, his disappointment palpable. "That's why I built this house. I'll do something else."

"You enjoy your work, and you're good at it." How could he consider giving up the job he worked so hard to realize? *What have I done to this good man?*

He calmly stated, "Would *you* give up Nora for a job?"

My stomach churned with trepidation as I struggled to find the right words to tell Jon some difficult news. He stood in front of me, and it didn't help that my body was betraying me— my entire person was hopelessly drawn to his strong, fit body. When I looked into his sad, blue eyes, they seemed to be pleading with me not to speak.

I swallowed hard and put it out there. "Jon, I've been see- ing someone." I willed myself to keep eye contact with him, as my senses screamed for me to look away.

He took a deep, troubled breath, and said, "That's what I've heard. I thought it couldn't be true, though, because you'd tell me, right?" He searched my face for answers, and I somehow managed to keep my expression even.

I loved Pierz, but small town gossip could be faster and crazier than the internet. My dad used to say if you fart in Pierz, by the time you got to Genola—a mile away—you've blown up the gas station. I powered through. "I've talked to him, briefly, a few times, but this week was the first time we met for lunch."

Jon's face was frozen in place as he asked, "Who is it?"

"Does it make any difference?" Oh, God, I didn't want to have this conversation. I couldn't stand to hurt him more than I already had.

Jon's voice was laced with pain. "It does if he's around my daughter." His eyes bored into mine, and it was all I could do to maintain the contact.

I tried to console him. "Jon, I wouldn't do that to you. He hasn't been around Nora. He won't be."

Jon's facial features tightened as he bit back an emotional response. He stated, in his best business-like tone, "I don't want him in my house." He was looking over the top of my head as he declared this.

"Okay," I said carefully, my discomfort getting the better of me. I could feel his anger vibrating under the surface. I suddenly had unexpected and unwanted visions of Jon becoming someone I'd never known. These flashes unnerved me, as I'd only ever known Jon as a sweet and kind soul—someone nearly incapable of violence. I was aware my trauma was probably messing with my perception, but still. It felt more real than I wanted it to. My muscles began to tighten reflexively.

It had to be confusing for Jon—this thing we'd been doing. And I didn't know what to call it, besides a "thing," because it was confusing for me, too. Jon asked me to sleep with him, and I did. If I was being honest, I looked forward to those times. But the reality was, it was too scary to be in a relationship with him—to love him like I had loved him. I couldn't live that way, feeling brittle and uneasy. My nights were filled with nightmares of being attacked by a psychopath; my waking hours were spent wringing my hands over whether Jon was going to be killed at work.

I could hear him swallow hard as we both unsuccessfully searched for words. I could feel his heart breaking, and I felt like the worst person who had ever lived. I wanted to take it back, but it was out there now, occupying the entire space between us. Maybe there wasn't room for words.

Jon stepped forward as if to hug me, and I closed my eyes and dropped my arms in anticipation. It was meant to symbolize a surrender to my fears, but he must have taken it as a rejection. Instead of hugging me, he stepped around me, and said goodbye to Nora, then headed for the door. It was typical of our communication, recently—when we weren't making love.

AFTER JON HAD DEPARTED and Nora was napping, Yesonia—or Sonia, as I was corrected—and I sat at the kitchen table and talked. I'd brewed some tea, for no other reason than to keep busy while my thoughts were swirling. Sonia was kind but unsure of herself, so I was shocked when she challenged me. "What is *wrong* with you?" Her timid demeanor hardened into something accusatory.

Taken aback, I asked, "What do you mean?"

Sonia seemed to hear herself and deflated into her chair. "I can't afford to get kicked out of your house because I have nowhere safe to go. So tell me if I should just shut up."

"Well, I'm not sure what just happened, but I'd like you to tell me what's on your mind," I encouraged her. I understood her emotional turmoil. "You're safe here."

Sonia began mindlessly spinning her cup of tea in slow rotations, not having taken a single sip. "Okay. Jon loves your daughter, and you trust him with her. And he loves you. And you light up like a Christmas tree when he's around—but, if I heard right, you just *dumped* him?"

I bristled. "It's not just about me anymore—you don't get it. I have Nora. I'm a *mother* now. I want her to feel, to *be* safe." I silently prayed I wouldn't have to explain all that had happened to me, hoping I could keep this conversation contained.

"What if Leah's killer maybe didn't shoot at Jon? What if he shot at me? Do you want me to leave?"

"Of course not."

Sonia prodded, saying, "Do you think Nora feels safer with you or with Jon? After watching him play with her, she seems to feel pretty safe." She took a sip of tea to make her point. I almost smiled at her grimace. Tea wasn't for everyone.

It was too much to explain, so I just said, "It's his work, Sonia."

Sonia pushed her tea away and stood up. She stalked away from the table and then returned with a restless fury. "Okay, I've got to say it. I'm *alive* because of Jon. *He* is the reason people like me don't get raped and murdered, and you're telling me you can't love him because of that?"

"It isn't that simple." I nearly heard my vertebrae click into place as my spine straightened defensively.

Sonia insisted, "Actually, it *is* that simple." She paused, tamping down her frustration, which I appreciated. "Evil is out there, and you've got a man with the balls to fight it, but that doesn't *work* for you," she sneered a little. "You do realize that bad things happen to people who aren't investigators. As a matter of fact, if something bad happens to you or Nora, it probably won't have anything to do with Jon's work."

The truth finally came out, "I'm terrified of losing Nora—and Jon. It's easier to be apart."

Sonia hesitated and then continued. "It's easier for you—not for Nora—and damn sure not for Jon. I would maybe understand if he did something wrong. Do you ever consider the misery he goes through for loving you? Or do you just focus on what *you* go through? What kind of mess would you be if the one person you loved left and took Nora? For nothing! That's what you did to Jon. So, if he seems scary, it's because he's *scared*. Jon would give up everything for you, and you leave him with nothing. I don't get it."

Sonia put her hand over her eyes for a moment and, as she lowered her head. She said, "Not having Leah to talk to anymore has taught me that time with some people is worth the pain. Jon's got a good heart. That has to count for something."

I had nothing to say to that . . .

9:05 P.M., SATURDAY, JULY 8,
BLOOMINGTON

SATURDAY NIGHT, I WAS RUNNING late for my standing date with Jon at the Radisson Blu. Nora was over-tired and refusing to cooperate with anything and everything when I was trying to leave. As I was finally ready to get out the door to bring her to my parents', she knocked a lamp over, so I had to stop and pick up tiny shards of glass and extensively vacuum.

By the time I checked into my room at the Radisson Blu, I was wiped out. When I reflected on my day, I couldn't say I was surprised to see my phone had gone dead. I wearily plugged it in and decided to take a quick nap before I contacted Jon. We had a lot to talk about.

JON FREDERICK
9:00 P.M., SATURDAY, JULY 8,
BLOOMINGTON

SERENA WASN'T AT THE HOTEL when I arrived. I had been waiting for an hour in the room, aimlessly clicking through TV channels and wallowing in shameful humility. I finally accepted the possibility that we were, truly, over, and quietly left the room.

I meandered back to my car in the hotel's colorless, cement-gray parking garage. Serena had told me she was seeing someone else. How much more obvious did it need to get? *What the hell am I doing?* I swore I'd never be the "other guy" in anybody's relationship.

I was about to start my car when I saw Serena running toward the hotel, adorned in a sundress with green-and-gold designs. A lightning bolt of exhilaration shot through me as I watched her long curls bounce against her tanned skin. And then I saw her face. It wasn't an *I'm so excited to see you* smile she once greeted me with. Instead, she looked stressed and weary, like a woman who felt an obligation to a man she once loved—a pretty woman who was offering herself out of kindness and a desire to never let me down. Serena stopped momentarily, hopping adorably on each foot as she pulled her heels off, then she started jogging in earnest.

I knew by the time I caught up with her, she'd be in the lobby. Not wanting to create a public scene, I called her phone— my call went directly to voicemail. I simply said, "I'm sorry for not letting go sooner. I love you so much. I need to do what's best for you, now. Thank you for caring, Serena. I wish you the best . . . I'm just so sorry." I hung up. Time for me to man up— her willingness to acquiesce didn't make it okay for me to keep asking her to do so.

I drove home and, still restless, took a long walk. I stopped at the Blarney Pub for a cold glass of Summit's Extra Pale Ale. It was refreshing, but I was generally a lager man. Lagers take longer to brew, but they're smoother and have a much longer shelf life. The anguished look on Serena's face replayed like an unwanted video clip through my mind, tormenting me. After three months of separation, I had called her to help with my sleep; I'd called her because I needed her. I did this even though she told me she needed time to heal. She suffered for it. The pub started to fill with young couples, so I slammed the bottom half of the ale and began the long walk back to my apartment.

After I'd clocked a mile, a black sedan pulled up next to me. The driver pushed the passenger door open. Inside, Jada Anderson mocked, "Hey, boy, want a ride?"

I stood for a moment, quietly considering what getting into that car meant. Maybe I just read too much into everything.

Jada looked good in her worn jeans and her baby-blue, over-sized Twins jersey. She had just left a promotion at a Twins game. I gave in and dropped into the passenger seat, allowing her to whisk me away. Before long, I was telling her of how my desire to reunite with Serena had finally broken—that even walls fall down.

Jada waited patiently until I was done. When she met my eyes, hers were full of compassion. "I think you're raging inside, like any normal person would be, but you're still trying to be a decent person to others. It's got to be exhausting."

I wasn't sure if there was truth to that, but I made a mental note to think it through later.

Jada continued, "You need a night out—just to get out of your head for a little bit. Right now, your head is a bad neighborhood, and you'd be ill-advised to go there alone."

When I opened my mouth to decline, she put a palm out in front of my face and effectively shut my argument down.

Jada drove us to the Azul nightclub where she had agreed to meet El Epicene. A young new rap band called Click Bait pounded out a diatribe against social injustice. El and I, the only white-skinned patrons, watched a packed dance floor, with supple African Americans oscillating and swaying to the beat. Watching Jada out there, waving her hands high above her head in pure joy, her body moving like a mesmerizing form of art, forced me to smile through my misery.

El studied Jada at least as intensely as I did. El was wearing something I wouldn't have worn, as a white person, into a predominantly black club—an oversized black Raiders jersey with a white Raiders cap on backwards and large, bright-white Nike tennis shoes, left untied. Picture a young Woody Allen in gang wear! I couldn't help thinking that, if El's feet were actually the size of those tennis shoes, she would have never been able to put Alan Volt's shoes on. Jada had laughed when El walked in. After offering El a pleasant greeting, she was swept out to the dance floor by friends.

This left me standing by her androgynous friend. In an attempt at wry humor, something I admit was unnatural for me,

I asked El, "Do you come here often?" It had to be her first time, as it would be all I could do to keep El from getting beat up by one of the bar patrons for the insulting clothing.

Barely able to hear me, she shook her head. Although I'd never excelled at lip-reading, I thought I could see her saying, "Jada *is* the music," as El wistfully stared on.

At one point, I stepped closer to El, and she yelled, "Ow! You purposely stepped on my foot."

I apologized. "I'm sorry." El's feet did full fit her shoes.

El muttered, "What's wrong with you? Jerk!"

I wanted to leave, but Jada kept glancing my way to make sure I was staying put. This wasn't an area for either Jada or El to walk to their cars alone on a Saturday night. I had an advantage, since a young, fit white male, in this club tonight, was interpreted by everyone as law enforcement. Well, almost everyone—at one point, an angry and intoxicated man of color walked by and muttered to El and me, "Slumming fucking crackers."

This misguided assumption brought a half-smile to my face. It was a free psychological assessment and somewhat accurate. I disagreed with the word "slumming," but I had to give him the other two. I did come from poverty, which could be referred to as white trash or crackers, and there had been fucking. But *slumming* implied white privilege. The concept of white privilege didn't occur to me when I was getting my ass kicked as a kid, or when we bought our groceries from a coin purse that held no bills, or when the bank foreclosed on our farm.

Still, I understand people had it worse, and that five percent of the people in every race were obnoxious, so it was best to accept that "two out of three ain't bad," and let it go. One of the young rappers from Click Bait approached me during a break, and we shared a pleasant conversation. We had worked at a charity event in North Minneapolis together last spring. El accepted my escort to her—his?—car, and when I returned to Azul, Jada was waiting for me. She asked in an alluring voice, "Do you want to get out of here?"

ONCE INSIDE MY APARTMENT, Jada moved close to me and purred, "Relax. Shut your brain off for a minute. We're both single, lonely people who were once pretty great together." She started to unbutton her Twins jersey, but I held her hands and stopped her.

Jada's every movement was seductive artistry, and painful to resist. She stepped closer, and with her glossy lips inches from my ear, she breathed, "Let go."

I nodded to the mirror on the wall. "Behind that mirror is a camera, one that records everything at the door."

Jada's laugh was rich and throaty, "You didn't change the locks?"

"No. I've been daring someone to enter since." I took a deep breath then, and succumbed to her invitation, but added, "We're not going in the bedroom."

Jada nodded, "I know."

I have a variety of odd rules I lived by. I only slept in a bed with one woman. I think sharing a bed is a big step, so before I invited a new person into my bed, I made myself buy a new mattress. It forced me to seriously consider the choice. Plus, I was, admittedly, a bit of a germaphobe.

I woke up with Jada snuggled against me on the couch. I got up and carefully covered her. I then went to sleep in my bedroom, leaving the door open so I would wake if we had a visitor.

6:30 a.m., Sunday, July 9

When I did wake, it was to the sound of the door of my apartment unlocking. Thinking Jada was leaving, I threw a t-shirt on and went to say goodbye. When I entered the living room, Jada was just stirring on the couch. Seeing my door come open, I quickly went for my gun.

I stood in boxers and a t-shirt, holding a Glock 22 pistol, facing Serena, who was walking through the door.

Serena looked me up and down, then glared at Jada. With the blanket still wrapped around her, Jada casually slid off the couch. She retrieved her clothes unapologetically and sauntered into the bathroom.

I asked Serena, "How did you just get in here?"

Dumbfounded, she responded, "I found my key. What the hell, Jon? I was waiting at the hotel."

I was tired of all of it. My pent-up frustration was now unfiltered and poured out. "Are you *kidding* me? You're seeing another man! It's really none of your business who's here."

I set my Glock down on the counter, but I wasn't done. "And you know what else? I'm broke. I've been sending you all my extra money to help take care of Nora and to make sure you get the help you need. I paid for a hotel room because you felt meeting me here compromised your freedom. I can't afford that anymore. Eventually,

211

I'll be walking around like I was in junior high—carrying a billfold with only a one-dollar bill inside."

Serena looked confused and stood mute, keys still frozen in her hand.

Jada was now dressed, and as she walked to the door to leave, asked me, "Are you okay?"

I nodded briefly, "Yes. Thank you for being there for me."

She responded, "Call me." Jada turned to Serena, "Don't worry, your bed is still yours." She exited quietly.

Serena glanced back at the door Jada had just exited and then turned back, "How can you afford to build a house, then, if you're so broke?"

I slowly responded, "It's being paid for by my private investigative work."

Shocked, Serena said, "You should have told me. I'll start paying rent." She made a move to reach in her purse.

Having purged my frustration, I felt contrite. I softly responded, "No, don't. Helping you and Nora is the one thing I've done right. I'll let you know when I need it."

Serena started to reply, but I felt the need to explain further. "You set your engagement ring on my dresser and walked out with our daughter, making it clear you didn't want me in your life. And now you're seeing another man? What did you expect? I waited for you for six months."

"I'm not seeing him anymore." Serena's eyes welled up, "Where is my ring?"

"It's on my dresser next to our engagement picture, right where you left it."

She turned away.

Sadly, for the first time in my life, I didn't want to console her. I wanted her to feel my sorrow—my hopelessness. I simply said, "I need to shower and then I'm going into work. Lock the door when you leave . . ."

28

JADA INSISTED ON STOPPING OVER. She believed if we were going to have any chance as a couple, we needed to discuss Saturday night, tonight. I honestly wasn't sure how I felt, but I did know a forced decision would guarantee failure.

Jada was clearly second-guessing this as well, and stood cloaked with uncertainly in the doorway. She hesitated when I invited her in, but relented and carefully perched on the corner of the couch.

She forced a smile. "The way you handled El reminded me why I'm attracted to you. El insisted we go to Azul. I ran into some friends there, and El shows up, wearing wannabe gangster clothing. I don't know what to compare it to—like a black man showing up to a redneck cowboy bar in a brand-new cowboy getup with shiny silver spurs."

I laughed, "El was worse. There *were* black cowboys, but there were no white gang members near Azul Saturday night."

Jada nodded with a soft chuckle. "I'm embarrassed to say it, but I just stayed away from El. I felt like she was making fun of us, even though I'd like to believe it was out of ignorance. And you just stayed right there—likely the only reason El didn't get an ass-kicking. I can imagine how painful it was, knowing she can't stand you."

I sat back at the other end of the couch, "She really likes you, though. That's got to get uncomfortable at work."

Jada considered this. "We work well together. El has good insight, and we both focus on the task at hand. This is what makes her oppositional dress style so weird. Part of me feels El has to know that the clothing choices she makes are offensive to some people."

I knew Jada wasn't here to discuss El, so I waited quietly as she began to pick nervously at the frayed openings on the knees of her jeans. She was wearing a sleeveless white blouse, and her arms rippled with tension as she continued picking.

Jada looked up and gave me a small smile. "I feel the need to clear up a conversation we had a couple years ago. I've never been comfortable with the impression I might have left. I told you people are too sensitive about the way some black parents discipline. What I meant was, the dangers in some neighborhoods are so great, with drugs and gangs—parents need to respond in a fervent manner. I'm not an advocate for hitting children."

Jada had been raised in Chicago by a father who was a maintenance worker at O'Hare Airport, which is a job that, even now, only pays twelve dollars an hour. Her mother cleaned houses for types like the Mayers. They wanted better for their children, so socked their wages away to give their kids a better shot than they'd had. What they couldn't afford was a move to live in a better neighborhood. So, while saving, they survived in an environment fraught with gang activity and the temptation of drugs, with claws that were always beckoning to unhappy adolescents. Jada's parents—along with others in the community who wanted better for their children—came down on their children harder and with more aggression than I could justify. While I once resented, and later forgave, my father for his over-the-top discipline, Jada vigorously defended her parents. Jada felt I'd never be able to understand—growing up where I did, with the parents I had, and with the color of my pale skin. We had ended up in a pretty heated discussion about child-rearing when we were dating. I believe that over-the-top punishment contributes to violence rather than preventing it, and what she was seeing was that children who received excessive punishment fared better than children with no discipline. Both of us parted in frustration with the other, but I think somewhere in there, we each silently acknowledged we couldn't possibly understand each other on the subject.

I nodded.

Jada continued, "We still have the same issue, Jon. I'm not going to take time off and have a baby right now, but I've hit thirty and am honestly not sure what the future holds. I've always made it clear I want to take my career to the next level before anything else."

I leaned toward her, elbow on knees. "I have a child, and I don't ever want to be less involved with her."

Jada reached over and placed her hand on my knee. "I'm okay with that. I know I can't replace Serena as Nora's mother.

I can be a gracious aunt, though, and allow you whatever time you need with your little girl." She gave my knee a quick squeeze then sat back. "But I need to know where I stand. I loved it when I could stop over anytime, day or night, and it was just us. I don't want to do this if Serena's going to be in and out of your life— and your apartment."

She paused for effect, then said, "I guess I'm telling you that you need to get a new bed."

Jada was a great model of a strong, independent woman for any girl, but my partner still would need to be a mom to Nora. I responded softly, "I'm not ready."

Jada groaned in frustration, "I don't have *time* to develop a relationship with your daughter. I've been talking to WGN in Chicago, and they may offer me an anchor job on the nightly news if my work on this investigation continues to go well. So, either we're doing this, or I'm gone."

She grasped my hands excitedly. "Come to Chicago with me, Jon. Start over."

I shook my head. "Jada, I'm moving to Pierz, so I can be close to Nora. I'll take whatever work I can find." Sadly, I literally and figuratively pulled away from Jada in that moment, knowing there was no resolving the differences in us that were so absolute and inflexible.

"I shouldn't have come here tonight." Jada inhaled deeply through her nose and abruptly stood up. She said, not without anger, "Just like that, we're over." She snapped her fingers close to my face, her lovely features becoming hard. "You know how many dates I've turned down in the last couple months—thinking we might get back together?"

Chastised, I nodded, "I would imagine many."

Jada quipped, "None." She smiled, effectively keeping me off balance. "Okay–many." She spread her hands in surrender, then said gently, "Jon, you can't keep your life on hold waiting for Serena to make up her mind."

"I'm not waiting—this *is* my life." I tried to explain. "I'm a single dad working every minute I'm not with my daughter, so I can survive and support her in every way possible. It's not what I wanted, but it's what my life has become."

I scratched my forehead, replaying recent events in my mind like fast-forwarding through a movie. "There was nothing wrong with my taking the side job for the Mayers, but I should have told Maurice Strock before I accepted the lead investigator role. Now I can't get out of it, because Maddy's out, and it's exactly what the killer wants." I leaned heavily back into the couch, my frustration momentarily overwhelming me.

Jada said, "Let's finish this. I can accept that we're over, if I have to. Are you good working with me yet?"

"I have no problem with it. We're still just two people who used to have a relationship."

Jada wasn't happy, but she resolutely nodded and stood to leave, and I stood with her. We hugged at the door, and Jada clung a little, whispering, "We can still be pretty damn good, can't we?"

I nodded, knowing any words would fall short. I thanked her for her caring support over the last few months, then wordlessly walked her to her car.

29

MADDY SAT PRIM AND PROPER, fingers laced and locked in her hospital bed, anxious for her possible release at the end of the day. She was still in her pale-blue hospital gown, with a big white bandage covering the wound on her neck, but she had showered and put on some makeup. Her street clothes were folded neatly on a chair near the bed, shoes under the chair, ready to be thrown on the moment she got word she could go. She wouldn't be back to work soon, but she had healed enough so she could go home. The bullet had passed through her neck without significant damage. Her doctor said it wasn't the first time he'd seen this, but she was still incredibly lucky.

I settled into the chair next to her bed, and she took my hand, "Thank you for saving my life. If you wouldn't have gotten me to the hospital as fast as you did, I wouldn't have made it. Aiming the flashlight at the shooter was ingenious."

I smiled. "I have my moments."

"I'm done being mad at you," she said with finality, and punctuated it with a shake of our enfolded hands before she let go.

"Now," she continued, "I want to talk about the case, but I'm not coming back anytime soon."

"In the past week, I've been to the top thirty industries in the Minneapolis/St. Paul area with Ava, including Toro, Hormel, 3M, General Mills, Land O' Lakes, Ecolab, Valspar, and a couple dozen others. She still hasn't recognized that smell."

"Lying here day and night has given me a lot of time to think about this." Maddy added cautiously, "This could be a woman in a relationship with someone in law enforcement."

She meant Jada Anderson but didn't want to say it. The coincidence of Jada just happening by as I was walking home Saturday night wormed its way into my thought process. But it couldn't be Jada. El? I dismissed this and interjected, "Or maybe he just watches a lot of investigative shows. Definitely accesses porn."

Maddy agreed. "Yeah, that's how you find BDSM couples. And Ava claims they met on the Backpages of Craigslist—a sex trafficking site."

Maddy glanced over at me and said carefully, "Even when I want to clear Ava, I'm never able to, Jon. She doesn't have an alibi—I called her bodyguards. She eluded them two hours before Bo Gere's murder and didn't come home until the next morning. Nobody but Ava has seen her attacker, *and* she can't identify him—she's not even sure of her attacker's gender."

I told her, "There were no prints, other than Yesonia's and the victim's, at the last scene. Leah's ex claimed they had an argument. She left and went to the bar. The story fits, but it doesn't take a lot of time to kill someone, so I haven't completely ruled him out. There's DNA we're testing. We don't have the bullet that went through my car window to match to the murder victims." I sighed in frustration. "We couldn't find it. My best guess is, somehow, it got embedded in the car I met. The owner may not even know it." I needed to find out where Ava was when Bo was killed.

8:30 P.M., TUESDAY, JULY 11,
EDINA

CLAY ROBERTS INVITED ME into his medieval-looking home, which featured dark woods and rustic metal ornaments. We sat at his square, African walnut kitchen table. Clay was barefoot and his hair was in disarray. His t-shirt and jeans looked rumpled and hastily thrown on.

Somewhat irritated, Clay asked, "What do you need?"

"I need to know who you were with on Thursday night, June 22."

"Good luck." Clay glanced surreptitiously toward his bedroom, then snarled. "Let's see, where did I file those bar receipts?"

I followed his glance with a sinking feeling in my stomach. "Ava Mayer doesn't have an alibi for the night Bo Gere was killed."

As if on cue, Ava came strutting out of the bedroom in a gold, oversized Minnesota Gophers jersey, bare-legged and barefoot. Her hair was a tangled mess. She remarked, "I've decided to stop being mean to Maddy. So why tell her I was with Clay? He is sort of my bodyguard."

She crawled possessively into his lap and passionately kissed Clay. I watched them blandly, suspecting Ava's shameless display was as much for my benefit as Clay's.

Clay patted Ava on the bottom and casually said, "Get dressed. I need to take you home."

"Boooo," Ava protested, but she ventured back to the bedroom.

Clay's smile disappeared the minute Ava was out of sight, and he seriously addressed me in a lowered voice, "You can't tell Maddy. I like Maddy. I swear, this was my last time with Ava. Maddy is someone I could develop a long-term relationship with."

I knew the answer, but asked anyway, "If you feel that way, then what's Ava doing here?"

"It's always been the same. You need a reason to have sex. I just need a place," he said impishly, always reminding me of the kid living inside his grown-man's body. "Maddy's family keeps dropping by at the hospital, so it's weird for me to be around her now. I don't know how to be around family."

"Learn." I reminded him, "Maddy's a *mother*. You know what it's like to have a mother who's messed up by a guy."

Clay didn't argue. "Yeah." He glanced back toward his bedroom. "I'm getting sick of my life. I want something real."

"Then you need to stop playing. I'm not going to lie for you to Maddy, but I'm not going out of my way to tell her, either. Just get this mess cleaned up." I left him at his table, lost in his internal conflicts.

30

SERENA WAS STIRRING A POT of jambalaya when I returned home. I quickly registered that she was wearing her engagement ring but said nothing. Baffled by the unexpected sight of her in my kitchen, I asked, "What are you doing?"

Her response was timid, "Please hear me out. I need a night to talk this through—c'mon, Jon—you've got nothing to lose." When I didn't respond, she teased, "Maybe it's only a moment—maybe the time of your life. Since money's tight, I thought I'd just come here."

The aroma of Old Bay seasoning, shrimp, Thielen's andouille sausage, fried peppers and onions, was tantalizing. Serena made an amazing jambalaya. I approached for a glimpse, and she gave me that sweet smile. Trying to resist, I painfully commented, "I thought you were seeing someone."

A shameful sadness washed over her, and she busied herself over the pot. She sipped from an oversized spoon to test her roux, then glanced at me and said, "I'm not. I ended it." After a pause, she wiped her hands on a nearby towel and finally met my eyes. "I don't even know what that was, other than a mistake. I'm so sorry."

I know I should have said something in response, but I was drawing a blank. I didn't know what she needed from me in that moment, so I opted not to speak at all.

She misinterpreted my silence, "So are you with Jada now?"

I softly said, "No." I wanted to touch her, but still feeling some resentment, and now guilt, I didn't. Conceding made me feel so weak—it was easier to just be angry. I had spoken to a therapist at CORE in Sartell during my time off, who advised, "Your partner never comes back from a separation full of re-morse for having hurt you. A lot of rationalizations go into a separation, and they only slowly dissipate when you offer com-passionate forgiveness."

Serena's big green eyes seemed to skewer through me. She switched gears, "There's something else we need to talk about," she said in a grave tone. "I think I was drawn into your case."

"My current case?" I was off balance already, and this was unexpected.

She gently pressed her hand to the small of my back, and guided me to the kitchen table where we sat down. "Before I left, I thought I was going crazy. I kept hearing this creepy voice whisper my name, from my laptop. Sometimes a picture of Alban Brennan would flash on the screen out of nowhere."

My heart constricted, thinking how frightening that had to have been for her. "Why didn't you tell me about it?"

"I couldn't ask you to stop working and stay home to take care of me—which is exactly what you would've done. I was recovering from postpartum depression, and I was afraid if you spent any more time around me, you wouldn't trust me with Nora. I knew I needed help, and my mom's as good as anybody can be with Nora."

She looked at me evenly, waiting for me to contradict her concerns. When I didn't, she continued, "I've since discovered that my thyroid was underactive, which contributed to my depression and lethargy—so I'll likely be on levothyroxine for the rest of my life. But it wasn't just one thing. I needed counseling and I received it. When I went off the grid, it all slowly went away. I stopped feeling crazy. Now that Sonia has been telling me about this killer hacker, I'm wondering if some of this was part of his game."

If Serena would have asked me to stay home, I wouldn't be on this case. This could have been the killer's intention from the very beginning.

My phone's ringing seemed unnecessarily loud in the silence that had had fallen between us. When I answered, Marcus Mayer barked, "Ava's disappeared. And she has my brand new forty-five with her . . ."

31

AVA MAYER IS BACK ON THE GRID. It almost makes me giddy, and I have to keep my emotions in check so I don't overreact. Snapchat places Ava at the Embassy Suites on Earle Browne Drive, in Brooklyn Center. I start on my way to Minneapolis, to pick up my killing clothes. I store them in a locker at the Heritage Facility in the Warehouse District. *Do I risk going to her room, or is this a setup? It has to be a setup.*

Women with Ava and Leah's beauty are pure eye candy. Maddy looks pretty damn good, too. And still, they need me to *save* them. Ava allowed a man to tie her to posts. Leah allowed a man to abuse her. Maddy Moore was seduced by a supervisor to betray her marriage. She has now ended the affair, though—I didn't want Maddy to die. I just wanted to get Jon Frederick off the case. I thought maybe by scaring Serena a little, he'd step back and take care of his family. Instead, he's spending day and night on the damn case.

I'd like to find out who pulled him into this case. To Layla Boyd's credit, she left Asher and didn't come to save him, so we're done. As far as Nina Cole goes, I could have walked into the house and had sex with her with no ether, and she was so strung out she wouldn't have known. That lesson may prove worthless for Nina, but to the world's benefit, Bo is gone, and I'm stocked with ammo. Leah Hartman couldn't be saved, but I have hope for Ava. She keeps jumping in and out of her safety net. I will have her yet . . .

32

I PULLED AVA'S LOCATION UP on Snapchat and headed to the Embassy Suites. She didn't answer my calls, but I spotted her Infrared sport Lexus in the parking lot. After considering Maddy's past accusations of my involvement with Ava, I decided it was best if I didn't enter this hotel alone, so I called for backup and waited in the parking lot. The only parking spots open, other than the handicapped ones, were in a lot fifty yards to the side of the hotel.

Out of the corner of my eye, I saw Clay Roberts follow a hotel guest through a side door. I yelled, "Clay!" He ignored me, and I swore.

Forgetting about my backup request, I ran toward the hotel. I then realized Clay had driven a car other than his own. He must have known Ava might have law enforcement tailing her. Clay had pulled up and parked illegally next to a side door. By the time I reached the hotel door, it was locked, and there wasn't another guest close by to unlock it. I ran to the main entry and found out which room Ava was staying in. I hurried up the steps to her room on the second floor, praying I wouldn't hear gunshots. When I arrived outside of her room, I paused before entering. The door was propped open, so I stepped close and listened.

Ava was shrieking at Clay, "You can't go back to Maddy!"

Clay responded cautiously. "Do you mind if I sit on the edge of the bed? I just came from work and I'm tired." I knew Clay well enough to detect fear in his tone, but he was masking it well.

Ava's voice was shaky, bordering on hysteria. "I'm not putting the gun down."

I removed my gun from the shoulder holster under my shirt and took it off safety.

Clay calmly said, "I don't care. I'm just tired."

"Maddy's old enough to be your *mom*," Ava spat. "That's just gross."

Clay said wearily, "She takes better care of her body than I do mine. She's fifteen years older than me. I'm ten years older than you. So, we're about the same. Look—you're where I've been for a decade, and I'm tired of that life. I'm tired of the attention, the bars, and the hangovers. I'm just tired."

Ava's tone softened a bit, "Maybe we want the same thing."

My hand tightened uncertainly on the door handle, as I anticipated the proper moment to enter.

Clay countered, "Maybe. But I'm not the one who's going to get you there. I need someone who's already there. Is that selfish? Probably."

Ava dramatically expressed, "Men *hate* me."

She wasn't going to out self-pity Clay. He responded, "Yeah, they hate me too—probably more. And my family's like cactus—all pricks." I relaxed a bit. Clay might just have this under control.

"What does Maddy have that I don't?" Ava's voice ratcheted back up toward shrill, and I tensed again.

I heard Clay's simple response. "Stability."

Ava reminded him, "You better be nice to me. I could blow your brains out! Everyone thinks I killed Alan. Why wouldn't I kill you?" Uncertain where this was headed, I was ready to spring.

Clay took his time before responding. "Let's just summarize what we got here. You're beautiful and you're smart. I drink too much and am generally unfaithful. You're going to shoot me and spend the rest of your life dating those pock-marked meth heads in prison? Is that what you're going for, here?"

The silence that followed seemed endless. Ava finally said, "Okay. Here—shoot me."

She must have handed Clay the gun. I readied myself to intervene. I quietly opened the door further. I couldn't see Ava's face, but I could see she was wearing a sheer black dress with a slit up the side that went all the way to Canada. I gratefully watched Clay unload the Colt 45. He threw the bullets toward the garbage can. Two of them clacked into the plastic lining the can. The others landed on the carpet nearby. Protocol would have had me march in and cuff Ava, but Clay was handling this well. I wanted to give him the opportunity to end this properly.

Clay shook his head sadly, "No one's getting shot today,

Ava. You're twenty years old. If you're like me, you have another decade to mess up before you consider making the right decisions. If you're like Jon, you'd be considering them right now."

Clay's statement made it clear he was aware of my presence. I remained out of Ava's sight.

Clay continued, "You could kick the whole bag of us all day and never kick the wrong one. Jon's in love with Serena, but she just wants to punish him because she's not happy. You act like you're in love with me, and somehow you've turned that into a need to punish me. Maddy's in love with an ex she pretends to hate, who's now in love with his new wife. And I'm in love with whoever's behind door number three. So if shooting me can resolve all *that*, you can have the gun back."

Apparently struggling with a response Ava yelled, "Dammit! I can't do anything right. If that guy who raped me would have showed up, I would have dropped him! Instead, I'm just pathetic." After a minute she whimpered to Clay, "Well, don't just sit there like a dumbass. Hug me." I watched Clay open his arms in resignation.

33

UPON ARRIVING AT THE EMBASSY SUITES, I called the desk for Ava Mayer's room number. I managed to get it by claiming to be a police officer. I used the steps to make my way up to her room. The steps provided a warning that you may encounter someone. With gun in the back of my pants, and ether in pocket, I'm ready to roll. I open the door to the hallway, just a fraction to make certain the coast is clear. And there stands Jon Frederick holding a door partially open, peering into a room . . .

34

ZEKE ABBAS ARRIVED AT MY SIDE to assist me. I motioned him to walk down the hall with me, out of Ava's earshot. I told him quietly that Ava had brought a gun to the hotel, and Clay boldly came here and talked her down. Zeke agreed the situation was now under control, so he left. I called Angela Mayer, and she agreed to come and pick up her daughter.

AFTER AVA HAD DEPARTED with her mother, Clay and I stood in the hotel parking lot.

I turned on Clay, "What the hell just happened? Do you have a death wish?"

Clay looked away, more shaken than he was going to admit. "Probably. She called me and told me she had a gun. I decided it was time for me to start taking responsibility for my behavior. I knew she was a mess when I slept with her, but I did it anyway. I didn't want some cop shot trying to talk her down."

He met my eyes and nodded, "This one was on me."

I squeezed his shoulder. "I hate to compliment you, but you were pretty damn impressive."

"What you *should* do is buy me a beer," he awkwardly tapped my hand on his shoulder, then casually shrugged it off. "Staring down the wrong end of a gun makes a man thirsty."

I smiled. "I'm not sure what I *should* do anymore, but I'm trying to figure it out. Serena stopped by and she's still there, so I need to head home."

I advised Clay, "I think you should go visit Maddy. You had the guts to tell Ava you care about Maddy. Maybe you should tell Maddy that."

Clay looked a bit more scared than when he had a gun pointed at him. "That would be the right thing to do, wouldn't it?"

"Yes." I met his eyes and tried to will strength his way. I felt a stirring of hope that he was finally growing up.

Clay gazed into the distance. "How come that occurred to you so naturally, and it never occurred to me?"

"I think it did. You just prefer to take the easiest route."

Clay threw me his million-dollar grin and said, "Another time, then." He slid into his borrowed car and tore out of the parking lot. As I watched after him, I had no idea if he was going to see Maddy.

3:00 A.M., THURSDAY, JUNE 13, MINNEAPOLIS

SERENA AND I HAD A NIGHT of honest sharing, which vacillated between being uncomfortable to painful, but there wasn't any arguing—just disappointed sighs and acceptance. I massaged her feet, and we slept in the same bed. In the middle of the night, I woke to Serena crying. I put my arm around and her and asked, "Hey, what's wrong?"

She shook her head, indicating she didn't want to talk about it, and then slid over to me and I cradled her into my chest.

I whispered as I smoothed her hair away from her face, "It's going to be okay." I wasn't sure if that was true, but it felt like the right thing to say. Maybe sometimes it's more important to give someone hope than to waste time trying to figure out if there is any.

35

WHILE LYING IN BED, I thought I heard someone in Jon's home, so I gathered my courage and went to check it out. I'm better now. I can do this. There stood Clay Roberts, his tight pecs bulging through a white muscle shirt.

Swiping back a shock of streaked hair, he said maliciously, "I know exactly what you are. I'm the one person you will never fool."

I felt naked in my thin t-shirt and underwear, yet I was inexplicably rooted to the floor.

Clay approached me and, without a word between us, began touching me. As I stood silently being groped, I was ashamed, embarrassed, and aroused all at the same time.

I woke up lying with my head on his chest, angry I'd ruined everything—and for what? *Okay. Take a deep breath and pull it together.* As I separated from him, I realized I was lying next to Jon. Clay had been just a dream or, rather, a nightmare. I sighed in relief and snuggled back against Jon. I'd learned I couldn't be responsible for my dreams. They emerged from my torments and shame. But I was accountable for my actions when awake.

As I ran my hand down Jon's strong body, I realized he was thinner than he should have been. I felt a pang of guilt, but it was soon replaced with an intense, loving arousal. He responded and I removed my shirt . . .

THERAPY ALLOWED ME to forgive myself for my own bad choices, and to stop blaming Jon for not protecting me. The edges of those jagged pieces of ice in my head that caused so much pain had been melted and smoothed. I would never forget what happened, but it would never bother me as it did, again. I was a protective parent, and I had an almost raw appreciation of those who had stuck by me. The possibility that I might not be able to salvage what Jon and I once shared was devastating. I'd received help from so many different sources. One of my most powerful experiences occurred when I saw an eight-year-old girl who had been a victim like myself—she was laughing and enjoying a game with a friend. If she could do it, why couldn't I?

SERENA BELL
5:30 P.M., FRIDAY, JULY 14, 2017,
COUNTRY MANOR IN SARTELL

NEEDING SOME GUIDANCE, I stopped to talk to Tony Shileto after work. With his unexpected free time and personal struggles over his disability, Tony had recently resumed religious involvement.

I wasn't sure how he was going to handle my news. It was a pleasant, warm summer evening, so I wheeled Tony onto the lush, green lawns. He was slowly looking healthier, but his hair held a little more gray. I relaxed in a chair next to him and kicked off my shoes to enjoy the warm grass beneath my bare feet. A cool breeze brought with it the sweet smell of fresh-cut grass, and added to the peaceful serenity of the moment.

Tony eased into the conversation with a sardonic smile. "So, you want some relationship advice from a man who hasn't been on a date in years." With a low chuckle, he put a hand to his chest. "I'm sure I, alone, hold the secrets to eternal love."

His face was open and trustworthy and I felt a sense of relief simply being in his presence. I briefly recalled a very different, harder Tony, when I first met him. His injury seemed to have softened his demeanor in a way that had allowed us to become very close friends.

Knowing he had heard just about everything, I didn't sugarcoat my dilemma. "I haven't told anyone this, and I'm going to trust your confidence." Still, I took my time with it, watching the green shoots of grass spring back into place when I ran my feet across the lawn below me. "I'm pregnant again and will be showing, soon. You know Jon and I aren't even engaged, anymore." I didn't look at him right away, knowing I couldn't bear to see disappointment flicker through his eyes.

Tony momentarily took my hand, and held it gently until I looked up at him. "I can top that. I'm an investigator who gets sores on his body from sitting in bed too long. Honestly, Serena, another person like you in the world can only be a good thing—congratulations!"

Tony was positively beaming, and for the first time, my angst over the situation was threatened by hope. It was such a relief to have unloaded my burden. I felt a visceral weightlessness. I especially appreciated his not going all fire and brimstone on me.

He asked, "Is Jon the father?"

"Yes. I ended the engagement, but we didn't stop—" I just left it at that, then continued. "I want to marry him, but after months of telling him I needed to be alone, I may have lost him. He's kind to me, but I feel like I irritate him. He doesn't love me like he did." I looked away as Tony patted my hand then carefully folded his hands together, as if in prayer. "The last time I stopped over, Jada Anderson had spent the night, and she's pretty tough to compete with."

He looked at me wearily, obviously disappointed in Jon.

I defended him. "I had told him I was seeing another man."

Tony gazed out at the long open yard as he shared, "There's a philosophical notion called the Thomas Theorum, which states situations perceived as real become real in their consequences. It means, for example, if you believe you've lost Jon, you won't make the effort needed to reconcile. On the other hand, if you believe you can change his heart, and risk showing him the change in yours, you could make it work." He turned to me and added, "Remember, there's a reason Jada is an ex." As he grew more serious, the lines of age deepened around his pained expression. He shared, "Resentment isn't going to change his heart, just yours."

I expelled a long breath. "I'll work on that. I promise."

Tony recited solemnly, "To paraphrase Corinthians thirteen, love is patient, love is kind. It does not envy. It is not proud. It keeps no record of wrongs. It always trusts, always hopes and always perseveres."

His words were soothing. I told him, "I'll try to make this my mantra."

Tony gestured toward my hand, "You're wearing your engagement ring."

"I want to ask him to marry me, but I want our marriage to be separate from my pregnancy." I extended my fingers and looked at the ring, a longing tugging at my heart. "I'm not going to tell Jon I'm pregnant until after he gives me an answer." It was not lost on me that I was once again in the same situation as when I became pregnant with Nora.

He remarked, "I'd use all the weapons I had available, and you've got a powerful one. Why shouldn't your pregnancy be part of his decision?"

"I want to know I can still capture his heart, rather than chase him into my home." I gave Tony a sad smile.

Tony spoke carefully, "I've been down this road. Too proud to share my feelings, I waited for her to come to me—she didn't. I still wonder what would have happened if I would've just opened up to her." He paused, lost in his regret for a moment, then continued, "I'm sure you were afraid on your first day of school. And I imagine you were afraid at your first ballet performance, and high school softball game. I'd bet you were afraid at your first day of work, and when you left for college."

He continued, "And now you're afraid of dying and afraid of marriage. You assume every situation will end badly because you see the risk but not the reward. I've been told that, above all things, God is kind. I need you to remember this," and he added dryly, "because I'm not always going to be in the mood to remind you. Every great relationship goes through tragedy, but, through it, you can achieve a resilient strength you didn't have before. You want to marry him, so tell him. His response is on him."

Needles of threatening tears prickled behind my eyes as he spoke, and with a shaky smile, I said, "You make it sound so easy." I considered the fact that a man who had lost everything was helping me.

Reading my mind, he smiled and said, "We're not human beings having a spiritual experience. We're spiritual beings having a human experience. This broken body of mine isn't who I am, and that broken heart of yours isn't who you are. Stop running from him and honestly tell him how you feel, and you'll be fine."

8:30 P.M., FRIDAY, JULY 14,
PIERZ

I FELT BETTER AFTER TALKING WITH TONY. I stopped at Coborn's and picked up some groceries, then drove to Bill and Camille's farmhouse to pick Nora up. Jon's parents returned from Sue's Drive-In with my little Nora, who was now wearing half her ice cream but tickled pink over her successful adventure. Bill started a campfire in the backyard, and we were joined around the fire by Victor and Yesonia, and Jon's older sister, Theresa.

Nora was tired and being entertainingly goofy from her sugar high. Theresa and Bill enjoyed a cold beer while the rest of us sipped various sodas. I loved this family. While I wasn't as close to Theresa, my mom had shared that Theresa vigorously defended me, even after my separation from Jon, when gossip arose in the small town.

Theresa was built like her brother—strong and thin, and not only dressed like Bill, wearing a flannel shirt and jeans, but also had some of his reckless abandon. There were always stories of Theresa when we were younger, like she was skinny dipping with a boy at Fish Lake, or making out with a guy right outside the Silver Bullet Bar in Genola, or was seen walking off the golf course with a boy late at night. Some of the stories were impossible, like the one where she and a boy were seen diving naked into the river at Pierz Park on an October night and then made love standing in water up to their necks. First of all, the dam boards were pulled in September, so the river was only two feet high, and second, the river water was so cold in October a guy would have to be dead and in a state of rigor mortis to maintain an erection.

Of course, none of the stories came from a direct eye witness, and instead originated from an alleged reliable source that preferred to remain unnamed.

When I was a God-fearing eighth-grade girl, I had volunteered to help the Fredericks set up for Theresa's outdoor wedding on their farm. I grew up only a mile down the road and already had a crush on Jon. I'll never forget when I was helping Theresa string lights, how she turned to me and said, "You know those stories you hear about me all over town?" Before I could tell her I didn't believe them, she laughed and said, "They're all true!" I had respect for her ability to disregard the gossip. We all need stories to laugh at, but I disliked it when the theme of the story was that we were somehow better than she was. I once asked Jon if the stories bothered him, and he said, "Yes, but consider this. Remember how pious my mom was when we were growing up? Camille and Theresa battled through Theresa's adolescence, so it's certainly possible that Theresa herself was the original source of some of those stories. Nothing could have infuriated my mom more."

Nora was tired, so I took her from Camille, while Nora pled with Bill, "Pa, it's not time for me to go to bed."

As I stood with Nora, with everyone's attention now focused on us, I told them, "I appreciate every one of you for always being so kind to me. I'm sorry I ever left Jon."

Theresa toasted her can of beer my way and humorously added, "So, you're thinking now, wherever Jon is, it's got to be better than here with the rest of us."

Bill replied, "Jon told us that if it doesn't work, we can only blame him, because you're the kindest person he's ever met."

It was just like Jon to take responsibility for everything— a man who saw it as his job to make the world better. I remembered him jacking Clay up once by telling him, "When you bitch about society, remember you and me, we're society. If you want it to be better then *be* better."

36

I SAT WITH TONY IN HIS DRAB ROOM at Country Manor. Despite encouragement from the compassionate nursing aides, Tony had refused dinner. He sat staring out the window in a white t-shirt with an orange stain of something down the front. Without looking in my direction, he complained, "Do you know what it's like to have a desert-dry mouth, and have your beverage sitting inches beyond your reach? The aides are nice, but I'm as helpless as an infant with no hope of getting better."

I didn't respond, because my empathy would have only agitated him. Looking around for somewhere to sit, I put myself into Tony's vacant wheelchair and scooted close to his bed. Something was bothering him. Silence was often the best way to get people talking, so I simply waited.

Finally, he sighed, "In the last couple hours I came to a de-pressing realization. You've given up on Serena. You wouldn't have allowed Jada to spend the night until you had abandoned hope."

I looked at him in surprise, wondering how he'd known about Jada. He quickly explained, "Serena and I are friends. She tells me things."

I finally nodded. "Serena was seeing another guy. Now, she says they're through. I never thought I'd say this, but it has stopped mattering. What's unfolded can never fold back. I'm just empty. She has stopped telling me, 'This doesn't change anything,' before she leaves, but those comments just wore me down."

"I think Serena intended to mean she still needed time, and you took her words to mean you're not good enough. Look—who the hell am I to give anyone advice, right? I know you're close to being filled with contempt for her," Tony acknowledged. "I've been down that road. I'm just asking you not to tear into her if—she asks you to marry her."

Shocked, I said, "Like *that's* going to happen."

"It's true." Tony raised his hand as if taking an oath on the stand.

I considered, "Serena does want me staying at my home, with her and Nora, when I'm in Pierz."

Tony interrupted, "Do you know Serena works as an administrative assistant just down the road from here? She checks in on me twice a week. She's got me into a routine and reading the Bible. There's a grace about her that makes me want to be better. You need to understand that, as painful as her past choices were, they were made out of a need for self-preservation, not malice. I know you're not in the same place anymore, but she's still a sweetheart. All I ask is that you keep an open heart."

With my love for Serena in a precarious state, dangerously close to descending into nothingness, I spoke of the case. "My supervisor's implying I'm incompetent, because I have *nothing* on three murders, and I've been shot at twice."

Tony finally turned my way and commiserated, "I don't imagine he offered any suggestions." His voice sharpened as he pulled himself out of his reverie. "I haven't been able to find anything in the videos. I don't think our killer drove into Princeton. I think he lives somewhere between St. Paul and St. Cloud on Interstate 94."

I feigned confidence. "Well I'm going to solve this. You may want to get healthy because I might lose my job in the process, so they'll be looking for an investigator to replace me."

I wheeled back and forth as I continued, and had a fleeting thought of gratitude, knowing I could stand up and walk away from this chair any time I wanted. "Thing is, Maurice is wrong. The DNA from Leah Hartman's murder matches the DNA from Ava's assault. Leah wasn't hunted down by an angry ex. It's this same Culhwch prick we've been chasing. And I've got the DNA profile back from Ancestry-dot-com."

Tony retorted, "As far as a replacement investigator for you goes, you obviously don't understand how helpless I am. I get open sores from doing nothing, and then I'm stuck in bed until they heal. Then I get to roll around in that thing," he nodded toward his wheelchair, "Which, I might add, I can do a lot better than you." He grimaced at my gracelessness in maneuvering his chair. "Do you have a name?"

I smiled, "We're in business, Tony! Our killer has a half-sister named Colleen McGrath."

"Well, enough olagonin'!" Tony perked up. "I'll go on Facebook and look for family members." With this, Tony flung back his bedcovers, and said, "Now, get outta my ride. I've got work to do."

37

TWENTY-EIGHT-YEAR-OLD SLY GRAHAM uses traditional brown rope to bind his pretty woman friend, Harper. Harper Cook is of mixed race (black and white) with straight, black hair. She is a thin and attractive eighteen-year-old who graduated from Robbinsdale Cooper last year. Sly was born in Milwaukee, Wisconsin, and took Interstate 94 to Minneapolis to escape consequences for two battery (assault) charges against his former lover, Brooke.

Battery is a misdemeanor in Wisconsin and doesn't warrant extradition. Sly has a tawny skin color, as a result of having one black and three white grandparents. He will be a challenge, even though he is only about 165 pounds, because he's a wired character. The advantage I have is that he tethers Harper after their Friday nights out at the Azul Nightclub. (Harper gets in because Sly knows a bouncer.) Sly has his own special way of tethering, which involves a combination of futumomo and a box tie. It requires over thirty feet of rope. While Harper is lying on her back, Sly starts by bending each knee until her heels are touching her rump, then her enfolded leg is bound tightly. With a series of ties, her legs are secured in a folding position called the futumomo. He then ties her arms behind her back, wrists to elbows, followed by extra rope wrapped twice around her torso above her breasts, and twice around her torso below her breasts. This is what's called a "Shibari box tie," in the BDSM world. Harper is completely at her master's mercy. I've seen their pictures online. You can't blame me for looking, when people invite me into their guilty pleasures by saving their pictures in online files. I may actually be saving Harper's life.

I'm in their house now. I search through the home—no guns to take. Sly's laptop is sitting on the kitchen table, plugged in and open. His security code is written on a post-it, stuck to the keyboard. People are so stupid. I had planned on delivering the next cypher, but I think I'll taunt the detectives by emailing it directly to Maddy Moore. Harper's fate will be dependent on how quickly Maddy accesses her email. I type the cypher in and send it.

> Boy, Sly couldn't offend his dear departed namesyke more. Graham barely cracker. Y does a man have a need 2 violate very woman whom once loved, too enjoy sex. Wy risk 9 lives they get 4 it. / Culhwch

I will never be caught because I'm not foolish enough to purchase anything I use in crime. Bo Gere's home was a treasure chest, as I walked away with a Browning hunting rifle with a thermal night vision scope, ammo, a nine-millimeter handgun with a build-in suppressor, a Taser bolt with replaceable cartridges, a hockey goalie, Jason-like mask (which I'm currently wearing), duct tape, and cuffs. So, when the investigators are out looking for where these items were purchased, it'll only come back to my previous victim. I keep a clothing change in my locker at the Heritage Facility so I never return home in my murder clothes. Now I just have to sit in Sly's house and wait . . .

I finally hear Sly and Harper approaching the house. Sly is slurring his words in his efforts to come on to her.

Harper jiggles the door handle. "Someone broke into your house. The door handle's been jimmied."

Sly gets brave and tells her, "I'll blow his fucking brains out!" I hear Sly stumble in and shout, "Come and get me!" He laughs.

People are such idiots when they're drunk. I wonder momentarily if he is carrying a gun. I step into the extra bedroom and, through the partially opened door, watch Sly stumble into the living room. He's got his back to me, and I'm relieved to see he isn't carrying. If he was, I'd just have to make sure I shot him first.

Sly yells to Harper, "The gaming system is still here. Laptop's still here. Maybe we chased them away."

Harper calls back, "Did you check the back bedroom?"

Sly runs his hand down his face in a drunken gesture of frustration, then lies, "Yes!"

Harper directs him, "Check our bedroom."

Sly laughs. "All right."

Soon I can hear Harper giggling. "No. I told you not to have that last drink"

Sly mumbles something inaudible, and Harper concedes, "Okay, but go lock the door." Sly stumbles down the hall, locks the front door and returns to the bedroom.

After several minutes of passionate groaning, Harper complains, "You always tie me too tight when you've had too much to drink. Get a knife and cut this."

Sly teases, "What's the magic word?"

"Cut it, or you're never touching me again," she warns.

Sly laughs. "That's magic enough for me."

It is time for me to intervene. I sure don't want Sly holding a knife.

When I step into the doorway, Sly and Harper both stop and stare, obviously disturbed by the Jason mask as much as my sudden appearance in their bedroom. Harper is bound on the bed, while Sly is facing me from the other side of the bed.

Harper screams, and Sly uses the distraction to pull a Colt 45 out from between the mattresses. Before I can turn and fire, Sly pulls the trigger. "*Click. Click. Click.*" He looks at Harper in disbelief as he realizes she had unloaded his gun.

"*Phhht.*" My silencer puts a bullet in his Sly's shoulder. I was aiming for his chest, but this could work better, since he can still walk himself to the car.

Sly screams, "We're dead!" He turns and yells at Harper, "You stupid bitch!" He hurls his gun at me and hunches over.

I easily dodge the flying forty-five, step around the bed, tase him, and watch him seizure to the floor.

Harper rolls off the bed, but because of her tethers, she's unable to stand up. I watch her frantically rub the rope against the metal frame of her bed.

I pocket the Taser and slip the gun into the back of my jeans. I quickly soak the ether rag and hold it over Harper's nose and mouth. In my hurry to shut her up, I may have used a little too much. She yells, "No!" Her next few gasps of air are ether-infused, effectively silencing her. Now I can take the Jason mask off.

Confused, Sly groans, "Why?"

I reply, "Well, I can't think when she's yelling, can I?" I need her to shut up and stop moving. When they're still, I can focus on what I want. When they move, I have to consider what they're thinking. She gave up the ability to protect her body when she agreed to be tied up. Who cares what she's thinking?

I help Sly to his feet and tell him, "You bound her like a hog-tied pig. No respect. Look at her—rope up and down her legs, across her stomach, above her chest—you're basically screwin' rope. What the hell is wrong with you?"

Sly pleads, "She was the one who wanted to try this Japanese bondage shit. She'd get rope drunk! I'm sorry! I'll never do it again!"

"Damn straight." To ensure his compliance, I say, "I need to get you to a hospital." I help him to his feet and tell him, "If you try to run, I'll tase you again."

With my guidance, but holding his shoulder in deep pain, Sly ambles along.

I grab the blanket, which was barely hanging on the bed, and walk Sly to his car.

He groans as he asks, "What do you need the blanket for?"

"We're taking your ride, and you don't want to get blood all over the seat, do you?"

It's dark outside, and no one's around to observe our awkward journey to his vehicle. Once at the car, I open the back door and help him in. I take the ether rag back out and shove it over his mouth. Sly attempts to struggle, but with his traumatized body, he is unable to resist my force. Once he's out, I push him over and cover him with the blanket. Being he apologized, I decided to make his demise less painful. I then fire the kill shot. *Society just got better.* Now comes the fun part . . .

38

JON FREDERICK
9:30 P.M., SATURDAY, JULY 15,
PIERZ

SERENA CALLED AND SAID we needed to talk—that it was important. I agreed, but told her I was close to breaking this case open, so I needed to spend the night in Minneapolis. Serena felt this was best because, although Nora was spending the night with my parents, Victor and Sonia were getting together at my house in Pierz to watch a movie. We weren't initially certain Sonia's sister, Leah, had been sexually assaulted when she was murdered, but now that we had the full coroner's report and the data from the lab, our suspicions were confirmed, and the family was notified. Sonia was struggling with periods of anger and bitterness, and I couldn't blame her. I didn't want to make Victor and Sonia reschedule their date. Victor apparently soothes her.

I picked Serena up in Pierz, and we headed south. About a half hour into our trip, Maddy called me from home and told me she had just received an email from Culhwch. I asked her to forward it to me. I pulled over and asked Serena to drive so I could work on the cypher.

Serena asked, "How do you solve a cypher?"

"If it's symbols, you can substitute. 'E' is the most common letter in the English language. Sometimes two letters often occur next to each other, like 'th.' But, here, I'm counting off letters."

I could tell Serena was frustrated. She wanted to talk, but now I needed to work. I thanked her as she silently drove while I focused completely on the cypher. When I focus, I don't think of, or hear, anything else around me. It's not a blessing for a relationship.

Ten minutes later, I looked up and said, "I got it."

Serena smiled, then reached over and put her hand on my leg. "Can you tell me?"

"It says, 'Body by Avon 94.' The significant letters are, once again, thirteen apart. As soon as I noticed the '9' and '4' were thirteen letters apart, I assumed the code was the same."

Boy, sly couldn't **o**ffend his dear **d**eparted names**y**ke more. Graham **b**arely cracker. **Y** does a man have **a** need 2 violate **v**ery woman whom **o**nce loved, too e**n**joy sex. Wy risk **9** lives they get **4** it. / Culhwch

When I called my supervisor, he told me Paula Fineday was on her way back from North Dakota and was close to the Avon area on I-94. Since I was now closer to Minneapolis, I was instructed to stop at our St. Paul office and pick up some equipment before I headed north.

I called the Stearns County Sheriff's Department and requested their assistance. They agreed to get on I-94 by Avon, and search all the exits for bodies or abandoned cars.

AFTER SERENA HAD HELPED ME load the equipment in my car at the BCA, I took over the driving, and we cruised I-94 through Minneapolis, heading toward Avon. I took Serena's hand and squeezed it. "I'm sorry. Looks like I have to work tonight." Serena wore a simple spring-green cotton top with the copper feather necklace I had given to her in better times. There was a pretty glow about her tonight.

Serena remarked, "You needed a driver."

"I'm sorry. I should have told you I was too busy." I blew out a frustrated breath.

Serena pulled my hand to her mouth and kissed my palm. "It's okay. I shouldn't have said anything. I'm glad we got some time together."

She was looking at the message I had jotted down with every thirteenth letter circled. She asked, "What do you think the original letter meant?"

"I honestly don't know, but I have a feeling it will become evident when we find this body."

"He loves his words," Serena mused, setting the cypher between us on the seat. "This is someone who is very adept at manipulating them. Maybe it's an interpreter, or a writer of some sort."

My phone buzzed, and I immediately responded.

Paula sounded terse. "I don't know if it's worth your trip to Avon. We can't find a body."

I remembered playing amateur baseball in Avon when I was seventeen. "They have a ballfield right off of 94. Have them check the dugouts."

"They have," she said, exasperated. "We'll keep looking, but sit tight. I'll call if we find anything."

When I hung up, I noticed Serena was frantically scrolling through the internet on her phone, so I asked, "What are you looking for?"

She continued to study the screen as she answered, "When you first told me the cypher, I wasn't thinking of the city of Avon. My mom used to buy Avon. According to the internet, there's an Avon store just off of 94 in Brooklyn Center. I think the store's closed now, but there's a beauty center still open in Brooklyn Park.

I considered this. "Which came up first in your search?"

"The Brooklyn Center one that's closed. It's right off of the 51 exit."

"Let's go there, first. I believe Culhwch gets his information from internet searches, rather than research."

As we approached the 51 exit off of 94, we spotted a metallic-blue Chevy Cruze pulled over on the shoulder of I-94. After I pulled behind it, I grabbed a pair of latex gloves out of the glove compartment and asked Serena to wait in the car. The front seat of the Chevy was empty, but I saw a gray blanket draped over something in the backseat. I could see what looked like a large bloodstain in the middle of the blanket.

Serena was now standing beside me with gloves on, so in spite of her consternation and distress, I told her to call nine-one-one, and request law enforcement and an ambulance.

When I lifted the blanket, I found a young man of mixed race bleeding from his shoulder but still alive. A second shot had grazed his forehead with minimal damage. In a weakened, barely audible voice, he whispered, "Help Harper. She's still tied up." Having delivered his message, he lost consciousness. Our killer left the car this time, so he wouldn't have to double back to his victim's home.

Her phone still to her ear, Serena told me, "There's a state trooper less than a mile away."

Although you never want to interrupt a crime scene, I carefully patted the man's pockets but found no wallet on his person. I quickly popped the glove compartment and, after rummaging through paperwork, found the title to his vehicle. I scanned quickly for his name and address. His car was relatively new, so I hoped the address was current.

Serena said, "We need to apply pressure to his wound."

"Could I get you to stay with him? The trooper will need to block off the scene and I have another victim to get to."

Feigning confidence, she replied, "Of course."

She quickly made her way around the car, opened the passenger side door, and used the blanket to apply pressure. I left my emergency kit with her and headed to Sly Graham's home on Fourth Street North in Minneapolis. It was only a little over a mile away, so I was likely the closest officer. On the way, I called Sean Reynolds and brought him up to speed on our crisis situation.

Once I arrived at the house, I pulled on fresh latex gloves before I entered, to avoid any cross contamination. Sly's door was open, same as Alan Volt's had been, back when this first started. I identified myself, to no response.

After a cursory search of the ground floor of the home, I located a young woman in one of the bedrooms, balled up on the floor. She had a bright red burn on her lips, and the tight brown rope had dug into her naked body. She had almost worn the rope through, but enough strands remained to squeeze her body in an unrelenting grasp. I quickly cut the remaining strands and freed her from her hemp prison. Her breathing was incredibly slow, and I feared it would soon stop. I immediately called for an ambulance. In addition to the chemical burn around her mouth, hives had formed on her chest, typical of an allergic reaction.

As the young woman was being loaded into the ambulance, Serena was dropped off by a state trooper. Her hair was windblown, and her spring-green top was now blood-stained. She was scrubbing her arms with antibacterial wipes. I could see the adrenaline was still racing through her system. She opened the passenger door of my car and sat inside, her legs hanging out the open door. Squad cars with flashing lights were now parked all around us. Serena appeared to be considering all the stimulation, as she commented, "No wonder you can't sleep at night."

I squatted in front of her and looked up at her, "Serena, you were amazing today. You saved a young man's life." I glanced toward the house, "I should stay and work—it could take hours."

Just then, Jada Anderson and El Epicene stepped out of the first news van on the scene. Jada registered Serena and me, and undeterred, went right to work, setting up as close as she could to where the police tape blocked out the public.

I asked Serena, "Do you want to take my car?" She was watching Jada and El in action, her expression unreadable. When she didn't respond, I asked, "I could see if Clay is headed back to Pierz to work on my house. Maybe you could catch a ride."

Serena scoffed, "I'm not getting in a vehicle with *Clay*. If it's okay, I'll go back to your apartment, take a long shower, and then I can come back and pick you up. I'm feeling pretty safe here—if you're not done when I get back, I'll lock the door, curl up and sleep."

A police officer walked by to make certain the media was keeping their distance. It occurred to me once again that our killer came and went without notice. This was why he understood how we approached crime scenes. I realized I couldn't trust anyone close to the investigation. It was not only possible, it was likely the killer was here, right now, undetected because of his role.

With a change of heart, I took Serena's hand and pulled her out of the car. "Come with me. We'll go over our statements one more time with investigators. Then I'm leaving with you." I needed to debrief her on everything she'd just experienced, even if it meant leaving my crew to work without me.

I was relieved to see Sean Reynolds emerge from a cluster of uniformed officers. He was dressed impeccably as usual, in a black suit and tie. His clothing hung loose on his muscular, six-foot frame. I thanked him for helping out and suggested, "Can we get the police to start from about a block out and then make sure to get the names of everybody on the scene right now? Everybody—even every officer. I think it's possible our killer is observing all of this."

Sean agreed, "I've been feeling the same thing. You've been shot at, twice, at crime scenes. I'm good with locking everyone down. At the very least, it'll ensure you walk out of here safe. This killer likes to watch. That's why he can spend so much time online researching his victims."

I asked, "Sean, would you mind if Serena stayed with you for a couple minutes?"

Sean agreed, and I walked directly to Jada.

Jada looked uncharacteristically nervous when I approached and said, "Let me see your phone."

El intervened, "Let's see your subpoena."

Ignoring her, Jada handed me her phone with apprehension.

I brought up her *Find my iPhone* app and saw she had been tracking my cell phone. This was how she knew where to find me the night I was out walking, and how she was first to this scene tonight.

Jada was abashed. "I'm so sorry. I was worried about you—you were such a mess." She held her hand out for her phone and added, "My intentions were good."

I said nothing, processing the feeling of violation I was experiencing.

Jada swallowed hard and revealed, "This was the only time I used it to find a crime scene." Jada took her phone back and, holding it up so I could see what she was doing, she deleted me from her app. "There. I promise I won't run this as the top story tonight. Please, forgive me."

El had been unusually nonverbal during this exchange, but now exclaimed, "What do you mean you won't run this as the top story? You have to!"

I turned my body so my back was to El, hoping El would pick up my disinterest in the incessant comments. "You put it on my phone the night my apartment was broken into—you made it look like you were just searching my call history."

Jada's lips puckered and twisted as she began to chew the inside of her cheek, always a giveaway when she was experiencing distress. Wordlessly, she nodded that I was correct. This was a betrayal, and Jada knew it. For me, it effectively closed the unfinished book of Jon and Jada.

El continued to interject static. "Jada, if you back off again, Jack Kavanaugh gets the exclusive. I swear, if we don't feature this, I'll go to Jack personally and tell him you backed off because your love life has taken priority over your news reporting." El's anger was palpable. "Remember when you told me shut down my love interest and focus on our work? Now I'm telling you."

Jada's eyes widened as she turned, experiencing her own betrayal for having confided in El.

I pulled Jada aside, away from the noise of El. "Be careful. This killer is very judgmental, and if he feels you violated some code, he'll come after you. El won't keep quiet over this."

Jada put her hand on my bicep, and then pulled it back quickly, having momentarily forgotten how our relationship had changed so dramatically in the last few minutes. She looked directly into my eyes and told me, "Please understand, I never intended to hurt you."

I nodded because I believed her, but good intentions didn't dismiss the betrayal. I turned my back to her and walked away. As I did, I caught a glimpse of Serena, realizing she watched the entire exchange between me and Jada. She had to have seen it wasn't a pleasant one, but looked a question at me, which I ignored for the time being. We had enough to talk about tonight without drawing this episode into it.

39

SERENA AND I SPENT MUCH OF THE NIGHT talking through the events of the day before, so we never got to her reason for asking to speak in the first place.

I explained the cypher to her: "Sylvester Graham was a nineteenth-century Presbyterian minister who believed lustful desires were harmful and could be controlled with a bland diet. The graham cracker was named after him. The victim you tended to in the car was named Sly Graham. He was mostly white, but not completely. That would explain the "barely cracker" part. Plus, it was a word play with the double meaning of cracker."

Serena tried not to smile as she commented, "So, next time I can't stop thinking of you, I should just eat a graham cracker."

I responded with mock seriousness, "No more s'mores when we're together," and she seemed to appreciate the reply.

Out of respect for Serena, I also shared the entire conversation I had with Jada. I had her drive me to the BCA office, and let her take my car back to Pierz. I would use a car from work, as I planned on working the rest of the day, and would retrieve my car when it became convenient. I met with Sean Reynolds to review what was uncovered at Sly Graham's home. Both Harper and Sly were at Fairview Hospital, still alive, and recovering. It bothered me that, before the homicide, Sly and Harper were at Azul, the very bar Jada had taken me.

10:45 A.M., SUNDAY, JULY 16,
FULTON NEIGHBORHOOD IN MINNEAPOLIS

I HAD A PRETTY GOOD IDEA WHERE I'd find Jada today. The murder of Sly Graham wasn't the lead story. Unrelated to our case, Justine Dammon, a forty-year-old Australian woman, was shot and killed by police officer, Mohamed Noor, age thirty-one, in Minneapolis after calling to report a sexual assault. When the squad car had arrived, Justine ran to it, slapping the back end, and from the passenger seat, a startled Mohamed shot her through the abdomen, killing her. The riots that follow the killing of innocents compound the problem. Since the Ferguson riots, enrollment in law enforcement programs was down sixty percent, which meant less-skilled officers were pushed more quickly into work in dangerous neighborhoods. Mohamed Noor was one of those police officers put on the street after only seven months of training, when two to four years was the past expectation.

Jada and El Epicene were somewhere between Washburn and Xerxes Avenue in Minneapolis, interviewing people close to the scene of Justine Damon's shooting. I managed to catch Jada standing next to the WCCO news van. She was dressed professionally, in a charcoal gray jacket and skirt, talking to a camera man next to the van.

Jada looked troubled, but she set aside what she was doing to speak to me. Downcast, she said, "Justine was a yoga instructor, just trying to help someone out." Her professional demeanor softened with her deflating posture, and when she leaned in for a hug, I complied.

As we parted, I told her, "Sly and Harper were at Azul last night. Were you there?"

"No," Jada responded defensively. Her eyes darted across my face, trying to read my expression.

I took a step back and sank my hands into my pockets, needing physical distance between us. "Why did you take me there?"

"El asked me to meet her there—ask her." As Jada gestured toward El and began moving in that direction, she quietly apologized again for tracking me.

I truly believed Jada's worry for me was genuine. But I couldn't let go of the notion of a secondary work motive. Jada steered me to El, who was sitting on a nearby park bench in an oversized, crisp white dress shirt, white slacks, and red tennis shoes.

As we approached, my curiosity got the better of me; I had to ask, "Why the bright white?" The neighborhood was mourning.

El responded, "She was pure . . ." I let El rant on. The harangue ended with El telling me she was changing her name to the letter L.

I finally interrupted, "Look, I don't care if you're a letter or a number, or simply the person formerly known as El. You were born Del Elliott and you had a difficult childhood. You're transforming—I get it. We all are, in one way or another. I need to know why you invited Jada to Azul."

El dismissed my response as irrelevant. Her face twisted into a sneer as she got to her feet. "Did it *look* like the first time Jada was to Azul?"

"But why that night?" Her attitude was not a deterrent, and I needed an answer.

"I got a tip that something big was going down. But nothing happened, other than some guy insulting you and your wimping out."

I almost smiled, remembering the insult was directed at both of us. "El, where did the tip come from?"

El turned on a heel and began walking back toward the news van, then said over her shoulder, "I don't have a need to share all my sources with you, like Jada seems to."

I countered, "Jada benefits from it."

El dismissed this, "Not like you do . . ."

40

O N A WHIM, I DECIDED to stop at Clay Roberts's home, before heading back to Pierz. Clay answered the door in jeans and a tight black t-shit. As he invited me in, he commented wryly, "Jon's gone cold and now you're back."

I put a hand up to stop his nasty words, "I didn't come here to argue."

Clay cocked his fists on his narrow hips and sneered, "I don't imagine you did. After Jon spent months waiting for you, I had to be the one to tell him about that pretty boy you were banging."

"I wasn't 'banging' him," I retorted in disgust. "I wish I'd never left Jon. There was a lot going on—I struggled with depression. I was being harassed online by some psychopath and I later found out my thyroid wasn't functioning right. I will make it right with Jon."

Clay laughed, "Good luck with that. If you were my woman and you pulled that crap, there would be no way I'd ever speak to you again."

I couldn't stop myself from saying, "If I was *your woman* that would be the best possible outcome."

Unfazed by the insult, Clay suggested, "You turned Jon into me—another guy who doesn't care. But it's been a good lesson for me. If any woman cared for me the way Jon's suffered for you, I've *really* been a jerk. So why don't you take that taut rump of yours back to Pierz."

Surprised by his correct use of the word, I was side-tracked for a moment. "Taut's a good word for you, Clay, even if I prefer you didn't use it to refer to me as a tight ass."

He then had to add, "I thought it meant taught by a lot of guys."

I stared at him blankly, just managing to stifle a laugh at his nescience. Changing the subject, I shared, "John, thinks this guy's going to kill Ava, but I don't think he is. I think this guy's en-amored of Ava, which essentially puts your life at risk. I couldn't leave without warning you." I turned to leave but couldn't without first trying to alter the way we interacted. I appealed to his sense of justice by sharing, "I'm trying to repair my life. Look, I'm sorry I came over that night. I don't want to have to feel sick about it every time we interact. When you and Jon have a conversation, he walks away with a smile—when you and I have a conversation, I walk away angry or hurt."

Clay remarked, "You think Jon and I don't insult each other?"

I swallowed hard and struggled to make eye contact with him. "But it's different. Every time we speak, you imply that I'm here to have sex with you. Do you have any idea how shaming that is? I have no interest in making that mistake again." I held my thumb and forefinger a quarter inch apart. "And it makes me feel this big. Can I just say, 'I'm sorry,' and be done with it?"

Clay turned his back to me and ran his hand through his long hair. "You think everything can be fixed. Some things just break, so you throw it away and move on."

"I can't—not without doing everything in my power to fix my relationship with Jon first. And that includes ending my antagonistic relationship with his best friend."

With his back to me, he said, "You've abandoned your religion?"

"No." It took me a minute before I realized his mistake. "Not 'agnostic'—'antagonistic' means hostile or difficult."

As I reached for the door handle, he turned and said, "Wait. I'm not great at explaining myself, so bear with me. Seeing you makes me angry—at me. Jon's my one friend. The one person, who has always wanted better for me. I've had a dozens of women like you. Why did I have to have you too? I wasn't feeling anything special—just curiosity."

"I feel this is on me. If I wouldn't have come over—"

Clay shouted, "Stop! You had no idea if Jon would ever be interested in you again." He took a deep breath, "But I did. I knew he wanted to find you and talk to you, but I didn't say a damn thing because I wanted to sleep with you."

It was difficult, but I asked, "Can we just move on, and not let our shame hang over every conversation?"

Appearing to have found some relief in unburdening his soul, Clay nodded, "I would be fine with that."

Now I could leave.

41

BILL AND CAMILLE FREDERICKS were in Genola, helping clean up after Freedom Fest. Vic and I had a blast listening to the horns of Brothers Tone and the Big Groove. This was the perfect time for me to go to the Fredericks' house and borrow Bill's Model 70 Winchester. He gave me the safe combination, so I could use Camille's rifle to practice hunting. Bill hid that rifle last week, commenting that I'd been "a little dark lately," so now I was taking his rifle.

I grabbed Bill's navy-blue camouflage jacket and loaded it with some Winchester brand 30.06, 165 grain bullets. I admit, I was feeling a little powerful and a lot scared. As I left the house, I was met by a man standing right in front of the door wearing a black t-shirt that read in white letters, "JUST SAY NOPE."

Victor brushed some of his scraggly blond hair to the side and asked, "What are you doing?"

Not wanting to lie to Victor, I said nothing.

Victor's blue eyes saw right through me, and, as he registered my intentions, he spoke urgently. "I love you Sonia. I will always love you. But if you hunt this guy down and kill him, I don't think I could ever live with you. You know I'm already a little paranoid."

Tears formed, but I stood resolute in my cause, brandishing the rifle.

Victor's family never gave him enough credit for his wisdom, but God bless him, he wasn't bitter about it. He told me they still saw his past craziness when they looked at him. He loved me because I didn't. Victor pointed out that, regardless of their patronizing manner, his family never excluded him, and introduced him at functions with a pride you'd expect to be reserved for a prince. You had to be patient to appreciate Victor. I told him, "I'm doing this. I made this decision before I ever met you."

His response was, "Three frogs are on a log and two decide to jump in the pond. How many frogs are still on the log?"

Confused at the purpose of his story, I said, "One."

Victor corrected me, waving three fingers in front of my face. "Three. Deciding to do something isn't the same as actually doing it."

42

JON FREDERICK

9:30 A.M., MONDAY, JULY 17,

BUREAU OF CRIMINAL APPREHENSION, ST. PAUL

TONY SHILETO HAD HELPED PUT ME on Colleen McGrath's trail. Colleen didn't have a legal history, which made her much harder to track down. She had joined the Peace Corps after high school and was now volunteering at a food shelf in Los Angeles.

Once I secured her phone number, I immediately called her. When she answered with a bright greeting, I simply said, "Colleen."

"Yes," she slowly responded, her voice lilting into a question.

"This is Jon Frederick. I'm a homicide investigator for the BCA, and I'm looking for a relative of yours. We have DNA evidence indicating you're a half-sibling to someone implicated in a serious crime, and we need your help to ensure no one else is hurt."

After listening to the long version of the "trials of Colleen" she finally revealed, "I was adopted at birth in a closed adoption." She added hastily, "My adoptive parents are amazing."

Frustrated, I crumpled up a training brochure on my desk and tossed it into the garbage can. *Are you kidding me? Now I'm looking at trying to get a judge to open up a closed adoption, and even if I find one of her parents, there's a fifty percent chance it's the wrong one.* And then Colleen gave me a gem.

"My birth mother contacted me a few years ago. Her name is Hillary Connelly. She's dried out now, so you might be able to have a conversation with her. She wanted to see if I'd ever come into money." Her sigh whirred noisily through the phone, but she added with some pride, "So, I got my opportunity to turn her away. It wasn't as gratifying as I had anticipated. I kept her number if you want it. Last I heard, she was still living in North Minneapolis."

The DNA of Colleen's mother, Hillary Connelly, was on file for a Manufacturing a Controlled Substance charge (methamphetamine), which landed her in prison. Our forensics staff was working closely with me now, as we all knew we were on the verge of identifying the killer. They were quick to inform me Hillary didn't have DNA in common with the I-94 killer. This meant Colleen and our killer shared the same father. A review of Hillary's past probation reports revealed a sordid history of addiction, abusive boyfriends, and children recklessly jettisoned into poverty along the trail of her life.

11:00 A.M., MONDAY, JULY 17,
BROOKLYN CENTER

I WAS INSTRUCTED TO WAIT FOR BACKUP, but, too obsessed and impatient to wait, I headed to Hillary's on my own. Hillary

Connelly lived in a cramped, lamp-lit apartment inside a filthy, white, stucco apartment building. She pulled open the door with such effort, one would think it was made of concrete. Hillary had choppy gray hair, and peered at me through heavily-lidded eyes, as if keeping them open was as difficult as it was to open her door. She was so frail, she was lost in her chartreuse housecoat—a color that did her mottled complexion no favors.

My background information put her at sixty-three years old; my face-to-face impression added another decade. Barely glancing at my badge, she allowed me in, and gestured toward an orange and brown floral, velvet sofa. The lamp on the end table had no shade, so the bare bulb was an additional insult to the already spare room. As she sat on one end of the sofa, she propped her forehead on shaky fingertips, as if the effort of holding her head up alone would do her in. Her voice was hoarse, like she had been screaming since birth. She spoke without making eye contact. "I'm glad Colleen did well, even if she doesn't talk to me."

Choosing to stand, I got directly to the point, "Hillary, I need to know the name of Colleen's father." I began to feel pressured, afraid she might fall asleep at any moment.

Hillary took a couple slow breaths before she finally met my eyes. "Bull was Colleen's father. He was the worst. He called himself the Brooklyn Bull, since he was raised in Brooklyn Park and Brooklyn Center. He was such a dick. He'd introduce me as, 'This is Hill. Not a mountain, not a molehill. Just a hill.'" A slight tremor shook Hillary's frame.

Brooklyn Center and Brooklyn Park were a couple of the tougher suburbs of Minneapolis, and I-94 ran through both. I'd heard them referred to as "Crooklyn Center" and "Brooklyn Dark," from the less sensitive living too close to the fray.

I asked, "Whatever happened to Bull?"

"When I got pregnant with Colleen, he stopped coming home at night. I tried to get him to stay by giving up our baby, but he left anyway." She looked up at me hoping for understanding. "I thought Colleen would be better off—Bull had a mean streak. After he left, I told social services I needed my baby, but there was no going back."

I finally perched next to her on the edge of the grimy sofa, and asked carefully, "Did Bull ever tie you up?"

Hillary's back stiffened. Her breaths were labored as I waited. "Why do you want to talk about that?" She reached for a tattered gold throw pillow and pulled it into her lap as if she could hide behind it.

I softened my tone in hope of lowering her defenses. "Bull has a son—not your son—who we're looking for regarding an assault."

Hillary said, "Well that must have been after we were together. Bull didn't have a son when I was with him."

"I need to know Bull's real name."

Hillary was silent as she busied herself trying to pull apart the clumped fringes on the pillow. I didn't allow myself to wonder what exactly had caused the fringes to stick together so firmly. When she finally spoke, there was more strength in her voice than I'd heard since I arrived. "In the assault—was the girl dressed?"

Energized, I now knew I was on the right track. "No, she wasn't."

Her eyes were rheumy when they finally met mine, and I could see I had clearly triggered memories. I could sense she was shutting down. Through yellowed, clenched teeth, Hillary muttered, "I'm not a snitch."

"You must realize you're not the only woman he's done this to." I put a hand out toward her forearm to offer comfort, but she flinched away and drew further into herself.

I softly pleaded, "Just a last name. You could save another woman from being raped."

Hillary spat out, "Bull Martin. Bull *is* his real name." Hillary pulled the pillow closer to her chest and looked sightlessly at the arm of the worn sofa, lost in the events of her past. She didn't even bother to glance my way when she said, "I think you need to go now."

On the back of my business card, I wrote down the name and phone number for a clinic that addressed trauma. I carefully tucked the edge of the card under the lamp base, encouraging her to talk to someone about it. As soon as I was in my car, I called Sean, and then Tony, and reported my new lead.

Law enforcement staff shared information with Tony, likely due to his devastating injury in the line of duty. The truth was, he wasn't appreciated as he deserved, prior to being shot. It wasn't long before Tony called me back and told me Bull Martin was living at a place that housed offenders transitioning from prison to the community, called the Dream Center, in St. Cloud. I drove north on I-94, and took the Clearwater exit, which brought me into Clear Lake. This felt right.

As I turned on Highway 10 to St. Cloud, I received a call from Sean Reynolds. He said, "I just had an odd encounter. I picked up the *Minneapolis Tribune* and spent the morning in Harper Cook's hospital room. When she came to and saw me,

Harper demanded I leave. I asked if the assailant was black, and she said, 'No—just go!' Her vitals escalated and I stepped out. Once she recovers, I'm going to ask a nurse what might have triggered the panic attack."

"Your guess is as good as mine," I said. "Is Sly talking?"

"Sly isn't a man who likes talking to anyone associated with law enforcement. He claims the guy wore a white hockey mask the whole time. I'm not buying it, but I think he'll come around eventually . . ."

2:15 P.M., MONDAY, JULY 17,
THE DREAM CENTER IN ST. CLOUD

THE DREAM CENTER IS A BOARD and care place in the Pantown area of St. Cloud. Bull Martin was a bald man who was aging badly. His baldness was not trendy, as there were still thin, dirty-looking wisps of hair above his ears, circling around the sagging skin at the back of his head. He sported a beer belly, faded tattoos about his neck, and full sleeves of images inked onto his arms.

I used Bull's pending probation violation hearing, for testing positive for marijuana, to motivate him to talk to me. Bull didn't want to go back to prison, and he knew his cooperation with a BCA agent would be viewed favorably at his hearing. He would rat out his own kid in a heartbeat if it would save him from one more day of incarceration.

We sat outside on a metal bench facing the brick 810 office building on Germain Street. It was hot and sticky, and the underarms of Bull's black, Jack Daniels t-shirt were darkened with sweat. The air around us was sour. He pulled out a pack of Camels and smacked it violently against the heel of his hand. He produced a beaten-up Zippo and lit a cigarette.

As we discussed his past relationships, Bull complained heartily. "They were a bunch of lyin', cheatin' whores. And now, not one of them has room for me. I took them in." He jutted a grime-encrusted thumbnail toward his chest, then took a hard drag off his cigarette and blew it out through his nostrils. "Felt sorry for them, even when they'd get pregnant and bitchy. I'd hang in there for a while, but there's only so much a man can take." Bull rested his crossed arms on his bulbous stomach, tapping ashes onto the ground as he did so.

I had read through Bull's probation history. He worked only sporadically, living like a parasite off women who received public assistance. I interjected, "So who were you with after Hillary Connelly?"

Bull smiled greasily, watching a Mustang full of young men cruise by, blaring rap music so loudly the bass rattled our bench. "Hill's bills," he said, blowing a plume of smoke above our heads. "Hillary should have come with a warning label. She was like a doorknob—everybody got a turn. I don't think Hill kept the kid."

He scratched his chin, "After Hill, it was Jade something. What the hell was her last name? She had a boy. Claimed it was mine, but a guy never really knows. I mean, I've been with some married women who ended up getting pregnant."

He attempted to give me a knowing wink, but after receiving my flat expression, took a another drag from his cigarette. "I don't like talking about Jade." With a grunt, he hauled himself up and wandered to an outdoor ashtray on the top of a garbage can. He stubbed his cigarette out more aggressively than was probably necessary.

"Why not?" After no response, I tossed a thought out I knew he'd respond to, even though I had no idea of to its accuracy. "I've heard she was pretty hot in her day."

Bull was hovering over the bench to sit back down, the seams of his Levis threatening to give, but straightened as he growled, "Where the hell did you hear that? She was a small-town girl from somewhere in the holy land over there—St. Anna, St. Stephen, St. Wendell, St. Joseph. I couldn't get rid of her." He lowered himself to the bench now, sitting forward in a way that accentuated his protruding belly. "I tied her up and did another woman right next to her, and she still didn't leave. It's like, you never lose a cheap pair of sunglasses," he chuckled mercilessly, "just the nice ones."

I swallowed my revulsion, knowing my gut reaction would shut this conversation down, and asked as casually as I could, "What happened to her? Where does she live?"

For a moment, there appeared to be a glimpse of grief in his eyes. He exhaled a stream of rank breath. "She died of cancer right after Christmas. She'd been at St. Benedict's nursing home in St. Cloud. I probably should have visited, you know. She never stopped loving me."

"What was her boy's name?" My muscles began tensing as I was putting pieces together in my mind. *A young boy, perhaps through a door with a hole in it—from a fist being punched through—witnessing his mother being humiliated.*

Bull struggled to recall the memory. "I'm not sure. Maybe the boy's name was Jade. It may have even been a girl. There were so many, and I was using heavy. I think there was a small A in the last name."

I was barely breathing as I suggested, "Like Anderson?"

"Maybe. I was thinking more like 'Catsandjammer' or something like that. Or, it's nothing like that and my brain is just messing with me. It does that sometimes." He huffed and turned to me impatiently, "Are you going to say I cooperated?

"Yes, but we're not done yet." I asked, "Where was this child when this crazy sexual stuff was going on?"

Bull laughed through his nose, "Always on the computer. The kid's probably the next Steve Jobs . . ."

AFTER LEAVING BULL, I immediately called Serena. She still had contacts in healthcare and would know how to find a woman named Jade, who died in a nursing home in December of 2016, much quicker than I could. She may even be able to find the name of a surviving descendant.

Within an hour, Serena called me back, "Does the name Jane Peterson mean anything?"

"No—do you have anything else?"

Serena hummed as she searched, "How about Jane Kelly?"

"It's Irish—that might mean something. There were two Janes who died at St. Benedict's in December of 2016?"

Serena paused, "Oh, St. Benedict's? I thought you said *any* nursing home in St. Cloud. Okay . . . hold on." I heard the clicking of computer keys through the phone. "No one died at St. Benedict's Center in December of 2016, but a Jade Kavanaugh died in November of 2016."

My enthusiasm became a tangible force as Serena continued, "The executor of her affairs was her son, Jack. She didn't really have anything. It was more a matter of closing accounts."

It made perfect sense. Jack Kavanaugh was a writer—a *wordsmith*, as Serena affectionately referred to those with extensive vocabularies. I mentally began clicking the puzzle pieces together. Jada said she had been talking to other reporters at a table the same night Maddy Moore was sedated after leaving the bar. I'd bet Jack Kavanaugh was one of those reporters. Jack was the one who got Ava to backtrack on her initial impressions of her attacker. And the third cypher was sent to Jack, sky-rocketing the ratings for his article. Jack's name was on the list of people identified at the last murder scene, but because he was the crime reporter for the *St. Paul Pioneer Press*, he wasn't considered out of place.

As I hung up with Serena, a call came through from Sean Reynolds. "We caught a break, Jon. Harper Cook wasn't freaking out over me—it was the fact that I was holding the *Trib*. It turns out she's allergic to newspaper print. If the killer had some on his clothes, that would explain her hives."

I told him, "I'm sure he did, Sean. The killer's Jack Kavanaugh . . ."

Ava's bodyguard, Jeremy, called and reported tersely, "I've been trying to get ahold of you for a half hour. Ava ditched me this morning, which isn't all that newsworthy. I can't follow her into places when she's trying on clothes. She came back on the grid briefly, about thirty minutes ago. At first, I thought she was headed back to your parents' place, but she's just sitting at this address—30409 County Road 34, 93rd Street, Pierz. It's in the middle of nowhere, east of Buckman."

I plugged the address into my GPS to see exactly where

it was. It was the old Giadowski farm. When I was about to make the cut from Highway 10 to Monticello, to get on I-94, Sean Reynolds called to tell me Jack Kavanaugh wasn't around. He wasn't at home, and he'd called in sick to work.

He said, "There's nothing in Jack's home that looks suspicious. So, I got to thinking, why would a writer smell like ink? He doesn't deliver the paper. The *Pioneer Press* isn't even printed in St. Paul. It's printed by the Minneapolis Tribune at the Heritage printing facility, in the Warehouse District in Minneapolis. So, I asked if Jack ever visits the print site. I was told he does, in fact, and even has a locker there. I'm on my way to the Heritage Center with bolt cutters now."

I did a quick U-turn and headed toward the abandoned Giadowski farm. Ava wasn't answering her phone. Something about this didn't feel right.

While racing to the farm, I called Serena to make sure she and Nora were safe.

Serena was laughing with Nora as she answered the phone. They were home. Her voice was light and joyful when she said, "Sonia left earlier. I think she was going to sight in her rifle with your dad."

Any other time, I would have been more careful with delivering news like this to Serena, but in the interest of time, I got right to it. "The killer is Jack Kavanaugh, and right now, we can't seem to find him. I'd like to see if Clay's in the Pierz area and have him stop over with a loaded rifle, to sit with you until this is resolved. Would you mind if I did that?" I couldn't take any chances.

"Not Clay," as if a switch was flipped, Serena's tone darkened with urgency that matched my own. "I'll call my dad. And I'll see if my cousin's around. She's a better shot than both of them, anyway."

I heard a rustling through the phone as Serena's movements increased. I could almost see her, phone snugged between her shoulder and ear, as she used both hands to make sure the doors were locked—the knobs, the deadbolts, and security chains. I knew she'd continue working her way through the house until every window and door was secure. She asked, "Is there any reason Jack would come here?"

"No. There has been nothing posted online about the location of our home. I just want to make sure you're safe—I'm not taking any chances." The rustling continued as I spoke, so I ended the conversation. "Text me after you've got the place locked down and the security system on."

I was comforted knowing Serena was at my home—our home. It was brick with wood shutters for the windows that locked from the inside, and I'd had a state-of-the-art security system installed just a few weeks earlier.

I tried calling Sonia, but her phone went directly to voicemail.

I then called Bill and asked, "Dad, are you with Sonia?"

Bill replied, "No. Did you try her cell?"

"She isn't answering. Serena thought Sonia was sighting her rifle with you."

With consternation, Bill shared, "I hid the 237 she's been using last week, and told her we needed to take some time off. Sonia's been madder than the snake that married a garden hose since hearing her sister was assaulted before she was murdered, so I thought she needed to take a break from firing a rifle. Your mom and I are in Genola now, but we can head home if you're concerned."

"I'd appreciate it if you would try to find her. We have just discovered that Jack Kavanaugh is the I-94 Killer, but we haven't located him yet. I want to make sure Sonia's safe." Then I asked, "Can you think of any reason why Ava would head to the old Giadowski farm?"

"No. Camille and I walked through the woods with her on their land and shared some of the stories. Ava's only called once or twice since she left."

"Snapchat places her at the farm right now."

Bill harrumphed, "Well I wouldn't know about Snapchat. Ava did joke that the only way she'd spend a night out in that hunting shack was if she live-streamed it to her friends as her own personal episode of *Survivor* . . ."

43

IT IS PARTLY CLOUDY TODAY, with the sun painfully bright when it appears, and uncomfortably cool when clouds impede the sun's presence. I take 20oth Street West, off 169, and head into the woods of rural Minnesota. I consider myself fortunate to maintain cell coverage. I turn right on Sage Road, past Gottwalt's store.

I should clarify that this isn't a town. It's a country store that could be from the old west, in the middle of nowhere. I close in on Ava Mayer's GPS location. Her obnoxious Infrared Lexis is sitting at the end of a long dirt driveway, which is mostly grown over with weeds and scrub grass. There's a barn that's completely collapsed to the ground, but no house left on the property. There are no other vehicles around. I drive a hundred more yards, park my car on a field approach and walk back toward my prey. There are no other cars around.

Dead leaves crunch beneath my hard rubber soles as I make my way to Ava. I finally spot a weathered, white hunting shack set off to the side of the property, with haphazardly boarded windows. I carefully study the woods before approaching, and there are no signs of human activity. There's just enough space between the decrepit boards to allow me to see into the shack.

Inside, there sits Ava, in her perfectly applied makeup, roughing it—Ava style—she's wearing an obviously new army t-shirt and camouflage-print sweats. She's is perched on the bottom of a cheaply constructed bunk bed, her hair pulled back into a tight, stubby ponytail. She's got burning candles set about the floor, and is oblivious to the world, wearing headphones and focusing intently on her tablet. I carefully make my way around the shack and peer in from each side. There's no one else there. My excitement intensifies as I consider the possibilities. Should I knock, or just kick in the door? *Ava, this time you've wandered too far from the safety net. I'm going to break you in like a wild horse.* She will be my Olwen—my Layla. I'm kicking the door in.

As I feel for my ether rag, the shack's door suddenly bursts open, and, with a primal scream, Ava explodes through it, breaking into a sprint toward the woods. She must have caught a glimpse of me. Ecstasy rushes through me as I match her pace, noisily plowing through the brittle leaves and dried brush. *It was finally happening—again!* Ava runs as if her life depends on it and, well, it *does*. She is only twenty feet ahead of me, now. I'm not the flabby man I was two years ago—I've trained for this. My new strength certainly surprised Leah Hartman the second time we met. My ability to overpower her was exquisite foreplay.

With nothing to lose now, I can do as I choose with Ava. I close to within fifteen feet. Ava glances back in fear. I can hear her breath coming in gasps as she pushes herself over the earth. I am now within twelve feet of her. Checking on me had slowed her down, and I would have caught her if I hadn't stepped into a dip— I stumble for several steps before righting myself. Ava is headed for an open field just thirty feet ahead. I have to close quickly, to keep her in the woods. I take three large steps and hit her with the Taser. Ava's petite body shakes violently to the ground. As she lands, the rough smack of the impact knocks the wind out of her.

My Ava now lies beneath me. I remove the hooks, crawl on top of her, and soak my rag with ether.

JON FREDERICK

5:00 P.M.

I RACED DOWN SAGE ROAD to Ava's last GPS location. Her scarlet Lexus came into sight, almost offensively bright against the colorless landscape. It was parked on the edge of the road, so I pulled over behind it. The car was empty. I sprinted into the woods chasing the location of her cell phone.

Making his way around a dilapidated shack, my father called out, "Jon!" As he caught his breath, he explained his presence. "After you called, I went home and found my rifle missing, so I called some friends and headed here. They should be here any minute."

As Bill spoke, I could see half a dozen hunters emptying out of several vehicles along the road—women and men in camouflage, all friends of my parents, all ex-military. As my father and his comrades were assembling to make a plan, the crack of a gunshot ripped through the dense woods. We looked at each other for a split second, then all took off running toward the sound.

Dry branches tore at my clothes and face like claws of the dead as I raced toward the sound of the shot.

SONIA HARTMAN
5:00 P.M.

I WAS PATIENTLY WAITING BEHIND a couple six-foot pine trees by an open field at the edge of the woods. Cloud cover stole the sun's warmth, leaving my fingers cold and shaky on the barrel of this large Winchester rifle. I put the clip in the rifle and slid a lever back to chamber the first bullet. I had one shot, so I needed to make it count.

Bill Frederick told me the kick of his rifle would knock me on my ass, but he took the 237 I usually practice with, so the Winchester was my only option. Ava should be running out any moment. I'd been ruminating over avenging my sister's death since the night she was murdered. It was a continuous loop I could only periodically distract my attention from. Everybody had loved Leah—not just me—everyone she interacted with. Her boyfriends were jealous because they knew anyone who spent any time with her wanted more. But to be honest, my desire for revenge had been gradually dissipating—like a fall leaf that was once green with life, then red with anger, and now had dried and was crumpling into nothingness.

Suddenly, the clouds passed, and the warm bright sun embraced me. I took off my jacket and surrendered to a pleasurable cascade of warmth. Leah was telling me she's okay. I didn't have to do this. She was setting me free. I set down my rifle and looked to the sky. I thanked Leah for relieving me of my burden.

CULHWCH
5:04 P.M.

WHILE AVA WRITHES IN PAIN beneath me, I hold her arms, savoring the moment. Tears stream from her eyes as she gasps, "I don't want to die! Please don't put that rag on me—please! I'll do whatever you want."

I pull my gun and touch the barrel to her temple. "Then lie still and let's get down to business," I say as I reach to unbuckle my belt.

Ava is compliant, extending her arms above her head, and I yank her army green shirt off with my left hand. "Time for another lesson, Ava!"

SONIA HARTMAN
5:05 P.M.

AWASH WITH RELIEF AT MY DECISION not to kill, I began walking toward the woods. I'd get him to surrender at gunpoint. I suddenly heard Ava scream. I picked up the Winchester and ran toward her cries. At the edge of the woods, she was sprawled on her back on the ground, and a man was straddling her with a gun to her head. I stopped, and without thinking twice, I raised the rifle to my eye and fired. *CRACK!!!*

JON FREDERICK
5:07 P.M.

I BROKE INTO A CLEARING AT THE EDGE of the woods and there was Ava, in a sports bra and camo pants. She was standing over

Jack Kavanaugh, kicking him ruthlessly in the ribs as he coughed up blood.

I raced to her side, kicked away the gun discarded near his body, and pulled her back. Ava's eyes were bright with fury as she struggled against me. I looked up to see Sonia walking toward us, her small frame nearly lost in my father's jacket. Her dark hair was woven into an intricate braid. She was carrying a 30.06 Winchester rifle and, with her free hand, was rubbing her shoulder from the kickback of the shot I realized she'd just fired. She stumbled a bit and looked at me vacantly, as if she couldn't quite make sense of what had just happened.

Bill had caught up to me, and immediately called for help on his cellphone.

Once I felt Ava wasn't going to continue her attack of Jack, I released her and stepped out of her way. She aggressively picked up her shirt and pulled it on, oblivious to nature's detritus clinging to it. Her wild eyes were only for the figure on the ground, and the rage emanating through her body was palpable. She moved to resume her attack, but as she ran toward Jack, a large, bearded man stepped in front of her, and pulled her into a bear hug to keep her from doing more damage to the wounded man. Ava's screams of anger, fear, and impotence ripped through her and filled the woods. She pushed and beat against his chest, but he held on patiently. Spent, she finally collapsed into him in tears, surrendering to his comfort, as if he was the tender father she never had.

Bill made his way over to Sonia and gently pried the rifle out of her hands. A fifty-something, gray-haired female hunter approached and carefully took Sonia's face in her hands, forcing her to make eye contact.

She asked Sonia softly, "Are you okay?" Sonia's composure collapsed at the woman's kindness. Her body followed suit, and when she sank to the ground, the woman knelt beside her, speaking warmly and reassuringly.

I was crouching like a catcher by Jack Kavanaugh.

Through gurgles of blood and strained breaths, Jack attempted to order me, "Arrest them."

I didn't look at him as I continued to take in the scene unfolding around us. I answered coldly, "Jack, everyone now knows you're the I-94 Killer. Investigators are headed to your locker at the print shop as we speak."

I was an amalgamation of emotions. I was angry that he assaulted Ava again, angry, too, about this whole setup Ava and Sonia apparently concocted. But I was also relieved it was over, and both Sonia and Ava were still alive. The manner in which the hunters stepped into comfort Ava and Sonia was heartwarming.

There was little I could do at this point. The cavitation done by a high speed bullet, mercilessly flattening as it worked through Jack's body, was lethal. It left an exit wound the size of an orange. I took off my shirt and used it to pack the exit wound, pressing it against the ragged edges of his flesh, trying to delay Jack's demise.

Noticing my state of undress, my dad brought me his dark leather jacket, which had the large, gold Guinness logo on the back (a harp). I quickly shrugged it on and let it hang open as I spoke flatly to Jack. "The closest ambulance is a half hour away. You're not going to make it, Jack. Do you want last rites?" Not everyone gets the Viaticum.

Barely conscious, Jack grumbled, "I don't believe—" Then stopped himself, and said, "Yeah."

I finally met his eyes, "The first step is confession. If you don't want to talk to me, I can have someone else kneel by you."

Fear played across his features as reality settled into his being. He was struggling with words, now. "Is this a trick?" Threads of blood from the corners of his mouth were smudged into a gruesome mask of violence I wouldn't soon forget.

"No, Jack. You've been around dying people before. Can you taste metal?"

He nodded affirmatively. "Those pigs drove my mom crazy. They beat her and tied her up." With every word that required his lips to come together, a spray of crimson settled over his neck and chest. I found myself pulling back to avoid getting splattered.

I cut in, "Confession first. You don't have a lot of time."

Jack coughed some more, choking on the life flowing out of his body. When he caught his breath, he shook his head back and forth, his eyes no longer focusing on me. "I shouldn't have killed Leah. I became Bull. I always wanted to be him, and I never wanted to be him. He was always in control—but such a ruthless ass."

I added, "And you shouldn't have killed Alan, or Bo, or Asher. And you shouldn't have shot Maddy or Sly. You shouldn't have raped anyone!"

"I never wanted to kill Maddy." Jack took a ragged gasp. He suddenly focused, looked me hard in the eye, and spat, "That one's on you—you ducked." Jack slipped into unconsciousness and never returned.

The presence of others kept me from saying what I wanted to, out loud. In my mind, I spoke to him: *Jack, you can be damned to hell. Even facing death, you're still too self-centered to take responsibility for your behavior. The damage you've done isn't repairable—nothing brings Leah Hartman back. Maddy's twelve-year-old boy now has to worry she's going to get shot every time she goes to work. Maybe the problem was you never meant something to anyone. Now, the solution is making sure you will never get to mean anything to anyone again. You're done, and I'm done thinking about you. Let your ashes fall where they may—it's not my call to make.*

My dad had been standing beside us, hands sunk into his pockets, silently watching the last conversation Jack Kavanaugh would ever have. I looked up at him, and he lamented, "I gave Sonia the combination to the gun safe because I trusted her." He swiped beads of sweat from his forehead and waved toward Ava and Sonia, who were now standing close. "Evidently, she and Ava had their own plan."

I nodded, "It's okay. You had faith in her, and she needed that."

My dad patted me on the shoulder, and then walked away toward the other hunters. He made a circular motion above his head, and said, "Let's go—we have no business here." The small army departed, and I made no effort to stop them. They hadn't really done anything. I appreciated his effort—if the killer had been on the run through the woods, the hunters would have been useful. There was no doubt in my mind these people would have tracked him down.

This left Sonia, Ava, and me standing about twenty feet away from Jack Kavanaugh's body.

Sonia stood emotionless while Ava squeezed her shoulder in congratulations. "Great shot . . . he caught me before I got to the opening. He was faster than we both thought, and I didn't expect him to have a Taser."

Ava then turned to me excitedly altering her story. "He was chasing me—I was just lucky Sonia was there. She saved my life!"

Sonia silently observed the lie.

I turned to her, "So, what's your story?"

In an effort to rescue Sonia, Ava interjected, "I called your parents one day, to thank them for letting me stay, and Sonia answered. I realized we had this killer in common, so we periodically got on the phone and comforted each other."

I noted to Ava, "And you managed to pop up out of nowhere, conveniently in an area where Sonia was learning to hunt. Instead of contacting authorities, you led Jack right to where Sonia was waiting with a hunting rifle." I turned to Sonia, "Talk to me."

Sonia shivered, "I wasn't going to kill him. But when he put the gun to Ava's head, I just fired."

Ava added, "You had to."

Sonia turned to me, "I'm never picking up a gun again."

I stepped toward her and put my arm around her shoulder; she leaned into me. "Okay. So, the two of you were out here to enjoy some peace and quiet. You took a rifle and walked to an area where you've target-practiced with my dad. Ava stayed back at the shack and relaxed by playing with her electronics. When Ava heard a man outside, she went running to you, and when you saw Jack put a gun to her head, you shot him."

Ava brightened, "That *is* what happened!"

Sonia didn't confirm or deny the story, but said, "I need to apologize to your dad." She thought for a minute and added, "And I need to talk to Victor."

The woods fell silent for a moment, and then the sound of sirens emerged in a progressively collapsing distance.

Sonia, Ava, and I each made our statements to investigators from the Morrison County Sheriff's Department. Maurice Strock then arrived with the BCA crew and interviewed us again. With his white hair blowing in the wind, Maurice left in a huff. He was concerned over the criticism he would receive for our failure to bring the suspect in alive.

Sean Reynolds approached me and said, "Game over Jack! Kavanaugh kept black sweat suits in a locker at the printing press. I believe he discarded them after each murder, and changed into a new pair next time. Storing the clothing by the press gave it a unique smell. There was also a laptop in his locker, which I imagine will prove valuable."

We watched as both Ava Mayer and Sonia Hartman were finally allowed to leave the scene with their parents.

Sean gave me a knowing look. "I think we both have a pretty good idea of what happened here. You have to give Sonia and Ava some credit. They got tired of hiding and finally said, 'Come and find me.'"

I told him, "Honestly, I believe Sonia. She told me she wasn't going to shoot him."

Sean nodded, "If your brother doesn't say anything contrary to that, I don't imagine there will be any charges."

Surprised, I asked, "What does Victor have to do with this?"

"Apparently Victor spoke to Sonia right before she came here. So Maurice is picking him up and bringing him in for questioning."

As a result of having worked successfully with the Morrison County Sheriff's Department in the past, they allowed me to step behind the mirrored glass and watch Maurice Strock's interview of Victor. Victor wasn't being accused of anything, but Maurice was concerned Victor might have some information that could result in manslaughter charges being brought against Sonia. A bible sat on the table between them.

Victor's long scraggly hair, moustache, and "JUST SAY NOPE" t-shirt made him look like a guitar player for a 1970s southern rock group.

Maurice set a bible in front of Victor and said, "I want you to appreciate the seriousness of this statement. I know you come from a strong Christian family, so I imagine swearing on the bible is significant to you."

Victor replied, "It is." Victor voluntarily placed his hand on the bible.

I considered intervening and requesting Victor lawyer up, but I didn't. My fear was it would just lead to a subpoena. Victor was honest to a fault.

Maurice stated, "Victor Frederick, do you swear to tell the whole truth, and nothing but the truth?"

Victor glanced toward the door and, realizing he wasn't going to be saved, said, "Nope."

Shocked, Maurice retorted, "Your hand is on the bible. You need to be honest."

Victor said, "I am. I don't know the whole truth. All I know is what I've seen and what I heard. Isn't it your job to determine what the whole truth is?"

Maurice nodded, "Okay. Just be truthful. Do you know Yesonia Hartman? I believe she goes by 'Sonia.'"

Victor smiled, "She invented flowers."

Behind the glass, I was grinning. You had to understand the language of Victor. This wasn't a psychotic statement. When someone exudes love, Victor says, "She invented flowers."

Frustrated, Maurice pushed his wire glasses up the bridge of his nose as he contemplated the benefit of proceeding. Maurice finally decided to surge forward. "Okay. We're telling the truth here. Did Sonia tell you she was going to shoot someone?"

Victor looked up at the ceiling as he considered this.

Maurice ultimately glanced up also, to see if something had captured his attention.

Victor finally returned his gaze and said, "Nope."

Maurice suggested, "Let me ask the question in another way. Did you have the sense that Sonia Hartman was going to shoot someone when she left your home with the rifle?" It was the last straw for Maurice. If Victor didn't bite on this one, there was no case to be made against Sonia.

Victor's response was, "There were still three frogs on the log, so no."

With both hands waving Victor away, Maurice shook his head and said, "I have no more questions for you. Just go."

On the ride home I told Victor he couldn't have answered the questions better. As a man who struggles with underlying paranoia, he anticipated being incarcerated, so he was now in a great mood. After some small talk he asked, "Can you tell me how to talk to Sonia about sex?"

I didn't want to have this conversation, but I was likely his only resource. "What seems to be the problem?"

Victor shared, "I just kinda go along with everything. I really like most of it. But some of it's uncomfortable. I don't know how to tell her there are ways she touches me I don't really like."

"You do know how to tell her."

Confused he said, "I do?"

"Think of it like thanksgiving dinner. What do you like at the thanksgiving meal?"

Victor smiled, "I really like ham."

"Okay, so when she's doing something you enjoy, you tell her you really like it, and you could take more of that. What do you think about yams? You usually don't take any."

"I don't like yams. It's a texture thing. Yams remind me of spackle. And then they put marshmallows on it. What the hell? It's like here's some broccoli with a gummy worm on top."

"You see, you already have the skills to say no. If she's doing something you don't like, you tell her, 'I don't want any of that,' or 'That makes me uncomfortable.'"

"Do you like cranberries?"

Victor said, "Sometimes, but not all the time. I don't like it when it's still in the shape of the can."

"I've watched you. You don't always take them. So you tell Sonia, 'I'd like this now, but not all the time.' Or 'I don't want to now, but I do like it sometimes.' You have the skills."

"How does mom get turkey so dry? It tastes like desert sand. But I do eat a little, for her sake."

"There you go. You have all the skills."

Victor thought for a moment, "I get it. And if it's dry, the gravy is like lotion, and I can just say—"

I interrupted, "Okay, you get it. This conversation is over."

Victor asked, "Do you want to talk about dessert?"

"No!"

44

I USED THE FOB KEY TO OPEN JON Frederick's apartment door one last time. I slipped my shoes off and quietly made my way to the bedroom. The door was open. I carefully sat on the edge of the bed looking around. There was a black Ripsaw t-shirt folded on the nightstand. Ripsaw was the name of Jon's uncle's rock band in the 1980s (before our time). When we were together, we watched them perform a reunion concert as a fundraiser at the horseshoe arena in Genola. I smiled at the thought of his uncles, in their forties, rocking out. It seemed actually young for a classic rock band today. The folded t-shirt on the night stand meant Jon had worn the shirt but didn't consider it dirty. I held it to my chest and lay back on the bed.

Jon wasn't home, and this wasn't my bed. Honestly, this wasn't Jon's home anymore, either. He was home, in Pierz, with Serena. I understood his desire to be close to his family. I was ready to go home, too. I had accepted a job as a news anchor in Chicago.

I shouldn't have burned Serena's letter. Last night, I burned my letter, too. Our ship had passed. He didn't board, and I held the rudder due east, refusing to disembark.

I sat up and decided I was keeping the t-shirt. I went back to the kitchen and pulled out a pen and paper. I wrote:

Sorry for lying about the key! I plugged in the toaster as a joke. I thought you'd know it was me, from always leaving it plugged in when I used it in the past. I didn't realize I'd left your extra set of keys on the counter also, until you pointed it out. I thought this case had the potential to get me to an anchor spot, but I needed you to work it. When I realized I could use the suspected break-in to get you to work the case, I just went with it. My thinking wasn't all self-centered. From the little I heard, I knew Ava Mayer was in a lot of trouble, and I could trust you to get to the truth. I also thought it would help you out of the funk you were in. I only tracked you because I was worried for your welfare. You take dangerous risks when you feel lonely and I wanted to be able to find you and help. I wish you and Serena the very best! I've accepted an anchor position in Chicago. I've always said I would leave when I had the opportunity to report in a larger venue. The time has come.

Take care, Jada

I walked in front of the hidden camera Jon had placed facing the door, did a brief 1920s flapper dance in front of it, and walked out the door. After I locked the door, I slid the fob back under it. Jon had forgotten that I hadn't returned the key when we broke up. It was time to leave it, now.

45

JON FREDERICK
6:30 P.M., SUNDAY, JULY 30,
PIERZ

JACK KAVANAUGH WAS DEAD. Ava Mayer had found a new, up-wardly mobile professional to torment. Harper Cook and Sly Graham had been released from the hospital and were recovering together. Nina Cole had relapsed and almost overdosed on oxy-contin last weekend, but she was back in treatment again. Victim's services were involved with all of them, although not surprisingly, Ava was the least cooperative.

Sonia Hartman was returning to the University of Minnesota in the fall. She had moved back home for what was left of the summer, but still visited Victor daily. I honestly didn't picture it working out, simply because Sonia was so much younger, but at the present time, they were good for each other. Her parents loved Victor because he was kind, respectful, and nothing like Leah's abusive boyfriends.

When I told Maurice Strock about my plan to leave the BCA so I could be closer to my daughter in Pierz, he requested two weeks before I turned in my resignation. Before the day was over, Sean Reynolds asked me if I would stay with the BCA if my position was transferred to St. Cloud (a thirty-minute drive from Pierz). I couldn't help but smile, and told both I'd get back to them after this weekend.

Serena rubbed lotion on her recently shaved legs. The contrast of her tanned skin against her white sundress was sensuous. We finally had time for our conversation.

Serena left to wash her hands and returned with her acoustic Martin guitar. I hadn't heard her play since before she was assaulted. She sat on the soft carpet in the living room—barefoot in her white dress, with long dark curls cascading over her shoulders. She strummed minor chords as she softly sang her version of "I Love You," by Aimee Belle. I'd never heard it sung so heartfelt, and any animosity I still harbored was melted away by the insecure quiver in her voice. Music has always had an overwhelming power to bring my emotions to the surface. Serena sang of her despair over the things she put me through. Above all, she wanted me to know that now, and from this point forward, her heart is with me, loving me.

A nervous secret glistened in her green eyes and she bit her bottom lip. Before I could soften her tension, she knelt in front of me and asked, "Will you marry me?"

My head and heart swirled with conflicting emotions—unconditional love, concern, anger, then love again. It wasn't like Tony hadn't warned me, but I hadn't anticipated being so overwhelmed with emotion. Carefully, I asked, "How can you be so certain you will love me for the rest of your life, when weeks ago you didn't even want to speak to me?"

Serena sat back on her heels. "I've learned pain is inevitable. Suffering is optional. I'm not going to stress about what could happen—I'm going to enjoy us, moment by moment. I want our life together. I want you. I've thought about what it must be like for you to live with me. You never say anything, but with your obsessiveness, it has to drive you crazy that I always have a pair of shoes sitting in front of the door, and a day's change of clothing on the bedroom floor. I'll try to be better."

I shook my head, "None of that matters. I'm less obsessive when I'm with you. But I don't know that I could handle you leaving again."

Serena's big green eyes fixed on mine, as she softly assured, "I'm not leaving again. There will never be another person, but you, for me. Even when you're gone working, I want you to know I'll always be here for you. The mistake I made by leaving scares the hell out of me, now. I came too close to losing you." She shuddered, "I want us back."

Serena got up and retrieved a purple Sharpie marker and asked, "Do you mind if I write a word on your back? When I'm done, you can write whatever you wish on mine."

I removed my shirt, and soon felt the cold tip of the marker as she wrote on my skin. Not able to see it, she explained it read, "Numquam Solus." She kissed my shoulder blade with full, warm lips that lingered. With sincere devotion, she said, "It's Latin for 'You will never walk alone.' You will never be alone again. I will have your back—always." Serena came around and faced me before she added, "I don't want you to stop being an investigator. As a matter of fact, I want to work with you."

I stood there motionless, trying to make sense of what she was proposing. She set the guitar aside and folded her legs under her. I slowly lowered myself down beside her.

She leaned forward, and her passionate energy was contagious. "Keep your job, and we'll do some private work together until we build up our business or get a great case. You can keep doing the hands-on work. I like the research and talking to you about the possibilities. I love our children, but I need to be part of the world beyond them, too. It's our world. Let's make it right. At least the best we can in our little corner of it."

I lovingly caressed her, "Yes, I will marry you."

Only hours earlier, I had watched Serena carefully piece together a Rey outfit (the heroine from *Star Wars*) for our daughter as Nora gazed on, in belief that the outfit would transform her into a superhero. I admired Nora, but Serena was the real superhero. It would be impossible for me to observe someone loving my child so intensely, and not love her.

I took her face in my hands and added, "But here's the deal. We marry right away—a small wedding with just a priest and our parents. I don't care if anyone else even knows. No more uncertainty—just done."

Serena curled her fingers around mine, holding my hands in place. She interjected, "I'm fine with this. But I want to plan a large wedding to follow, so the community can celebrate our marriage with us. Pierz is our community, now—again. Let's celebrate us!"

I smiled as I pictured Victor having the chance to stand up at a wedding. Nora will celebrate our day with us, in her own special dress, dancing on the wooden floor of the Pierz Ballroom . . .

After a brief, gentle kiss, I pulled away, "Wait. You said children. Specifically, 'I love our children.'"

Serena placed her hand low on her stomach. Smiling provocatively, she picked up her phone and played "Sharing the Night Together" by Dr. Hook on the Beats Pill. She stood up and took my hand, pulling me up to dance as she whispered, "Would you mind sharing the night," with the music.

9:45 P.M., SUNDAY, JULY 30
PIERZ

THE MOON GLOWED CONFIDENTLY as Serena and I relaxed on our porch swing. There were no houses visible from our back porch—just room for Nora to play, a garden and trees. It was a warm July night and the combination of her pregnancy and an evening's passion had exhausted Serena's tender heart. I heard an owl in the distance and considered that maybe a mile or so away, Victor and Sonia were hearing that same owl on their nightly walk.

Serena had finished her homemade chocolate chip cookies, but her glass of milk had now been abandoned on the stand by the swing. We had made cookies with Nora earlier in the day, "Sarah Kieffer style." (You slam the pan every two minutes after they start baking to get the chewy wrinkled caramelized texture.) I don't know that they taste any better, but Nora sure giggled as she helped bang the pan against the stovetop. After Serena's foot and leg rub, she had fallen asleep, lying against me in her thin pajamas. In physics formulas "K" refers to something that's constant, even when everything else changes. Serena and

I can deny our love for each other at times, but it just makes us fools in the midst of the omnipresent affection we have for each other—an endearment so clearly visible to everyone else—"K."

I still had a few sips of milk left, but I set my glass aside to write a note I would give to Serena with her breakfast tomorrow morning. I'd never been much of a poet, but I can rely on her kindness to appreciate the effort.

My Dearest Serena,

I want to trip over your shoes when I enter the door . . .

   To remind me to never walk by you without appreciating your presence.

I want to see your clothes strewn about the floor . . .

   Like the beautiful amber and scarlet leaves that will blanket our yard   next fall.

I want to be torn . . .

   Grounded in humility on earth over having lost you, yet my heart in the heavens and crazy in love at this very moment.

I ought to be committed . . .

   I am committed, as I need you to be, but still playfully provocative.

I am grateful to you, Serena, far beyond what my clumsy words

   profess . . .

For your warm comfort, wisdom, grace and delicious sensuality.

It's not by accident that we love each other,

despite obstacles, for our love just is . . .

Jon

I occasionally have lapses of resentment for having been abandoned, but I only let it last seconds. I've learned to understand love differently. Regardless of what anyone's been through, love is the only way out. Love is the action that reveals the beauty in others. It's by loving Serena that I experience her absolute affection.

The End

CPSIA information can be obtained
at www.ICGtesting.com
Printed in the USA
LVHW04s0704171018
593820LV00002B/4/P